A Danby dinner party turns deadly. . . .

Mr. Hayes leaned closer, and in the light of the candelabra on the table, Cecilia noticed a very strange thing. There was a large bruise beneath one of his eyes, half-covered by powder a shade paler than his sun-bronzed skin. Where had he got such a thing? And he smelled of wine and some lemony-green cologne. He reached for his glass for another long drink.

"I would like to propose a toast!" Annabel suddenly cried merrily. Annabel waved one of those heavy pieces of silver in the air, as if she would give a toast with her fish fork. Was it an American thing, then?

Lady Avebury studied Annabel with wide, startled eyes, her hand frozen on her own fork. Ladies did not give toasts at dinner parties!

"You've all just been so very kind, so marvelous to me, after my terrible, terrible ordeal," Annabel declared with a bright smile. "I absolutely must thank you all, thank beautiful Danby, my darling refuge. I could never have hoped to find a better harbor!"

Redvers and the footmen came in with the entree course, and the butler froze at seeing the unprecedented scene in his dining room. He glanced at Lady Avebury, who gave him a subtle little wave. He had Paul go ahead to the dowager countess with his silver serving tray of lamb cutlets, and the new footman behind him with the mint sauce.

Suddenly, Paul seemed to trip. He stumbled against the table, spilling some of the tray onto Lady Byswater's lap. She cried out, leaping to her feet, while Lady Avebury hurried over to try and placate her and Redvers pulled Paul back. Sebastian growled under the table, and the dowager laughed in delight at the silly scene before her.

"I don't feel at all well," Mr. Hayes gasped. Cecilia swung back around to face him and saw he had turned quite gray. He half rose to his feet, grasping the damask tablecloth in his fist. Cecilia, most alarmed, reached for his arm to try and steady him. But he fell sideways, taking the cloth, plates, and silver with him. He was ill all over the mess, a greenish, foamy sort of sick tinged with red blood, and seemed to tense into a convulsion.

"Oh, help, please!" Cecilia screamed. She knelt down by Mr. Hayes, trying frantically to pull him onto his back, but he went very still.

Lady Takes the Case

Eliza Casey

BERKLEY PRIME CRIME

New York

BERKLEY PRIME CRIME
Published by Berkley
An imprint of Penguin Random House LLC
penguinrandomhouse.com

Library of Congress Cataloging-in-Publication Data

Names: Casey, Eliza, author.
Title: Lady takes the case / Eliza Casey.
Description: First edition. | New York: Berkley Prime Crime, 2019. |
Series: A manor cat mystery; book 1
Identifiers: LCCN 2019022977 (print) | LCCN 2019022978 (ebook) |
ISBN 9781984803887 (paperback) | ISBN 9781984803894 (ebook)
Subjects: GSAFD: Mystery fiction.
Classification: LCC PS3613.C3226 L33 2019 (print) |
LCC PS3613.C3226 (ebook) | DDC 813/.6—dc23
LC record available at https://lccn.loc.gov/2019022977
LC ebook record available at https://lccn.loc.gov/2019022978

First Edition: November 2019

Printed in the United States of America
1 3 5 7 9 10 8 6 4 2

Cover art © by Alan Ayers
Cover design by Paul Castalano
Book design by Elke Sigal

Prologue

Spring 1912

When Colonel Havelock bicycled through the tall iron gates, past the gatehouse, up the long gravel drive, and along the lane of ancient oak trees, he found a scene of utter chaos. For an instant, all he could do was stare, openmouthed with astonishment. *Chaos* and Danby Hall were usually complete strangers.

But not tonight. The house, one of the grandest in the county, seat of an ancient and venerable family, was brightly lit from every window. All three stories, the Elizabethan center block of red brick, the pale stone Palladian wings stretching gracefully to either side, even the old medieval watchtower that soared up from the back, were glowing with brilliant amber light.

People dashed up and down the marble front steps, swirling like a flock of insects disturbed from their nests. Ladies in bright satins and chiffons, beadwork and diamonds flashing, fluttered and sobbed and clung to one another. Gentlemen in impeccably cut dark evening coats gesticulated wildly, demanding to know "what the deuce is happening!" Colonel Havelock glimpsed the Dowager Countess of Avebury, a formidable figure in Victorian black silk, waving her walking stick at a hapless constable.

It was like nothing the colonel had ever seen before—and he was a hardened veteran of the Boer War, local magistrate since his retirement, scourge of criminals. He mopped at his brow with his handkerchief and wished he could turn around and go right back to his cozy bed at Mattingly Farm, where Mrs. Havelock would have a nice pot of tea waiting.

Still, duty called, and he was never a man to shirk it. He steered his bicycle along the end of the drive, to where the graveled lane widened around a grand marble fountain that glowed pure white in the moonlight. The voices grew louder, a chorus of fury and woe, and a lady shrieked, "It's all ruined!" The dowager's Scottish terrier Sebastian, horror of all constables who encountered his strident bark and snapping teeth, growled.

"Hush, Sebastian," the dowager said. "And you hush, too, Annabel. This is no time for hysterics. Don't be so American about it all."

A tall woman in gold silk gave a wail and whirled around

to run back into the house. The colonel assumed she was the American.

"Surely, it is quite understandable, Mama," the current Lady Avebury answered her mother-in-law, in a quiet tone of resignation.

"Hysterics are *never* understandable, Emmaline, though I am not surprised someone of your scatty upbringing might think they were," the dowager said with a sniff.

Colonel Havelock stopped his bicycle and slowly dismounted, thinking that walking the last few feet might be more dignified.

"Hullo, Colonel," he heard a light, clear voice say. He turned to see Lady Cecilia, the daughter of Danby, sitting on the edge of the fountain, her satin-slippered feet dangling. Her pearly white gown blended into the marble. A large, handsome marmalade cat, whose fur almost matched her own strawberry blond curls, perched beside her. She didn't look hysterical, merely very interested in it all. "I'm glad you're here. If anyone can calm matters down, it's surely you."

"I'll do my best, my lady," he said, wondering what she could tell him about it all. Mrs. Havelock was on a couple of charitable committees with Lady Cecilia and often commented on how levelheaded and sharp-witted she was. "Just out of interest, did *you* see anything?"

Lady Cecilia frowned in thought. "Not really. I wish I did. It all seemed a rather ordinary dinner party at first. But then . . ."

A lady shrieked again, and Lady Cecilia grimaced. "You'd best go in quickly, Colonel," she said. "Her nibs won't be contained much longer, even by my grandmother."

"Her nibs?" Colonel Havelock asked, astonished that an earl's daughter would use such slang.

"Annabel Clarke. A guest from America. She's terribly prone to dramatics, I'm afraid." She gave him a sympathetic smile. "I'll talk to you later."

Colonel Havelock nodded and made his way into the house. The grand entrance hall, with its pale marble floor, its soaring blue-inlaid dome, was empty, but he could hear voices from the dining room beyond. The scene he found there was freezingly bizarre.

He had only been in there once before, for a military dinner hosted by the earl, but he well remembered the elegant dark-red silk walls, the buffet displaying old silver and fine old Chinese porcelain vases, the long table glittering with cut crystal, and the elaborate swags of the velvet draperies at the tall windows. All that was the same, but the elegant order had been upended. The damask tablecloth had been pulled halfway off the table, spilling wine and food, and a few chairs were overturned.

Stretched out on the red-and-blue Axminster carpet was a man in evening dress. His cravat was loosened, his face bright red and swollen beyond recognition. Dr. Mitchell, the local physician, knelt beside him, while a few constables milled about. Two footmen, tall, handsome men who suddenly looked very young and awfully frightened in their scarlet livery, hovered in the corner, along with the intimidating Danby butler Redvers. He muttered low, soothing words to the scared young men, but he looked rather discomfited. Not like the unflappable Redvers at all. Mr. Brown, the young vicar, muttered prayers in the corner.

Standing near the doorway was the earl himself. A tall, handsome gentleman just starting to turn a bit portly, his strawberry blond hair going a bit silvery and thin, he scowled in mingled concern and anger. Colonel Havelock remembered the gossip that had been going around the neighborhood, that Danby was losing money, and he was sure this was the last thing the earl needed on his overflowing plate.

"Oh, Colonel," he said hoarsely. "I am glad you're here. Such a rotten business! A guest in our own house. I'll never forgive myself."

"I'm afraid such things do happen, my lord, no matter where we might be. A sad truth of life," the colonel said carefully. "Who was the deceased?"

"Richard Hayes, the explorer. Maybe you've read about him? We didn't know him well, I'm afraid, but it's ghastly all the same. Dinner was going along just as usual, and suddenly he started gasping and choking. Fell right over in the mint sauce." The earl grimaced and gestured toward the wreck of the elegant table. "We called immediately for the doctor, but nothing could be done, I'm afraid."

Colonel Havelock carefully studied the scene again, the

red wine and champagne spreading stains on the white cloth, the overturned chairs. "A terrible accident, my lord?"

"I'm afraid not," the doctor said, rising to his feet. "Lord Avebury was quite right to send for you. This frothy discharge at the victim's mouth, along with the color of his skin, indicates poisoning. Strychnine, maybe. We will know more later, when I can more closely examine him."

"You mean—he was *murdered*? In my house?" Lord Avebury gasped, his face ashen. His son, Patrick, usually so quiet and inconspicuous, stepped closer and laid his hand on his father's arm. He looked calm, interested, concerned.

"It was meant to be me!" a woman cried. Colonel Havelock turned to see the American lady hovering in the doorway. She looked like she was playing out a scene onstage, tall and statuesque, her auburn hair falling from its diamond-tipped pins, her pale-gold gown disheveled. She pointed a trembling finger at the dead man.

"Someone tried to kill *me*," she sobbed, and promptly swooned to the floor.

Colonel Havelock sighed. The dowager was right about Americans. He had the terrible feeling it was going to be a long while before he saw his cozy teapot again.

Chapter One

A few days earlier . . .

Lady Cecilia Bates's bedchamber was tucked away in the quieter East Wing of Danby Hall, far from the grander suites of her parents but with the best views of the rose garden, the lawn, and the trees of the ancient park beyond. Even though it was on the smallish side, Cecilia had decorated it to her own taste, in sky blue, cloud white, and sunny yellow, the bed, chairs, and dressing table carved out of a pale, light wood. Satin-upholstered chairs were grouped around the white marble fireplace, with her books and sketch pads piled around them, and blue-and-white-striped draperies hid the morning light at the windows.

Cecilia loved her room. It was her quiet sanctuary, away

from the rest of the busy, bustling house. Best of all, it was away from her mother, and Lady Avebury's constant exhortations to find a "good husband" and marry soon. Her first Season was behind her now, after all, and she was not getting any younger.

Usually, when she swam up from a cozy night's sleep and snuggled deeper under her satin blankets for a minute, she was excited to face the day. A ride, breakfast, and she would be free for a few hours until she had to help her mother pay calls on the tenants and neighbors and write letters. But this morning, as soon as she opened her eyes, she growled and pulled the bedclothes all the way over her head. Today was going to be different.

Today, they had to prepare for the Heiress's arrival tomorrow. And the long house party would begin.

Cecilia sighed and rolled over to bury her face in the pillow. Nothing could block out the party. It was bearing down on Danby no matter what she did. Only days away, and the preparations felt like they had been going on forever.

The door clicked open, and she drew away from the pillow to see Rose, the young housemaid, tiptoeing into the room. A cup of tea was balanced carefully in her hands. She placed it ever-so-gently on the dressing table before she crept to the window and reached for the taffeta draperies.

"It's all right, Rose," Cecilia said. "I've been awake for ages."

"Oh, good morning, my lady," Rose said with a grateful

glance. The curtains opened with a swoosh, and pale morning light swept over the floral needlepoint carpet. "I do try ever so hard to stay quiet."

"I know you do." Rose wasn't meant to be a proper lady's maid. She'd only been an upstairs maid at Danby for a few months and was still young and uncertain. But Cecilia's maid had left, and her mother's maid, the dour, intimidating Sumter, had declared she couldn't keep looking after two ladies. So Rose was sent to deputize.

Cecilia's mother declared that she would only hire just the "right" lady's maid, and none was available at the moment. Cecilia was afraid she knew the truth. She had seen the paintings and ornaments missing from the corridors, the increasing shabbiness of the upholstery and carpets, her father's worried frowns. The bustle and consternation over the arrival of the Heiress. Danby was not what it once was. The estate had never quite recovered from the great agricultural depression.

But no one talked to Cecilia about such things, nor would they. She was left to worry in restless silence and to try to help a maid who really only wanted to go back to her regular duties.

"It looks like a fine day outside, my lady," Rose said, handing Cecilia the cup of tea. "No rain yet. Will you want to ride after breakfast? I think your boots are still being cleaned."

Cecilia sighed and drained the cup. Thankfully, it was

nice and strong. "I *want* to, but I imagine my mother will need my help."

"Oh yes. Mrs. Sumter says Lady Avebury was up before dawn."

"I can imagine." Cecilia had seldom seen her mother quite so excited as when she learned an American heiress was coming to stay. At least it turned her matchmaking attentions from Cecilia to her poor brother, Patrick, for a while.

Rose opened the wardrobe, sorting through the gowns and shawls and hats. "What will you wear for the morning, then, my lady?"

"The blue tweed skirt, I think, and one of the plainer shirtwaists. I can put on a jacket after, if I'm needed on an errand."

Cecilia reluctantly climbed out of bed and let Rose help her wash and dress. She sat down at the dressing table and watched in the mirror as Rose brushed and braided her thick, red-blond hair. The girl wasn't really very good with hair, a little clumsy, but she was kind and quiet, and Cecilia liked her easy presence. It gave her a peaceful moment before she had to go downstairs and face the day.

"You really are so kind to help me, Rose," Cecilia said, fiddling with the silver boxes and combs on her lace-draped table. "I'm sure we'll have you back to your regular job in no time." Once the Heiress arrived and saved them with her American gold.

"I don't mind at all, my lady," Rose said. "I like a bit of a change sometimes. But you'll want someone more experienced to help you with your party clothes this week!"

Cecilia thought of the new dresses that had just arrived from the dressmaker in Leeds, all pale silks and chiffons, with fashionable high waists and narrow skirts. She didn't know how they were all paid for, but her mother had insisted. Only the best, or the best to be found in Yorkshire, anyway. Danby was the seat of an ancient earldom, after all, and they had to look like it.

"I daresay that between us we will muddle along," Cecilia said. "I'm sure it makes extra work for everyone."

"We're all happy for a bit of excitement downstairs, my lady, to tell you the truth! There hasn't been a proper party in ever so long. Mrs. Frazer is beside herself with the new menus."

Cecilia laughed. "I'm sure she is." Mrs. Frazer had been head cook at Danby for as long as Cecilia could remember. When she and her brother were small, they would sneak down to the kitchens and Mrs. Frazer would give them iced buns. She was an excellent cook who did like a challenge, even as she moaned about it, and Cecilia feared the Bates family hadn't given her one in some time. Mama had even expressed worry that Mrs. Frazer might go elsewhere, since everyone in the neighborhood had longed to lure her away for years.

Especially their nearest neighbors and old rivals, Lord

and Lady Byswater at Emberley Court. They would love to steal away Mama's prized cook and her lovely Lamb Devaux, her very own creation, and raspberry tarts.

Cecilia watched in the mirror as Rose pinned up her braided hair in a tidy coil at the nape of her neck. Rose might not know the latest coiffures, but she was careful and neat. "You're sure you don't mind the extra work, then?"

"I heard the guests might bring lots of tips, my lady," Rose answered with a cheeky smile and a blush. "A few coins for my hope chest!"

"Rose!" Cecilia cried. "Are you engaged?"

"Not as such, my lady, not yet. But there is someone who—well, he's ever so nice."

"How lovely." Cecilia sighed, a little envious. All the young men she had met during her Season had *not* been "ever so nice" but completely dull. "I do enjoy a good romance."

"You won't tell Mrs. Caffey, will you, my lady?" Rose asked nervously. "Not until it's all settled?"

"Of course not." Mrs. Caffey, who like Mrs. Frazer had been at Danby for ages, was an excellent housekeeper and most efficient, but she was also rather old-fashioned. She wouldn't approve of the maids marrying. She was one of those who didn't realize it was the twentieth century now. "It will be our little secret."

All too soon her toilette was finished, and Cecilia had to leave the sanctuary of her chamber and go downstairs. She left Rose tidying up and made her way down the corridor, along the old Elizabethan gallery to the stairs.

The gallery connected the older part of the house to the Palladian mansion her several-times-removed great-grandfather had built when the Bates fortune started to catch up to its ancient name. Cecilia loved it, as it felt like moving from one time to another, a bridge between eras. It was also a splendid place to hide away and read on rainy days. She and Patrick had even raced their bicycles there when they were children, once they managed to obtain the precious and long-forbidden wheeled items.

One wall was all windows, curtained in heavy tapestry fabric, looking out to the ornamental lake, the marble folly made to look like a Grecian temple that had replaced an older watchtower, and the park beyond. The other wall was paneled in dark wood, with three grand fireplaces carved with fruit and grinning theater masks so overexpressive they had frightened her when she was a child. Hardly less frightening were the family portraits hung between them, along with old weapons and battle flags. Only the most ancient visages were kept there, Bateses who had served Queen Elizabeth and James I, solemn and fierce in their starched ruffs and pearl-edged farthingales.

Cecilia saluted them today as she made her way along the inlaid parquet floor, which echoed the old-gold coffered ceiling overhead. She paused to peek out the window and was glad to see that last night's rain clouds had indeed scuttled away, leaving a hesitant, watery-pale sunlight peeking into a blue sky. The weather would be one less thing for her mother to fuss about.

"Hello, Ralph, old man," she said to the rusting suit of armor just at the end of the gallery. She patted him on his creaking shoulder. "Still keeping watch on things, I'm glad to see."

Outside the gallery, she turned and found herself at the main staircase. Slightly newer than the gallery, but not as new as the main house, all the local history books called it "the best open-well staircase in the neighborhood." Cecilia had always thought it didn't quite look real, as if it belonged in a fairy-tale castle like Sleeping Beauty's; its dark wood was so thickly carved with cherubs and flowers and feathers, and Bs circled with wreaths. There were niches for sculptures and paintings, and at the landing, her grandmother's portrait by Winterhalter from when she was a young woman visiting the French royal court. Even with dark, lustrous hair and the wide, swooping pink satin skirts of her youth, she was formidable.

Cecilia wondered if maybe that was why Danby never felt like a comfortable *home* to her, except for her bedroom. Someone like her grandmother or the Elizabethan courtiers was always watching. And her grandmama hadn't looked any less intimidating when she sat in a summertime garden for Mr. Winterhalter than she did now in her dower house, and she was certainly no less farseeing.

Cecilia hurried past her grandmother's blue-eyed stare and turned again at the staircase hall. She could have gone through the monumental foyer into the staterooms, the White Drawing Room, the dining room, the Gothic library or chapel, but she chose a narrower hallway toward the smaller, octagonal breakfast room at the back of the house.

She had heard that in her grandparents' day, breakfasts were taken in the overwhelming grandeur of the main dining room, until Cecilia's mother insisted a smaller, more intimate chamber be constructed. Only one of the many lovely things her mother had accomplished as a young Lady Avebury.

Cecilia sighed. She wished her mother had such a distraction now, instead of bending all her formidable energy onto her children's marital prospects. At least this house party was focused on poor Patrick and not her.

The breakfast room was a lovely, serene space, papered in a blue-and-white floral pattern, the chairs cushioned in a yellow chintz, the needlepoint carpet a riot of yellow and pink roses and blue violets. The matching chintz curtains were back, letting the daylight shine on the silver warming dishes lined up on the mahogany buffet. A still life of fruit and roses hung above it, echoing the view of the terrace and rose garden outside the windows.

Usually, Cecilia breakfasted alone with her father, and sometimes Patrick, if he could be torn away from his botany experiments in the laboratory shed beyond the garden. Her mother took the morning meal on a tray in her room. It was a peaceful, quiet hour, her father usually buried in his newspapers. But today her mother was actually there, as if the countess's suite could no longer contain her energy.

She sat across from her husband at the round, yellow-draped table, a meager repast of toast on her plate, a stack of papers beside her. Lord Avebury tried to hide behind the *Times*, pretending it was a normal morning, but Cecilia saw him cringe with every furious rustle of her mother's famous lists.

Patrick was nowhere to be seen. Lucky chap.

"Good morning, Mama. Papa," Cecilia said, as cheerfully as she could. She kissed her father's cheek and hurried over to fill her plate.

Redvers, the butler who had served at Danby since long before Cecilia was born, lifted the silver cover from the dish of buttered eggs for her. "Good morning, Lady Cecilia. Would you care for a cup of tea? Or perhaps some chocolate is called for today." He raised his shaggy gray brow at her, making her smile.

He and Mrs. Frazer did know her sweet tooth too well. "Oh, chocolate, please, Redvers."

"Right away, my lady."

Cecilia added a dollop of kedgeree and some toast to her plate before she joined her parents at the table. A cup of lovely, frothy, dark chocolate soon appeared at her elbow. She had a feeling she was going to need it.

Her mother glanced up and speared Cecilia with a sharp glance from her sea-green eyes. Emmaline, Lady Avebury, had been a wondrous beauty in her youth, and everyone agreed she was still very lovely, with her tall, slim figure in fashionable gowns, clear roses-and-ivory complexion, and mounds of dark hair barely touched with silver. It was whispered that her great beauty was why the very eligible young Lord Avebury married her back then. So many young ladies clamored to be the Countess of Avebury, and Emmaline was from an old but poor family, mostly populated now by colonial civil servants in India and Africa.

Cecilia had often wished she had inherited some of her mother's dramatic looks, instead of the Bates reddish hair and freckles. She was sure her mother often wished that, too.

She sighed. Well, there was nothing to be done about her looks at such a late date. She went about buttering her toast.

"Patrick should be here," her mother said. "There is so much to go over before the guests arrive!"

"You know Patrick never pays attention to such things, Mama," Cecilia said. It was true. Her brother, though very sweet, was usually off in his own world. After taking a Second Degree in classics at Cambridge, he had come back to Danby to busy himself with what he really loved—botany. He had built himself a laboratory in the garden, behind the old stables, and everyone else stayed away from the strange smells that tended to emanate from it. One was lucky if he came to dinner in clothes not torn or stained.

"Well, he *should* care!" her mother cried, furiously shaking one of her lists. "I am doing all of this for him, for his inheritance. There have been Bateses at Danby for four hundred years, but that won't last much longer if Patrick doesn't make an effort. It will all be lost, and my hard work all these years will be for nothing."

Lord Avebury peered cautiously over the top of his paper. "My dear, I am sure that when it comes to it, Patrick will do his duty."

His wife shot him her most piercing glare. "Will he? I fear I am not as sanguine as you, Clifford."

"What are the planned activities, Mama?" Cecilia asked, desperate for the conversation not to be all about poor Patrick's shortcomings as heir.

Emmaline looked at the list crumpled in her hand. "Oh, the masked ball, of course. I have invited the whole neighborhood for that, and we shall be fifty for dinner before. I need to see if Mrs. Frazer has word of the lobsters and asparagus." She jotted a note with her little gold pencil. "A picnic luncheon, if the weather holds. Lawn tennis. I do hear that it's a favorite pastime of young people in America." She frowned. "Would an American want afternoon tea? A musical evening?"

"Oh, Mama, they are quite civilized now," Cecilia said cheerfully. "You know all those American duchesses at court! They're grander than anyone else."

Emmaline scowled. "That's what I'm worried about.

Danby must be seen at its very best. We can have no one else snatching Miss Clarke away. Should we bring the Garden of Eden tapestries out of storage? I'm not sure we have enough on display; it's been so long since we had a large party, and the tapestries were a gift from Queen Elizabeth."

Cecilia thought about all the paintings, sculptures, Chinese vases, silver epergnes, and Sevres clocks all over Danby, even after a few had gone missing. "How could anyone help but admire Danby, tapestries or not?"

Emmaline's expression softened. "That is true. It is still the grandest house in the neighborhood. Clifford, have you and Redvers ordered the wine yet?"

"I'm sure we have good enough vintages in the wine storage to impress an American girl," Lord Avebury said, turning the page of his paper.

Lady Avebury scowled again. "But not to impress Lord Byswater! Or Mr. Hayes. Mr. Hayes is a famous explorer, you know. He has seen the richest things the world has to offer."

Cecilia knew he had. For a time, the newspapers were full of nothing but the exploits of the famous Richard Hayes. He had been into the jungles of Asia, the darkest recesses of Africa, all over India and Persia, befriended kings and empresses and bishops. She didn't know where her mother had met him, or why he would be interested in coming to Yorkshire, but he had accepted the invitation.

"Why must you ask the Byswaters, anyway?" her father

demanded. "I get enough of their nosy questions when I meet them in the village."

Lord and Lady Byswater were Danby's closest neighbors and their estate the only rival in size. But unlike the Bateses, they were rolling in money, as Lady Byswater had been the heiress to a flour mill fortune. They were nice enough people, and said to be devoted to each other, but it was no secret they would like to acquire Danby and add to their acres. For a while, they had even seemed to hope Cecilia would marry their only son, but luckily, he was rather young for her and the scheme came to nothing.

"Because of exactly that, Clifford," Lady Avebury said. "They must see Danby as strong, and as Bates, as ever. Once they see Patrick with Miss Clarke, they will know they can't ever buy Danby, and they will settle down and be quiet again."

Cecilia's father didn't look entirely convinced. "Being quiet has never been the Byswater way."

"Who else is coming?" Cecilia asked.

Her mother turned back to her handy list. "My friend Mrs. Solent, of course."

"Oh, Aunt Maggie!" Cecilia said happily. Mrs. Solent was her mother's oldest friend; they had gone to school together as girls whose families were far away in India, and then made their debuts together, marrying in the same year. Now Mrs. S was a widow and spent her time traveling. Maybe she was the one who knew Mr. Hayes. "I'm so excited to see her again."

"I couldn't have a party without her help," Lady Avebury agreed. "And there are the Rainsleys . . ."

"Maud Rainsley and her mother?" Cecilia asked, surprised. Maud Rainsley, who was studying history at Girton College at Cambridge, had once hoped to marry Patrick. It had been no secret and ended with rather a fizzle. How could Maud watch now as Patrick was meant to marry the Heiress? "Really?"

Lady Avebury sighed. "I saw Mrs. Rainsley last time I was in London. How could I not ask her? We were with them so often during your Season, and they were so nice."

Cecilia did like Maud very much, but she still wasn't sure it was such a fine idea. But her mother was right. The Rainsleys were so kind, they couldn't cut them now.

"Then there's Lord St. John," her mother said. Lord St. John was quite well-known as a roué in London, but he was also a distant cousin, and had been heir to Danby until Patrick came along. Rumor had it he had been rather sour about being displaced, but family was family, and he had to be invited sometimes no matter how irritating he could be.

Her mother named a few others, all usual guests at Danby.

"Who are you putting in the Green Chamber?" Lord Avebury asked. The Green Chamber was the grandest room in the house, where the last king, Edward, had stayed when he visited.

Her mother gave him an aghast look. "Miss Clarke, of course! Who else? She will adore it."

Cecilia thought of the Green Chamber, which was beautiful to be sure, but also drafty. And Americans had all that lovely central heating and heavenly hot water. She did love Danby, but it had always been her home, what she was used to. Would an American heiress be impressed by it?

Then again, "Countess of Avebury" did have a rather nice sparkle to it.

Her mother straightened her pile of lists with a brisk movement. "I must speak to Mrs. Frazer about the menus, and then I will run some errands in the village. Cecilia, you will come with me."

Cecilia knew it wasn't a request. She gulped down the last of her chocolate for fortification. "Of course, Mama."

"And Clifford, you will see to the wine," Lady Avebury said.

"Of course, my dear."

Her gaze turned stern. "*Today.*"

He sighed. "Of course, my dear. Today."

Chapter Two

I don't know where I'm meant to get such supplies at the last minute!" Mrs. Frazer exclaimed as she looked over Lady Avebury's new menus. "Fresh raspberries, and turtles. Turtles! Why her ladyship has to change her mind, when the courses were all decided . . ."

"Have we even made turtle soup before?" Pearl, her head kitchen maid, asked, as she put the finishing touches on the mint sauce for the family's dinner. "I don't remember it."

"It's very fashionable now; they say they have it in America, at Newport, for every fine dinner," Mrs. Caffey, the housekeeper, said with a sigh. She, too, had an updated list, moving guests around between the chambers when it had seemed all was finalized days before. "I'm sure she just wants Miss Clarke to feel welcome."

Mrs. Frazer gave a snort. "And she wouldn't have felt welcome with my famous crab vichyssoise? I don't even know where to find this many turtles at the last minute."

"Perhaps Paul could be sent on the train to London tomorrow to make a last-minute order?" Mrs. Caffey suggested.

Mr. Redvers rushed into the kitchen with the evening papers in his hands, ready to iron the newsprint for Lord Avebury. His lordship liked to know all the very latest news and so was brought the papers as soon as they arrived, for a glance before dinner. Redvers frowned when he saw Mrs. Sumter, the lady's maid, was already at the iron with Lady Avebury's dinner gown.

"Paul and James, as head footmen, will be far too busy tomorrow when the guests start arriving, and they can't be spared for any jaunts to London," Redvers said.

"Then how am I supposed to make this bloomin' soup with no turtles?" Mrs. Frazer cried, slamming down the lid to a saucepan. "I can't be doing with all this nonsense at my age!"

"I'm sure Collins can go," Redvers said quickly, exchanging a long glance with Mrs. Caffey. They were long used to Mrs. Frazer's sudden tempers but also fully aware that she was always being lured by other employers. Employers who might have smaller households and offer greater freedom with menus, not to mention larger budgets. That couldn't happen, not when Danby was renowned for its good food. "Is that not what chauffeurs are for?"

Collins had not been long at Danby, only since Lord Avebury insisted on replacing the carriages with a new motorcar. It was still a controversial event belowstairs.

"He'll have to be on hand to fetch the guests from the station," Mrs. Caffey said. "I think the Rainsleys are due on the nine forty-five. Mrs. Solent is bringing her own car."

Redvers sighed. "I suppose Paul *can* go, then, if he takes the very earliest train and doesn't tarry. Will that give you time to finish the dish, Mrs. Frazer?"

Mrs. Frazer sniffed. "I suppose it'll have to. He can go to the greengrocer while he's there, too; there won't be enough raspberries in the village, and the pineapples from our hothouses are getting low."

"Where am I supposed to go?" Paul asked, coming in to look for his extra white gloves in the sideboard drawer. Paul, like most footmen, was tall and handsome, with glossy dark hair and broad shoulders, but he was sometimes forgetful. The rumor was he had once aspired to be a boxer, but his mother was ill and needed steadier financial support. It was also whispered he was courting Rose, but no one knew for sure.

"To London, my lad, but it's no pleasure jaunt," Redvers said sternly. "You are to fetch a selection of turtles for Mrs. Frazer's soup, and perhaps an order of fruit, and come right back. You'll be required to help with the luggage in the afternoon. And fix that loose button on your waistcoat immediately."

Paul looked rather cheerful at the prospect of a London trip, even if it was a flying one. Mrs. Sumter finished her ironing and held up the burgundy-red silk for a critical study.

"All done, Mr. Redvers," she said, just as the bell sounded for Lady Avebury's room, summoning her. "You should probably send Rose up to Lady Cecilia, too."

"I'm on my way," Rose cried, rushing past with a freshly laundered pair of evening gloves. She paused to throw a smile at Paul, who grinned back.

Mr. Redvers laid the papers out for a quick going-over with the still-warm iron. He gave Mrs. Caffey a rueful smile. "I do worry that we haven't had a large party here at Danby in some time. We're all quite out of practice."

Mrs. Caffey smiled in return. She and Redvers had worked together for years, since they were just footman and kitchen maid, and could usually read each other's thoughts. "It's true things have been rather quiet in the last year or so, especially since Lady Cecilia made her come-out in London and not here. But surely, it's like riding a horse? Once you've learned how, you never forget it. Or so I've heard. I don't think I've ever been on a horse."

"Don't worry, Mr. Redvers, we won't let you down," Paul said, sewing on his button with clumsy stitches.

Redvers scowled at him. "You certainly will if you don't

put that button right-side-up. The Bates crest is going in the wrong direction entirely." He bent his head back to his task—and suddenly froze.

"Is something amiss, Mr. Redvers?" Mrs. Caffey asked.

"I—what was the name of Miss Clarke's ship, Mrs. Caffey?" he asked in a strangled voice.

Concerned, Mrs. Caffey quickly shuffled through the papers in her pocket. "The *Galatea*. Why?"

Mr. Redvers held up the newspaper. The stark, black headline read—"*Galatea* Sunk!"

❧

Cecilia sat at the piano, trying to plink out a bit of Mozart as they waited for dinner to be announced. Music wasn't one of her favorite things, despite all her excellent governess's efforts, but there had to be something to pass the time. She didn't dare go close to her mother, who was muttering over her lists again. After a day of thinking about nothing but party errands, Cecilia wasn't sure she could face it.

She studied the room as she mangled a bit of the étude. Since it was only the family, they had gathered in the yellow music room before dinner rather than the grand White Drawing Room, which was being prepared for the party. Cecilia didn't mind at all; much like the breakfast room, the music room was smaller, more cheerful, especially with a fire crackling in the white-painted fireplace against the howl of the wind outside the windows. The yolk-yellow brocade walls and draperies were set off by yellow-and-white-striped upholstery, a coral-and-gold rug, and light flower paintings on the walls.

Besides the piano and a harp that Cecilia also could barely play, there was a backgammon table, card tables, and little nooks for quiet conversation. Her mother's portrait as a debutante hung over the fireplace, a fluffy confection of white tulle, pink ribbons, and pearls, topped with a twinkling smile. Cecilia glanced over at her mother now, with her beautiful face all worried, her hand tensely stroking the fur of her old spaniel dog, and wondered where that girl had gone. Cecilia sighed. No wonder she was so reluctant to get married herself. It just seemed to bring anxiety.

A log fell with a crackle in the grate, and the spaniel let out a great snore and rolled over on Lady Avebury's lap. Patrick didn't even look up from his book.

"Where are those blasted newspapers already?" Lord Avebury muttered.

"I'm sure they are on their way," Lady Avebury muttered distractedly. "Though why you want to ruin your evenings with bad tidings, I do not know. Patrick, darling, don't you want to look over the arrangements for the party? I should so like your opinions on the games I've organized. Are tennis, croquet, and archery quite enough? Miss Clarke can always borrow my mare, too, if she's inclined to ride."

Patrick blinked at her over the edge of his book, as if

she had just shaken him awake out of a dream. Poor Patrick, Cecilia thought. He usually did look like that, as if startled to find himself in the real world. He was certainly a very handsome young man, taking after their mother with his curling dark hair and pale, finely chiseled features. Between that and the Avebury title, it was no wonder girls so often mooned over him, even the very intelligent Maud Rainsley. But he usually lived in his own little world. It would take a strong wife to manage him and look after Danby.

Maybe American blood was just what he needed.

"I don't know why you ask me that, Mama," Patrick said. "You know that I have no idea about games. I'm sure your guests will enjoy whatever you choose."

"*Our* guests, darling," Emmaline said tightly. "They are to be *our* guests, especially dear Miss Clarke. Your father did work so hard to get her to accept this invitation."

Lord Avebury harrumphed. He had met Mr. Clarke, the famous Annabel's father, when the American banker had been on a visit to London and come to Lord Avebury's club. Clifford had said the man was rather a bore, could only talk about money and food, though he had a fine taste for a good claret. But Mr. Clarke was a widower from a place called San Francisco and had a motherless daughter who was eager to see England and "make new friends" there.

After a thorough investigation of the Clarkes, finding their finances to be sound and the family respectable, with only a few Clarke cousins who had vanished long ago in Canada, Lady Avebury had issued the invitation for Miss Clarke to visit Danby. And meet Patrick.

Their parents had not even tried to gain Patrick's enthusiasm for the plan first. Not that it would have helped if they did, Cecilia thought. Unless it was a rare plant, Patrick didn't even give it a notice.

"Where are those papers already?" her father growled again, just as the door opened and Redvers appeared with the newspapers in hand, as he did every evening.

Yet his face looked positively as gray as his hair, and he seemed reluctant to give over the papers.

Cecilia's fingers went still on the keys. "Why, Redvers, whatever is the matter?"

Lord Avebury pushed himself up from his chair. "Redvers?"

"I am sorry that the papers are late this evening, my lord, but have you heard of this?" Redvers showed a headline to Lord Avebury.

Cecilia's father turned pale, and even her mother finally looked up from her lists.

"Has it been confirmed?" Lord Avebury asked.

"I thought you would want to call the shipping office yourself, my lord," Redvers said.

"Oh, for heaven's sake, Clifford, what is it?" Lady Avebury cried.

Lord Avebury handed her the paper. "It seems Miss

Clarke's ship has met with a mishap. You are quite right, Redvers, I shall go call the shipping office at once. And perhaps a brandy should be fetched for Lady Avebury?"

Cecilia rushed to her mother's side as Lady Avebury gave a choked gasp. Patrick studied them warily from behind his book.

"I can fetch the brandy," he offered, and Cecilia waved him on his way. She picked up the paper and quickly studied the article for herself.

It seemed the RMS *Galatea* had encountered some sort of engine troubles somewhere off the coast of Ireland and gone down in choppy seas. There was time to launch most of the lifeboats into the cold night, but there were said to be casualties. The number and identity, though, were not mentioned.

"Oh no," Cecilia whispered. She thought of poor Miss Clarke, far from home, cast out on a cold ocean, maybe even hurt. How awful for her!

"All my plans," her mother muttered. "My lovely party . . ."

"Mama," Cecilia said, shocked. "I hardly think a *party* is the thing to worry about now."

Her mother gave her a stern look. "Cecilia. I have spent my whole life working in service to this estate. I will not give up on it now."

Patrick rushed back in with a glass of amber-colored liquid balanced in his hands. He looked very concerned but baffled, as he usually did.

"Perhaps you could send for Sumter, Patrick, so she could see to Mama?" Cecilia suggested. Once their mother had been led away by her maid, Cecilia sat next to Patrick by the fire in awkward silence. Neither of them was at all sure what to do next. Their organized, regimented lives had never encountered a shipwreck before.

"I'm sure Miss Clarke is quite all right and has just not had time to send a telegram in all the confusion," Cecilia said.

"Oh yes," Patrick agreed, in his usual affable but distracted way. "It does say they loaded most of the lifeboats."

"She will be here very soon, then." Cecilia kicked her shoes under the hem of her gown, listening to the crackle of the fire in the heavy silence, trying not to imagine how cold it must be on the open water. "Patrick, dear . . ."

"Yes, Cec?"

"Do you think—that is, do you imagine you might come to *like* Miss Clarke? Once she is here."

Patrick frowned as he seemed to think this over. "Perhaps. As well as I might like anyone else."

Cecilia thought of Maud Rainsley. "As you might have liked Miss Rainsley, before she went to Girton?"

Patrick frowned. "Maud is nice, but she has her own work to do. She wouldn't want to take on Danby."

Cecilia wasn't too sure about that. She had been rather sure Maud was quite fond of Patrick. "You think Miss Clarke *would* want to take on Danby?"

"Mama and Papa seem to think so. I guess we'll see

about that." He gave her a rueful, crooked smile. "We both know I'll need a solid sort to keep me tethered to the ground, Cec. I'd never be able to manage Danby on my own."

Cecilia feared that was true. Patrick was so often up in the clouds somewhere, or rather down on the ground with his plants. She gently patted his hand, and they sat in silence again until their father returned. His face looked tired but not sad.

"She is quite safe," Lord Avebury said. "And, it seems, insisting on taking the train here tomorrow as planned. Your mama's party can go on."

"That's good news, Papa," Cecilia answered. But from the look on her brother's face, she wasn't really so sure.

Chapter Three

Jane Hughes huddled deeper under the blankets of her train berth as she listened to the endless *clack clack clack* of the wheels, roaring onward into the night. She squeezed Jack, her new cat, closer, and tried to find comfort in his warm softness, his steady purrs. His presence was a small shield against the terrors of the night. Sleep was out of the question.

Had they only been put on the train a few hours ago? It felt like a hundred years, or maybe just a moment. Time hadn't made any sense at all since the ship sank and hurtled them all out in the endless, icy water in those tiny boats. It all seemed fragmented, like that old kaleidoscope her brothers had when they were small. One turn, and she was helping Miss Clarke change her clothes for bed. Another, and they were turned out of their berths by a great, screeching lurch. Another, and they were adrift in the night.

One more turn, and here she was. Plucked off the rescue ship in Liverpool and dropped onto a train, headed for Yorkshire. Who even knew where such a place was? It sounded like wilderness. Once, maybe last week, though it seemed so long ago, Jane had happily imagined herself exploring London. Parks, museums, Madame Tussauds, ghosts in the Tower, seeing the king and queen—how exciting it all sounded! Like a dream come true for a poor girl like her.

Now there was just the clack of this train, the dark night outside the window, the cold and damp.

"I should never have left New Jersey," she whispered to Jack, who rrr-ed softly in return.

New Jersey hadn't been so bad, had it? At least it was familiar. Dad's work at the greengrocer's, her mother's homemade dumplings, her brothers being pests. Even the job with old Mrs. Heseltine, before the hotel, hadn't been so bad. Jane had gone there after she left school, starting in the kitchen, and eventually becoming an upstairs maid until the job came open at a hotel in Manhattan.

She never would have gone so high or had so many chances in a proper Society house in Newport. She would have stayed a kitchen maid. But Mrs. Heseltine was quite elderly, living a quiet life in her old house bought by her late husband's steel money out in the countryside. She rarely gave parties anymore and never went out. She was a forgetful lady, prone to losing things, but nice. She told Jane stories of what life was like in olden days, when Mrs. Astor ruled New York City, and taught her about being a lady's maid. Dressing hair, choosing the right clothes. Keeping secrets.

Jane sighed and rolled over in her train berth. She'd certainly learned a lot from Mrs. Heseltine, and missed her, though truth be told she'd also been relieved when the lady decided to go live with her son and closed up the big house. It was time for new adventures. Full of excitement, Jane had headed for New York, even though her mother insisted she would do better to come home to the family apartment and find a nice boy to marry.

Jane didn't want to marry. Not yet. She was sure there were adventures to be had first.

And she had been right, just not quite as she had hoped. All the great houses of Manhattan already had plenty of maids. But Jane was able to find a place in a hotel. A nice hotel, solid and prosperous, but still a hotel. Sweeping up people's messes in the bath chamber, avoiding men's grabby hands in the halls, and carrying sheets and towels to the steaming laundry wasn't what she really wanted to do with her life. The only bright part was that she sometimes did the ladies' hair and helped them with their gowns.

Then Miss Annabel Clarke arrived.

Whispers said that her father was one of the richest men in San Francisco, all the way in California, into shipping and exports and imports, whatever those were. Everyone at the hotel was so excited when she checked in, waiting for her boat to England. An heiress, from the West Coast! They hardly ever had such glamorous guests. Most of those people went to the Waldorf or the Ritz.

The maids all crowded around behind the main staircase banisters to watch Miss Clarke as she swept in. She certainly *looked* glamorous, Jane had to admit, tall and slender, but with a bosom to be proud of. She had dark-auburn hair, piled atop her head in fashionable curls and topped with a giant, tilted blue satin and net confection of a hat. Her blue-velvet suit, trimmed in white-satin piping and gleaming with pearl buttons, was in the very height of fashion. Maybe even Parisian, Jane speculated, remembering what Mrs. H taught her about tailoring. The bellboys followed her with a small mountain of luggage on their carts.

But Miss Annabel Clarke did not look happy. In fact, she looked as if the entire world was conspiring to make her angry and spoil her day altogether. Her cheeks were flushed bright red, and not from rouge, in Jane's opinion. (Mrs. H had used *plenty* of rouge.) Miss Clarke yanked off her kid glove and rang the bell on the front desk several times, even though the manager was already there, bowing.

"My maid has left me," Miss Clarke declared, as if the girl was a real Benedict Arnold. "I require someone to help me with my clothes and fix my hair. Immediately!" Her voice was high, light, touched with a strange, flat accent.

"I—I'm not sure we have anyone like that available," the

manager stammered. They were, after all, a hotel that catered more to businessmen and Canadian tourist families than grand ladies.

Miss Clarke swept a glare up the staircase, making all the maids gasp and duck. Her green eyes glowed, hard like shining coals. "I'm sure you must have *someone* who can do it. I have had a very long journey, and I require assistance immediately."

So Jane came in. One of the other maids pointed out to the manager that Jane had once worked for a rich lady, and often helped guests with their coiffures, so she was sent up to Miss Clarke's suite. She had never felt so nervous before as she straightened her cap and knocked cautiously at the door.

Miss Clarke opened it herself. She still wore her velvet suit, but she had taken off her hat, and her hair fell past her shoulders in heavy waves. "Yes?" she barked.

"I'm Jane, ma'am," Jane gasped. "I was sent to serve as your maid?"

"Oh good. I'm hopeless at taking care of myself. I've never had to do it." Miss Clarke pulled Jane into the room and slammed the door behind her, as if Jane was truly caught. "I hope you know what you're doing. The last girl was utterly hopeless, and I do have standards."

And so she did. That first evening, preparing Miss Clarke's rose-scented bath, laying out her dinner gown, and fixing her masses of hair, made Jane feel more stupid and clumsy than she ever had before in her life. Miss Clarke rapped out orders and became angry when they weren't followed immediately. Even the act of choosing a pair of shoes required shouting.

Yet the next day, Miss Clarke asked for Jane again, and once she took up the lady's breakfast tray, things went a little smoother. Jane chose a morning ensemble that was deemed "acceptable," went shopping with Miss Clarke on Fifth Avenue, arranged for the packages to be sent back to the hotel, and helped Miss Clarke change into a filmy, pistachio-green chiffon tea dress for a repast in her suite. The dress had proved not to fit quite correctly over the shoulders or in the hem, and Jane fixed it, tending the delicate chiffon and lace so the stitches couldn't even be seen.

As she dressed Miss Clarke's hair that evening, the lady studied her in the mirror with those strange glowing-green eyes. "You know, Jane, I'm meant to be leaving for England on the *Galatea* in two days."

"Yes, Miss Clarke," Jane answered, trying not to burn off the auburn curl she had wrapped around the tongs.

"I'm meant to meet a great gentleman, a lord who owns a large estate, and see if I want to marry him. If he is handsome and charming enough, I might do it," Miss Clarke said. "But I need a maid for the journey and to go with me to Danby Hall. Would you do it? I don't have time to find anyone else."

Jane stared at Miss Clarke in astonishment—until she

smelled hair burning. Her, Jane Hughes, go to England? To a great lord's estate? So many wondrous images flashed through her mind then. She had read about England in borrowed books so many times! Of course, she wasn't entirely sure about Miss Clarke. She was bossy and persnickety. But when else would Jane have the chance to go to *England*? To see so much of the world?

So she said yes, and two days later was aboard the ship with Miss Clarke, her parents' warnings ringing in her ears. She was too young to go so far away! Only eighteen. What if she didn't like it there? What if she never found someone to marry?

But she had to go.

The voyage had been all right, after the initial queasiness. Jane tried not to look at all that endless water, tried not to really imagine where they were—in the middle of nowhere. She was usually kept too busy to worry about it all. Miss Clarke was a most exacting employer, very choosy about her clothes and inclined to shout and toss shoes when she didn't like something, which was all the time.

But an evening flirting in the dining saloon and cardroom always seemed to mellow Miss Clarke, and by bedtime she would tell Jane stories about the heir to Lord Avebury, who would soon marry her and make her the lady of Danby Hall. It all seemed like a fairy tale, one Jane got to play a tiny part in.

Finding Jack, a skinny, marmalade stowaway of a cat, in

the galley behind the second-class dining room, helped Jane feel less lonely on the ocean, too. He was adrift, just like she was, trying to find a place, and they took to each other right away. Miss Clarke didn't even seem to really notice Jane sneaking bits of food into her tiny cabin. Late at night, she would whisper secret hopes and fears to Jack as he purred peacefully on her lap.

She never expected for things to end as they had. For the fairy tale to go all awry. Jane squeezed Jack tighter as she listened to the mournful train whistle and closed her eyes.

"Jane," she heard Miss Clarke whisper. "Are you awake?"

"Yes, ma'am." Jane opened her eyes and peered down over the edge of her bunk. Miss Clarke slept in the lower berth, and Jane saw in the dim light that she had pulled the sheets up to her chin. Her braid of hair was dark against the stiff white linen.

Miss Clarke had loudly proclaimed her own fearlessness throughout their ordeal, being more angry about the loss of all her fine trunks than anything else. But Jane had noticed that, like herself, her employer wasn't sleeping much lately.

"I'm afraid I'll dream it all over again," Jane confided.

"It's all behind us now," Miss Clarke said firmly. "Danby Hall is ahead, that's all."

"Will you tell me about it again, ma'am?" Jane asked, hoping for distraction. "The lovely big house."

Jane knew Miss Clarke had never actually seen this Danby Hall, no more than Jane herself had, but she did tell the nicest stories about it. Its grandeur and history, its beautiful gardens, the glamorous parties it hosted. Parties Annabel Clarke would soon preside over. And Jane would be lady's maid to a countess. Someday.

When Jane closed her eyes, she was sure she could picture it all. A future that was not at all like what happened there on that dark sea. Danby Hall would mean beauty and, above all, safety. Jane was sure of it.

Chapter Four

Cecilia was very glad to escape the house early the next day, before her mother could track her down and make her help with those infernal lists. There had only been her father at breakfast; Patrick was wisely in hiding. Cecilia even had to slip through a side door, for Redvers was overseeing an army of maids and footmen as they put the finishing touches on the grand staterooms. The air of the house was thick with beeswax polish and the heady gardenias and white roses of the new floral arrangements.

But the breeze outside was fresh and clear, the dew of morning still on the grass of the lawn, an early mist clinging to the edges of the hedgerows. Cecilia breathed deeply as she hurried ahead on the path, trying not to break into a run. At least until she was out of sight of the windows, and any of her mother's ladylike-behavior spies.

She hurried up the winding gravel drive, perfectly laid out by her great-grandfather to reveal the house only in glimpses between trees and Italian statues, until a carriage turned one last corner and revealed Danby in all its pale stone and red brick glory. Even now, when more guests roared up the drive in motorcars than ambled along in carriages, the effect was stunning.

Cecilia didn't look back at it, though. She turned out of the wrought iron gates, gilded and topped with the Bates coat of arms, and went toward the village. The road was empty, except for the faint cheeps of birds hiding in the hedges, and Cecilia skipped a little, singing along with them. She was free!

At least for a little while.

She twirled around, until her blue beret flew off her head and landed on a low tree branch. She snatched it up and felt in the pocket of her tweed jacket to make sure the list was still there. The list of errands was her ticket to the morning's freedom. Nothing too complicated; a few foodstuffs Mrs. Frazer had forgotten, more flowers for the bedchambers, an advertisement to leave for a new footman. Maybe there would be time to stop at the bookshop. Usually, her mother would only order delicacies and blossoms from London, but the Heiress was truly arriving that day, and there was no time to lose to make everything perfect.

At the crossroads, where one direction led to the Byswaters' estate and the other to the village, she paused and studied the landscape around her. It was truly a lovely day, pale sunshine in a slate-blue sky, the fields stretching past stone walls in a patchwork of dark green and gray. If Miss Clarke didn't think the neighborhood was lovely, Cecilia didn't know what was wrong with her.

Cecilia frowned. Even if she and her mother sometimes argued, even if Cecilia chafed to be free, she did understand her mother's worries. Understood what drove her. Cecilia loved that land, too, loved their home and the history of it all. But surely, there had to be another way to save it all without sacrificing the Bates children's happiness?

She sighed, realizing she didn't have the answers. She didn't have *any* answers. Not yet. She only had her errands.

She spun around and hurried down the lane toward the village. As she drew closer, the road was no longer deserted. Other pedestrians, a few carts and horses, and one motorcar passed her, their drivers calling out greetings. Cecilia waved back and paused at the edge of the village green to double-check her list.

The green was the center of everything, with a granite obelisk of a war memorial surrounded by benches and pathways, and shops lined up behind it in winding rows of gray Yorkshire stone and slate roofs. Her first stop was to be Mrs. Mabry's grocery, to put in Mrs. Frazer's order for delivery.

"Oh yes, we have those in stock, luckily. Enough for one

dinner anyway," Mrs. Mabry said with her usual twinkling smile, studying the list. "I can have it to Danby this afternoon, my lady."

"Wonderful, thank you, Mrs. Mabry. You have saved Mrs. Frazer's canapes!" Cecilia said. "May I also put this notice in your window? Mama says we are in dire need of a new footman."

"Of course, my lady." Mrs. Mabry tilted her head thoughtfully. "Perhaps I could speak to my sister? She does say her son, my nephew, is looking for a position. He's a handsome, strong lad, if I do say so myself, and smart."

"That sounds perfect. Have him apply to Mrs. Caffey, the sooner the better." Cecilia left her notice and went to the florist's shop across the street. She could see that Mr. Smithfield was quite flustered by the last-minute order, and declared he would have no roses left after sending them all to Danby, but he could make the delivery by evening. By the time she left his sweet-scented rooms, the village was much busier, the window seats of the tea shop full, people streaming into the Crown and Shield pub for lunch.

The bells of the old Norman St. Swithin's Church tolled the hour, and Cecilia realized she did have a little time left before she had to return to Danby. She stopped to buy a currant bun at the Misses Moffat's tea shop and eagerly turned toward the bookshop.

Mr. Hatcher's shop was nearly her favorite place in all the world. Dimly lit, faintly musty, crowded with overflowing shelves and teetering piles of volumes old and new. She could happily get lost in there for hours.

But today she had only a few precious moments.

Mr. Hatcher glanced up from a crate he was unpacking, and a smile broke across his gray-bearded, bespectacled face. Mr. Hatcher always matched his shop—a bit shabby, a bit careless looking, his gray hair too long and unkempt, but with a mind filled with treasures.

"Lady Cecilia!" he said, dusting his hands off on his apron. "Such a nice surprise to see you here today. I didn't expect you with all the commotion up at Danby."

"Oh yes, there is much to keep us busy at home today," she answered with a laugh. "I managed to escape with a few errands. Anything new today, Mr. Hatcher?"

"I'm just unpacking this arrival from London. A fresh volume of poetry from Rudyard Kipling, and one from Ezra Pound, very new. Some of my customers think he is rather shocking."

Cecilia hadn't heard of Ezra Pound, but "shocking" sounded just like what she wanted to read. She knelt down beside the crate in a slapdash, unladylike manner she knew her mother wouldn't approve of and glanced through the books.

"I think you might enjoy Mr. Pound's work, Lady Cecilia. Much to ponder."

"Then I'll take it, along with the Kipling. Do you have any new studies on botany I could bring to my brother?"

They happily sorted through the volumes in companionable silence. "What's the news in the village, Mr. Hatcher?" She knew that Mr. Hatcher's careless exterior concealed a brain that missed nothing. From behind his dusty window, he saw everything that happened in the village. She did wonder what they all thought about an American as the next Countess of Avebury.

"Oh, very little, Lady Cecilia. You know us," Mr. Hatcher said. "Mrs. Mabry's terrier escaped, but he was found again, going for a swim in the pond at Mattingly Farm. Colonel Havelock wasn't best pleased. The draper's shop is expanding, which I'm sure Lady Avebury would appreciate, and a new shop is going in next door, but it's all very mysterious. And the Misses Moffat caused a scandal by serving blueberry buns rather than currant last week."

Cecilia laughed. "Shocking! I must buy several to take home today."

Mr. Hatcher suddenly looked serious. "I did wonder about something, though."

Cecilia leaned closer, intrigued. "What is it, Mr. Hatcher?"

"A stranger has been seen around, maybe two or three times, but that's enough to cause comment in such a small community. He bought some provisions at Mrs. Mabry's store, and even she could get no information out of him. He paid fully, in cash, and she thinks he has a West London accent, but he gave no name."

"A stranger?" They did sometimes have tourists in the

neighborhood, looking for relics of the Brontës, mostly, or to gawk at grand houses like Danby, but they were usually inclined to be talkative. "Is he not staying at the Crown and Shield?"

Mr. Hatcher shook his head. "No one knows where he's staying. But he's been seen at the Byswaters' and Mr. Jermyn the lawyer's office."

Was he involved in the Byswaters' attempts to buy Danby? "What does he do there?"

Mr. Hatcher shrugged. "No one knows."

"How strange." Outsiders usually did not stay in the neighborhood very long, or hide their business so well. They were a small neighborhood. "I will keep my eyes open, thank you, Mr. Hatcher."

When she left the shop with her new books, she glanced carefully around the green, looking for any spying strangers. She saw only the usual villagers, nannies pushing their charges in prams, men headed back to their offices. Mr. Brown, the young vicar, who tilted his hat to her as he made his way through the lych-gate of St. Swithin's. Not for the first time, she had quite lost track of time in Mr. Hatcher's bookshop and would have to hurry to get back to Danby before she was missed.

Outside Mrs. Mabry's grocery, a man stood in the doorway, his arms crossed as he studied the street. Cecilia almost stumbled on the cobblestones when she saw him. Surely, such a man was too handsome to be real? Too tall, too broad in the shoulders beneath his rough blue wool coat, too golden-blond, too—everything. More like a god in a Norse saga, or some European *duc* with dastardly designs in one of the romantic French novels Mr. Hatcher sometimes secretly ordered for her.

Wait a minute. Cecilia froze, staring at the man. What if *he* was the mysterious stranger lurking about the village lately? She had certainly never seen him before. She would most assuredly have remembered. Watching him carefully, she started to cross the street.

He stood up straight, his arms falling at his sides. "Lady Cecilia Bates?" he called, his voice cool and clear, slightly touched at the edges with a rougher accent.

Cecilia gaped at him. "Yes?"

He smiled, a warm, flashing, cheeky sort of grin. He seemed to have no sense of the awkwardness of the morning as he bowed to her. A few people had stopped on the walkway to discreetly watch.

"I'm Jesse Fellows," he said. "Mrs. Mabry is my aunt."

"Is she?" Cecilia said, puzzled.

"She said you might be needing an extra footman up at Danby."

"Oh yes! Of course." Cecilia suddenly remembered her earlier errand, to place the notice for a new footman. "We do have rather a lot of guests arriving soon."

"I can start whenever you like, my lady," he said with a smile, wide and white and distinctly un-servant-like. "I've been working waiting tables at a London restaurant. Surely, it can't be all that different."

"I'm not sure," Cecilia said uncertainly, a little dazzled by that smile. "You must ask to see Mrs. Caffey, then. She will put you to work right away." She gave him a quick smile, but she knew she had to run away. If she kept looking at his Viking handsomeness, she would break into uncontrollable giggles. "Just ask at the back doorway, through the kitchen garden."

"Thank you, my lady. Much obliged." His grin widened, turned cheeky. "May I say I have your recommendation?"

Completely at a loss for words, Cecilia could only spin around and dash as fast as she could out of the village, her cheeks feeling as if they were on fire.

❧

She was so distracted that she didn't even recognize until it was too late the unfortunate fact that her grandmother was outside the dower house at the edge of the village.

"Ladies do *not* run, Cecilia!" the dowager countess barked. "I know your governess was not the most attentive of souls, but she surely told you that."

Cecilia stumbled on the cobblestones, cursing herself for not paying attention. She knew better than to pass her grandmother's house without being properly prepared. She should never have let that good-looking footman distract her!

Cecilia pasted a smile on her face, prayed she did not

look *too* out of sorts, and turned to face her grandmother. The Dowager Lady Avebury had apparently been in the midst of lecturing her gardener, because the poor man was now tiptoeing off around the side of the house with a most relieved look on his face. The dowager was making her way to the low stone wall of her front garden, all gray silk, gray pearls, gray pompadour of hair, waving her walking stick at Cecilia.

Anyone who did not know her would surely look at her and think, *What an adorable old dear!* Petite, plump, dressed in the lace and pearls of her Victorian youth, she looked so harmless. So sweet.

But Cecilia knew better. Her grandmother was sharp as a razor, and she knew *everything* that happened in a fifty-mile radius. She probably even knew everything that happened in London, as long as it had to do with people in Society.

"Grandmama," Cecilia said, still gritting her teeth in a smile. "You look well today."

"Do not try to cozen me, dear. Where are you off to in such a hurry?"

Cecilia knew she couldn't escape. She kissed her grandmother's powdered cheek over the wall. "I was late returning to Danby. Mama sent me to the village on an errand."

"Ah yes. I hear all is in confusion today, everyone racing about like rabbits. In *my* day, discipline was more strictly enforced. All was in readiness at a moment's notice. Your mother's nerves are affecting her again, I suppose." The dowager studied Cecilia carefully with those bright turquoise-blue eyes that saw everything. "Has our Miss Clarke arrived yet?"

"Not yet. Later this evening. And I don't think she's *our* Miss Clarke. We haven't even met her."

Her grandmother pursed her lips. "Oh, she will be ours soon enough. No American could resist Danby in full fig. And Patrick always does what he is told, I'll say that much for the boy. I just received a note asking me to come to luncheon tomorrow for a look at the girl." She gave a deep sigh.

"You don't have much hope for Miss Clarke, do you, Grandmama?"

"My dear, she is an American. I remember well their last invasion, Consuelo Marlborough and their ilk. How loudly they laughed! It still makes my head ache."

Cecilia thought of the missing artwork on Danby's faded silk walls, the leaking patches of the roof, the overgrown gardens. No matter how loud Miss Clarke's laugh might be, Cecilia was sure it wouldn't matter. "Perhaps she will be nice."

The dowager snorted. "Nice! Oh, Cecilia. You always were far too optimistic for your own good in this world. You must take your grandmama's advice—go to London as soon as possible, and find a suitable match for yourself. A good, strong, steady Englishman. You won't want to live at the mercy of such a sister-in-law when you are older."

Cecilia rather thought she didn't want to live at the mercy of *anyone*, but there was not much she could do about it at the moment. "Thank you, Grandmama. Solid advice, indeed."

The dowager rapped her stick against the wall. "Don't be cheeky with me, young lady! You know I am right. You are not a child any longer, Cecilia." She handed over a basket filled with her prize-winning pink and white roses. "Now, give these to your mother and tell her to put them in Miss Clarke's chamber. I assume she is in the Green Chamber? We might as well put our best foot forward. They are blooming early this year, thankfully."

"Thank you, Grandmama. They are exquisite, as always." Cecilia buried her nose in the heady, velvety scent, and she suddenly remembered what she had heard in the village shops. "Grandmama, have you perchance seen a stranger around the village lately?"

Her grandmother's blue gaze sharpened, and her nose quivered as if she scented gossip on the breeze. "What manner of stranger?"

"Mr. Hatcher said he has been seen about, just watching. Dressed respectably, London accent, but no one knows his business or has seen him before. It seems he isn't staying at the Crown and Shield. I just wondered if any of your friends had a son or nephew visiting the neighborhood."

The dowager frowned in thought. "Not that I know of, though I can certainly ask Lady Lortmane or Mrs. Williamson when next we play bridge. What on earth would someone be doing lurking about here? No one comes to this village on purpose."

"I just thought it was a bit odd. Well, I must be going, Grandmama. I will see you tomorrow at luncheon."

Cecilia kissed her grandmother one more time and hurried away, back toward Danby. She wondered about someone lurking about the village, their business unknown. Mrs. Mabry's handsome nephew suddenly appearing. Miss Clarke arriving. Strange things did seem to be afoot lately at Danby.

Chapter Five

Aunt Maggie!" Cecilia cried as she stepped into the music room and found that guests were already arriving at Danby. At least Mrs. Solent, her mother's best friend, was already there, sipping tea with Lady Avebury. "How wonderful to see you."

"And you, Cecilia darling," Aunt Maggie said, kissing Cecilia's cheek. Like Cecilia's mother, Aunt Maggie was tall and slim, but her life of travel left her skin slightly touched with gold, her hair lightened to a gray-touched honey-blond. Her dark eyes sparkled from under her large brown-velvet hat. "My, but you are quite blooming since I last saw you! How quickly you have grown up."

"It's been ages since we've seen you! And speaking of blooms . . ." Cecilia handed her mother the basket of roses, only slightly tousled after her quick run home. "Grandmama sent these. She says you must put them in Miss Clarke's room."

Her mother scowled, as if the fragrant blossoms were moldy leaves. "But I have already put orchids in there!"

"Ah, English roses." Aunt Maggie sighed. "How it makes one think of home. I've missed their perfume this year. These must be early. How clever of the dowager countess."

"Where have you been traveling this time, Aunt Maggie?" Cecilia asked eagerly. She sat down and reached for the teapot, excited to have a drink and hear all about Aunt Maggie's adventures. They were always so wondrously different from the restricted routine at Danby.

"Cecilia, you have no time for tea," her mother snapped. "Go and change your clothes. Miss Clarke will be here at any moment."

Aunt Maggie gave her a sympathetic smile. "I have been to Egypt, my darling. And to Moscow. And then Greece. I will tell you all about it later. And I might have left you a wee giftie on your dressing table."

"Oh, Aunt Maggie, thank you!" Cecilia took one gulp of tea, shoved a raspberry biscuit in her mouth, and rushed out of the room before her mother could reprimand her. Behind her, she heard her mother say, "Is it true that you met Mr. Hayes on your travels, Mags?"

Aunt Maggie laughed. "Oh, Emmaline, my dear, you have no idea! *Such* a rascal. I saw him on a *dahabiya* on the Nile . . ."

But Cecilia had no time to eavesdrop on delicious gossip about their guests. She had to hurry if she was going to be presentable for the Heiress.

The *shipwrecked* Heiress. Danby was just going to be full of adventurous tales in the next few days.

Rose was waiting in her chamber, laying out a pale-green and cream-lace afternoon dress. Cecilia found Aunt Maggie's package on the dressing table and eagerly tore off the tissue paper. It was a small alabaster statue of one of the maidens of the Erechtheion near the Parthenon, her tiny face and the drapes of her chiton perfect.

"Lovely." She sighed. She set it carefully next to a vase of violets and wondered wistfully if she would ever see such places herself. Ever go anywhere or discover anything.

"Are these shoes the right ones, my lady?" Rose asked.

Cecilia sighed and turned away from the thought of exotic travels. "Yes, quite right, thank you, Rose."

Rose had barely fastened her into the dress, and started to tidy Cecilia's windblown hair, when a knock sounded at the door. "The car has just turned in at the gates, my lady," Mrs. Caffey called.

"Thank you, Mrs. Caffey, I'll be right there!" Cecilia grabbed up her pearl necklace and clasped it around her neck as she dashed out and down the gallery. She barely had time to salute Ralph as she ran by.

The grand foyer was empty as she hurried through, but

she could smell the fresh scent of lemon polish, covered by the perfume of lilies and carnations, as if the servants had just bustled out.

The foyer, almost more than any other part of Danby, seemed to have been built expressly to awe guests, and it was polished to within an inch of its marble life for the Heiress, after being rather neglected for months. The pale, carved stone of the walls gleamed, the blue inlay of the dome as fresh as the sky, and the Bates coat of arms over the door was regilded to shine. By the door to the drawing room, the tall blue-and-white Chinese vases brought back by her great-great-grandfather stood sentinel.

It was all chilly, pale, wintry grandeur. Cecilia almost felt sorry for Miss Clarke, stepping into such a cold place after being lost at sea.

Cecilia hurried outside to where everyone was gathered on the marble steps, the maids and footmen in their best crisp black-and-white, Redvers inspecting them carefully. Her parents and Patrick were at the foot of the curved steps, next to the red carpet laid out for Miss Clarke. Lady Avebury straightened Patrick's cravat, frowning as she studied his appearance.

"You look quite nice, Patrick," Cecilia said as she joined them. And he did, in his dark-blue suit and burgundy waistcoat that was far nicer than the old tweeds and patched dungarees he usually wore in his laboratory.

Patrick fidgeted as their mother smoothed his hair, just as she had when they were children and were presented to her at teatime by Nanny. Nanny's standards in tiny children's hair had never been high enough for Lady Avebury.

Then she turned her attention to Cecilia. "Is *that* what you are wearing?"

Cecilia was rather stung. The green dress was quite a favorite of hers. "I suppose so, Mama, since I'm here now."

Lady Avebury shook her head. "Oh, it's too late now. Just stand up straight, Cecilia, and smile. Everyone smile!"

Just as they snapped into place, with even Patrick pasting a rather worrying semblance of a grin onto his face, the car rolled into view. Cecilia nervously smoothed the lace of her sleeves as she watched it lurch to a halt. Collins, the chauffeur, opened the back door.

The lady who stepped out fit her role perfectly. Cecilia wasn't sure she had ever seen someone so beautiful off the stage. Miss Clarke was statuesque, with masses of glossy auburn hair piled high and topped with a black velvet toque. Her skin was all pink and white, and she had bright, catlike green eyes that narrowed as they swept over the house. She wore a purple suit trimmed with black braid and held a small leather case under her arm. That seemed to be her only luggage.

A smaller young woman, with pale-blond wisps of hair escaping from under her brown felt hat, wearing a simple pale-blue dress and brown coat, hurried to her side, lugging a covered wicker basket. She looked rather lost, and Cecilia felt a spasm of sympathy for both of them.

"Miss Clarke, my dear," Lady Avebury said, coming forward with her most gracious smile. She kissed the Heiress on the cheek. "I am Lady Avebury, but you must call me Emmaline. We are so happy you have arrived unharmed."

"Unharmed!" Miss Clarke exclaimed, in a strange, flat voice, but with a lilt of an accent at the end of her words. "I should say not. I have lost all my luggage. Twenty trunks of gowns and furs, my jewel case, all my hats. It has been quite the trauma. All I have is what I stand up in. There was simply no shopping to be had in Liverpool. I have been utterly crushed by it all."

Cecilia rather thought that being cast adrift on an icy sea at night, seeing people drowned or injured, might be worse than losing a few gowns, which surely a lady like Miss Clarke would only wear once. But there was no accounting for how people behaved when they were in shock, as Cecilia imagined Miss Clarke must be.

"We will call Mrs. Ripton in the village to come in right away and make you a few things while we send for a real couturier from Leeds or even London," Lady Avebury said soothingly. "Mrs. Ripton isn't Paquin, of course, but she is quite clever with the most stylish colors. And you must take all the time you need to rest here at Danby."

Miss Clarke nodded and let Lady Avebury take her arm. "Now, let me introduce you to my family," Emmaline said, her well-practiced smile never flickering. "Lord Avebury you know, or rather your father has met him. We did send him a telegram right away, of course, letting Mr. Clarke know you arrived in England safely."

"I am so pleased to meet you at last, Miss Clarke, and so relieved at your arrival," Lord Avebury said with a small bow. Miss Clarke smiled and batted her enviably sooty lashes at him.

"And this is my daughter, Lady Cecilia," Lady Avebury said. "I am sure you will be the best of friends. I fear I know little of what young people are interested in these days, and Cecilia will be glad to be of assistance!"

"I am sure we will be friends indeed," Miss Clarke answered without much interest.

"I should so love to hear all about America," Cecilia said. "I hope to visit there one day."

"Really?" Miss Clarke gave her a puzzled frown. "Why?"

"And my son, Patrick, Viscount Bellham," Lady Avebury said quickly. With her free hand, she tugged Patrick forward, so fast he stumbled a bit. His face looked rather red as he studied the beauty before him.

"H—how do you do, Miss Clarke?" he stammered.

Miss Clarke quite transformed as she curtsied to him, giggling and tucking in her chin to peek up at him from under her lashes. "I am so very pleased to meet you, Lord

Bellham. Perhaps later you could show me around these beautiful gardens? I am *longing* to know all about your lovely house. So much marvelous history, I'm sure. Where I am from, everything is horribly new."

Patrick swallowed hard and reached up to loosen his cravat. "O—of course. Miss Clarke."

Lady Avebury gave a smug little smile. "Shall we go in? I've ordered some tea, Miss Clarke, and then will show you to your chamber. My friend Mrs. Solent is here, but no one else is due to arrive until tomorrow. That should give you some time to purchase a new dress or two and get some rest."

"This is my maid, Jane," Miss Clarke said, waving a black-gloved hand toward the pale blonde who hovered near the car.

"Mrs. Caffey will see to her," Lady Avebury said.

"Come, miss, let me help you with that," Collins said, taking Jane's wicker basket. She gave him a shy smile in return and pushed some of her frazzled strands of hair back under her felt hat.

Cecilia let her parents go inside first, with Patrick following with Miss Clarke on his arm. Cecilia glanced at the maid as she turned to follow Collins toward the servants' entrance. Jane was staring up at the house with wide eyes, reluctantly handing over her basket. Cecilia glimpsed a pair of green eyes peering out between the slats.

"Oh, a cat," she whispered. How she loved cats! Yet she had never had one, being told cats belonged in the stables, or that they couldn't get along with her mother's spaniel or her father's Labradors. Cats certainly wouldn't get along with Sebastian, her grandmother's terrier-terror.

She would have hurried over for a closer view, but her mother called, "Cecilia! Hurry up, now."

"Coming, Mama." Leaving the cat behind, Cecilia followed the others back up the steps. The heavy front doors closed slowly behind her.

Jane had never seen a place like Danby Hall before, not in real life. It was like something in a storybook, all dark and towering and grand. Everything was marble or gilt or carved wood, with portraits of stern people in glowing satins staring down at her. There was even a suit of armor, lurking in the shadows like something about to come to life and clank through the cold corridors.

Jane gaped at it all, curious and frightened and excited all at the same time. She knew she shouldn't be where she was. After the brisk but kind housekeeper, Mrs. Caffey, showed her to her room in the servants' wing—her very own room!—Mrs. Caffey had taken her to Miss Clarke's chamber to unpack her mistress's meager luggage. Miss Clarke's lodgings were those of a princess—no, a queen. The Green Chamber lived up to its name, with an enormous bed on a platform at one end, all draped in forest-green brocade trimmed with swags of gold fringe. The walls were covered with more green silk, with green-and-cream-striped window draperies, and gilded chairs and settees dotted over the ivy-patterned carpet. A landscape of a forest glade hung over the green granite fireplace. Across one corner stretched a dressing screen painted with green orchids and ribbon swags.

"The Green Chamber," Mrs. Caffey said, casting a careful eye over the arrangements, the green-edged stationery on the desk, the fire in the grate, the perfect fall of the gold-fringed cords on the curtains and the draperies around the tall bed, the orchids and roses. "King William IV stayed here once, as well as Queen Victoria herself, and Edward VII in the last reign. The state bed is two hundred years old."

"It's amazing," Jane gasped. Just think—kings and queens had slept right there!

Mrs. Caffey smiled. "Do come back downstairs when you've finished, Miss Hughes. We have our tea in the servants' hall before serving dinner upstairs. I've brought two or three of her ladyship's gowns that might suit Miss Clarke for dinner. I'm sure you can take in any little modifications that might be needed. I also have a nightdress and dressing gown, and a day dress for breakfast tomorrow. Miss Ripton should arrive quite early in the morning, and she does work swiftly. Now, I will leave you to unpack. Let me know what else Miss Clarke might need."

But it hadn't taken Jane long to unpack the one case, and only then did she realize there was no bathroom attached to the beyond-grand chamber. She knew Miss Clarke would want to wash and would throw quite the fit if hot water wasn't immediately available. Jane peeked outside the door, but she saw no one. She couldn't even hear an echo of a voice anywhere. It was as if she was all alone in that castle of a house.

She ventured out, hoping to at least find a footman to give her directions back to the servants' stairs, but there was nothing. She tried to find her way, but all the carpets, the portraits, the velvet chairs, and Chinese vases all looked alike. That was how she found herself in a sun-washed gallery, and she knew she was utterly lost.

But she couldn't help stopping to stare around her in awe. The tapestries that lined the walls, the portraits of people in embroidered velvets and lace ruffs, the pikes and swords and battle flags, the immense fireplaces and suit of armor, it was like falling back in time.

"Oh, I say, are you lost?"

Startled by the sudden sound of a voice in that empty place out of time, Jane whirled around. A lady stood at the far end of the long, narrow room, tall and slim, almost gawky, with reddish-blond hair falling down over the shoulders of her pale-green gown.

It was Lady Cecilia, the daughter of the house, and she had caught Jane nosing about where she shouldn't be.

"I—I'm sorry, my lady," Jane gasped, bobbing a wobbling curtsy, just as she had been taught. "Yes, I'm afraid I am. Lost, that is."

The lady laughed and hurried closer, her green satin shoes clicking on the wood floor. "No wonder at all. I'm afraid it's all too easy to take a wrong turn. I've lived here all my life, and I still get lost. I'm Lady Cecilia Bates, by the way."

"I'm Jane, my lady. Jane Hughes."

"You're Miss Clarke's lady's maid, aren't you?"

"Yes, my lady."

"Then they've surely put you in your own wing, in that ridiculous Green Chamber. No wonder you got turned around."

"I was looking for a bathroom. Miss Clarke likes a warm bath before dinner."

"Wouldn't we all?" Lady Cecilia said with a laugh. "I'm afraid the closest bathroom is at the opposite end of the corridor from the Green Chamber. When my mother first came to Danby as a bride, she tried her hardest to bring the house into the twentieth century, but she only got so far. It's better, though; there was only *one* bath in the whole house before then. But perhaps Miss Clarke can install one en suite someday? Come on, I'll show you."

Jane followed Lady Cecilia out of the gallery, past the suit of armor. "That's Ralph," Lady Cecilia said merrily. "Never mind him!"

"Begging your pardon, my lady, but what sort of room is this one?"

"This is the oldest part of the house. It was part of the Elizabethan manor house that was originally Danby Hall, or rather Danby Priory, but none of the priory is still here except the chapel, and we seldom use it. Queen Elizabeth gave it to my ancestor after he fought in Ireland. The earldom came later. Part of that house was knocked down in the eighteenth century to make the Palladian residence you see in the front."

Jane shook her head in amazement. "Where I was born, an *old* house might be a hundred years old, and there weren't many of those."

Lady Cecilia gave her a curious glance. "You're American, too, like Miss Clarke?"

"From New Jersey. I worked in Manhattan for a time, but I've never been abroad before. Or anywhere farther west than Pennsylvania!"

"And such a terrible experience, to be shipwrecked on your very first voyage."

Jane shivered, remembering being shoved into the crowded open lifeboat, the icy wind, the screams and shouts, the endless dark of the night. Jack's comforting mews from his basket. Miss Clarke making the two of them row until their hands bled. "It was—not exactly a tea party."

A frown flickered over Cecilia's face. "I would imagine

not." They went down a short flight of stairs and turned onto the corridor leading to the White Drawing Room. "That's my grandmother," Cecilia said, waving her hand at a portrait on the wall. The dowager's painted eyes watched them with disapproval. "Did I see you had a cat earlier? In that basket?"

Jane was nervous. Were they going to make her get rid of Jack, her friend, after all they had been through? "Is—is that against the rules?"

"Not at all," Lady Cecilia said quickly. "Guests bring pets all the time! You should have seen the most ill-tempered Pekingese the Duchess of Salmotran brought! She quite chewed the legs off a Grinling Gibbons table, horrible. I just—well, I love cats, and I've never been allowed to have one, no matter how much I beg." She glanced down to fiddle at her silk skirt, looking far more sad than any girl with a silk skirt had a right to be.

Jane was startled anyone that had the things Lady Cecilia possessed could be sad, but people were people. And everyone deserved a pet to love. "His name is Jack. I found him on the ship. He's very quiet, and smart, and I promise he hardly eats anything."

Cecilia's eyes shone with eagerness as she turned to Jane. "Do you think maybe I could meet him one day, Jane?"

Jane hesitated. Jack was hiding in her room, safe for

now. Should she risk letting him out, letting him be discovered? But Jack might be lonely, too, just like Lady Cecilia. Just like Jane herself. "I think Jack would like that. He's friendly."

"Oh, wonderful!" Lady Cecilia opened a hidden door at the end of the corridor. "Here you are, then, Jane. A bit of a trek from the Green Chamber, but the soaps and bath oils are made right here on the estate, and mostly from my grandmama's own prize-winning roses. I do hope Miss Clarke won't mind."

Jane was afraid Miss Clarke *would* mind. She had put up such a fuss in America when the bathroom wasn't to her liking, and here it was way down the hall. But the towels were thick and perfectly white, the soaps smelled heavenly, and the claw-footed tub was huge. Maybe Miss Clarke would deign to use it. But Jane couldn't say that to this nice young lady, who was working so hard to make even an American maid feel welcome. "It's lovely, Lady Cecilia."

"Now, the Green Chamber is just at the end there; be sure to turn right and not left, or you'll end up in the gallery with Ralph again. You can see it there, just across from that statue of Artemis with her bow? Then when you want to find your own room, just turn right, and across from the staircase is the door to the servants' stairs. It's rather easy to miss, but if you come to the tapestry of the fall of Troy, you've gone too far."

Jane's head was spinning. "Thank you, Lady Cecilia."

"I do hope we'll meet again soon, Jane!" Lady Cecilia waved and hurried away in a flurry of cream lace and lilac perfume, leaving Jane alone in that endless, unknowable house.

Chapter Six

When Cecilia arrived in the White Drawing Room the next day for preluncheon sherry, she found most of the guests were in place. She had skipped breakfast and gone off riding early and missed their arrival, so for the house to be suddenly filled with people was a bit startling. But nice, too; she couldn't remember the last time Danby seemed so alive.

She paused in the doorway, studying the gathering. Miss Clarke wasn't there yet, nor was Patrick, but Redvers and the footmen were passing around tiny glasses of sherry to the various groups, and the room was filled with lively chatter and movement. The laughter blended with the popular music hall tunes Aunt Maggie was playing at the piano, which had been moved in from the music room, making it seem even more like a party atmosphere. Only her grandmama, sitting alone by the window, frowned as she watched it all.

The White Drawing Room was the most formal room in the house, built to greet and impress royalty. True to its name, the paneling was painted pure snow-white, with plasterwork details of palm fronds, swags of ribbon, and fruit spilling out of cornucopias gilded to stand out. Cherubs over the doorways held up the Bates coat of arms, along with those of various Avebury countesses, and a van Dyck of an earlier Bates family hung over the red marble chimneypiece. The sofas and chairs were upholstered in crimson Venetian cut velvet, matching the window draperies.

Usually, the room was shuttered and closed, quiet. Almost haunted. Today, all of that was banished, thanks to the arrival of Miss Clarke.

Cecilia's mother held court in a velvet armchair near the piano, talking to two men who stood beside her. One was Philip Brown, the vicar of St. Swithin's. He was rather young for such a living but was the nephew of a viscount friend of Cecilia's father. He had sent feminine hearts fluttering since he arrived to make the sermons the year before, as he was quite tall and good-looking, with thick, curling light-brown hair and a kind smile. His sermons were short and rather funny, too, always a plus.

The other was a man Cecilia had never met, but she was sure he must be Richard Hayes, the explorer. She had seen his grainy photograph in the newspapers. Very tall and very lean, his skin was sunbrowned and his shock of blond hair bleached almost white, as if he had indeed spent long years trekking through deserts and over tundra. His eyes were a light blue against his bronzed skin, the lines around them carved deep as he smiled. He was dressed differently than the other men, too, in a pale-cream suit and spotted cravat. He laughed loudly, his teeth alarmingly white, and drained the tiny glass of sherry.

He *was* handsome, Cecilia decided, and surely had lots of fascinating tales to tell. But also rather full of himself, as if he was quite sure everyone was watching him.

Her father sat by the fireplace with Mrs. Rainsley and her daughter, Maud. Mrs. R chatted and laughed, oblivious to everything around her except whatever she was saying to the earl, but Maud looked distinctly uncomfortable. A tall, always slightly awkward young lady, not entirely at ease with herself despite the fact that she had lovely golden hair, a clear peaches and cream complexion, and a dazzling intelligence Cecilia very much envied. She was shifting on her feet as she half listened to her mother, fiddling with the trim of her mulberry-colored dress, seemingly deep in her own thoughts. Cecilia remembered that Patrick had said he and Maud could never have made a match. But did Maud agree? Or had she been more fond of him than Cecilia's oblivious brother ever knew?

The music stopped, and Aunt Maggie called out, "Any requests?"

"'Be My Little Baby Bumblebee,'" someone answered with a hearty laugh.

Cecilia turned her head to see Lord and Lady Byswater in the window seat. He was the one who requested the rather rakish song. Cecilia knew that her mother had invited them, of course, but she hadn't quite believed they would come. Not that the Byswaters would ever be rude, certainly not; neighborhood harmony among the gentry must always be preserved, and they seemed like nice people.

But as the Bates fortunes had stumbled, a series of lucky investments had bolstered the Byswaters. Cecilia had often peeked over the hedges at the edge of their adjoining parks as a new, gleaming roof went up on their house, a new wing was added, along with new garages to house gleaming new motorcars, and a stylish Oriental teahouse appeared on a hilltop. Lady Byswater hunted on the most gorgeous strawberry roan, and they had spent last winter in Egypt, cruising the Nile on some City millionaire's yacht.

And it was certainly no secret Lord Byswater wanted to expand—by buying Danby land. Cecilia was sure that if they could, they would have found a way to marry into the Bates family, but their only son was still a child, too young for her. Cash for land was the only thing they could do, and Cecilia knew that her father, hard as he tried to conceal it, would soon have had to put such a sale into consideration.

Why were the Byswaters there, then? To see if the American marriage was likely to go through? To make Lord Avebury an offer? They gave no sign of being discomfited today, even though the Clarke millions might take away their expansive ideas. They were beautifully dressed, Lady Byswater in a gorgeous caramel-colored suit that went perfectly with her dark-red hair, and smiled and chatted with everyone around them.

Aunt Maggie laughed at Lord Byswater's cheeky smile. "Oh, you *are* naughty, Harold! But I do think Strauss is more the order of the day, don't you?" She trailed her fingers lightly over the keys, launching into a polka.

"Turning into a wallflower now, Lady Cecilia?" a voice asked, and she spun around to see that Lord St. John had crept up behind her.

Timothy St. John was their distant cousin, and had once even been heir to Danby, but Cecilia had somehow never much liked him. He was too prone to standing close, or pulling a girl too tightly when he danced with her, too fond of insinuating conversations she was sure she didn't quite understand—or *want* to understand. He was handsome enough, with pale hair and dark eyes, if getting rather stout in his close-fitting suits and his silly green cravat. He certainly didn't look or smell as if he needed any sherry right now. He swayed a bit on his feet as he peered down at her from reddened eyes.

He leaned closer, and his touch lingered on her arm a shade too long as she stepped back. "Cousin Timothy. It's been a while since we've seen you."

"Oh, I've been very busy indeed in London," he said with a grin. "Making useful friends and all that. And I had my trip to America last year, ghastly old place. And you, dear little Cecilia—how much you have grown since last year. How old are you now?"

"Just now nineteen." She took another step back. She had heard a few whispers about his London friends. Card players, business speculators. Even Germans. And now Americans? "If you will excuse me, Cousin Timothy, I must go and speak to Miss Rainsley."

"We should have a cozy little chat very soon, just you and me," he said with a wink.

When pigs take wing, she thought, but she just nodded and smiled. She whirled around and hurried to where her father sat with the Rainsleys. Maud smiled happily and kissed Cecilia's cheek.

"My dear Cec, how lovely to see you again!" Maud said.

"And you, Maud. I am quite longing to hear what life is like at Girton. It must be terribly exciting!"

"Oh, it is absolute heaven." Maud sighed. "My tutor is quite the expert on Italian Renaissance history. I've decided to make it my own specialty. I am learning so much!"

"But nothing as useful as coming to London for the Season would be, Maud dear," her mother said with a strident laugh. "The girls are kept quite separate from the young men just across the green, as bad as novices in a cloister. How will she ever meet a nice suitor that way? A waste of time."

Maud rolled her eyes. "Yet my uncle does not think so, or he wouldn't go on paying the tuition."

Mrs. Rainsley's plump, rosy face hardened under her up-sweep of elaborate, too-golden curls. "And what will happen when his generosity ends and you are nothing but an old blue-stocking? Young people, they never think ahead. What are *your* children doing with their lives, Lord Avebury?"

Cecilia's father looked startled by the sudden question. "Oh—er, Patrick has his scientific work, you know."

"And you, Lady Cecilia?" Mrs. Rainsley demanded. "What are you doing with your time? Not frittering it away with books like Maud, I hope."

Cecilia exchanged pained, helpless glances with Maud.

"I believe her mother is making arrangements for the Season," Lord Avebury said. "Such things are always better left to the ladies, I find. Much too complicated for me."

Mrs. Rainsley gave a giggling laugh. "Quite right. The late Mr. R was hopeless at any social arrangements. Why, I remember one year . . ."

"Shall we take a turn about the room, Maud?" Cecilia asked desperately. "I am quite longing to hear more about your studies."

Maud quickly took Cecilia's arm, and they rushed off as fast as they politely could, strolling around the edges of the drawing room, beyond anyone else's hearing. "I don't see the guest of honor," Maud said.

"Mrs. Caffey said she wasn't at breakfast, either. I'm sure she's still exhausted after her ordeal."

"Oh yes, the shipwreck. It must have been so awful." Maud glanced back at her mother, who was laughing loudly at something the earl said. "I do hope luncheon is soon, though, before Redvers can bring Mother any more sherry!"

Cecilia giggled. "Oh, Maud. How is Girton, really?"

Maud gave a happy sigh. "Utter bliss, Cec. Reading and conversation all the time! My tutor thinks I might even be able to teach there myself one day, if I can obtain the proper credentials."

Cecilia was quite envious. She doubted her parents would ever let her escape someplace where she could read all the time. "It does sound splendid."

"You should try it for yourself!"

"I'm not clever enough."

"Of course you are! You're far better read than I am, and you know so much about art and history."

Cecilia shook her head. "Studying something for myself isn't the same as what you do."

"No, at university it's even better, because there are

other girls to share it with. What else are you going to do? The Season again?"

Cecilia frowned as she thought of what last year, her first Season, had been like. Endless rushing around, changing clothes, pained conversation over dinner with young men who only wanted to talk about cricket. "Mama wouldn't let me."

"That's what I thought about my mother, but once I persuaded my uncle to cover the tuition, she came around. You would love it."

Cecilia studied Maud closely. Her friend really did look happier, more at ease. "So you really don't care about Patrick?"

"Your brother?" Maud's brow arched in thought. "I confess I like him better than your usual lot of titled young men. He has such unusual interests, and I—well, I suppose I thought he understood me. But needs must in life, yes? I have no fortune for him." She smiled brightly, but Cecilia wasn't quite convinced.

"Aren't these pretty?" Maud said, turning toward a case of snuffboxes. The silver and enamel and tiny jewels of them gleamed behind the glass.

"Yes, my grandfather collected most of them," Cecilia said, happy to go along with the change of subject. "That one once belonged to Marie Antoinette."

"And this one?" Maud pointed at the box in the center,

beautifully engraved gilt and silver crowned with a large cabochon emerald.

"Some czar or other gave it to him. When I was little, I wanted that emerald for my play-princess crown, but I was never even allowed to take it out of the case!"

Maud laughed, and they chatted about the history of the various boxes for a few moments until the "guest of honor" made her appearance on Patrick's arm.

It looked like the dressmakers were already hard at work, for Annabel wore a gown of black-and-white-striped mousseline trimmed with embroidered Battenberg lace. Her auburn hair was piled high and held with white ribbons, gleaming in the dusty light from the windows. Patrick stared down at her as if he was dazzled, or stunned.

"I am so sorry we're late!" she said with a trilling laugh. "Patrick here was showing me his adorably clever botany experiments."

Maud's face froze in its smile, and Cecilia took her arm.

Annabel studied the room like a queen examining her court, perfectly at ease. But Cecilia noticed that her bright smile faltered for an instant, and a dark-red flush touched her cheeks. Cecilia tried to see what flustered Annabel so, but everything in the drawing room looked just as it had before. Aunt Maggie played the piano; Lord Avebury chatted with Mrs. Rainsley; the Byswaters were rising from the window seat; and Lady Avebury was sitting with the vicar, Lord St. John, and Mr. Hayes.

When Cecilia looked back to Annabel, the Heiress was smiling up at Patrick as if nothing at all had happened.

Lady Avebury rose to her feet with her "pleasant hostess" mask firmly in place. "Shall we all go in to luncheon?"

Chapter Seven

Cecilia stared out her chamber window as the sun sank beyond the Danby gardens, turning everything to pale gold and rosy pink. It had been such a long, odd day, the Heiress's second full day at Danby. After breakfast, Lady Avebury and Patrick gave Miss Clarke a tour of the house followed by an elaborate luncheon in the garden with many of the neighbors invited.

Annabel seemed excited to meet everyone, regaling them with tales of her ordeal at sea, flirting with Patrick. But in the afternoon, when Cecilia's mother had organized a croquet game and tea on the lawn—Annabel vanished. Lady Avebury was livid, though she covered it with bright smiles and loud laughter at Lord St. John's jokes.

"You know, Lady Cecilia," Mr. Hayes had said as he

whacked at his croquet ball, "I've seen so many countries, so many dwelling places. Persian palaces made of lapis and gold that you wouldn't believe could be real; Spanish gardens that smell of orange blossoms and jasmine all year around. Chinese throne rooms of red and black lacquer. Greek villas about to tumble into the sea."

Cecilia felt a twinge of envy. "How grand it all must be!"

He gave her a crooked smile. "Of course it is. But what you have here is just as lovely, just as special. It *is* England. Your family should protect it. Be careful not to sell it all too cheaply."

Before Cecilia could answer, he chased after his croquet ball into the hedges. She turned his words over in her mind now as she watched the sunset creep over the gardens, painting everything in misty pastels. Danby was indeed special. She had always known that, even at the times she only wanted to escape from it, see the world as Mr. Hayes did. It was her home, built up by generations of hundreds of people who loved and cared for it. It was a living thing, really.

Yet now it was fading, unless something was done quickly to revive it. Something drastic. Was Annabel Clarke really the only answer? Would she, could she, love it as Cecilia did, as her mother and grandmother did?

Cecilia hadn't known Miss Clarke long at all, of course, and their only conversation had really been about all the lovely clothes Annabel lost on the *Galatea*. Cecilia didn't know about her home or her life before, books she had read or hopes she had dreamed, but surely, Annabel's American life was quite luxurious and easy. Fun. Danby was many things, but "easy and fun" almost never. It was all about duty, family, obligations, routines.

And then there was Patrick. He deserved to be happy. He needed a lady who understood his eccentricities and could help him fulfill his duties. Above all, Cecilia longed for someone who would be kind to her sweet brother. He had watched Miss Clarke all through dinner last night and luncheon today, hanging on her words, his eyes wide, dazzled. Cecilia had never seen him that way before. Then, when Miss Clarke disappeared that afternoon, he looked crestfallen. Maud tried to talk to him, to draw him out about his latest botanical experiments, but it was quite hopeless. He barely muttered answers.

He had known Miss Clarke for such a short time. Was she already bruising his heart? Where had she gone all afternoon? When she returned, she had seemed distracted, distant. Was there an escape somewhere for any of them?

A knock sounded at the door, and Cecilia was glad to get out of her gloomy thoughts. "Come in!" she called.

To her surprise, it wasn't Rose who came in, but Jane Hughes, Miss Clarke's maid. She wore a new, crisp black dress, her wispy blond hair pinned neatly back in a ruffled white cap, but her eyes were wide and shy as she glanced around.

"I'm sorry, Lady Cecilia, but Rose was needed to help

reorganize the drawing room, so I was asked if I could help you this evening."

"Oh yes, Mama was planning charades for after dinner," Cecilia said, remembering her mother's newest scheme to entertain the elusive Miss Clarke. It required making stage room in the White Drawing Room, though she was surprised Redvers would allow the maids to touch the velvet furniture. "That is very kind of you, Jane. Are you sure Miss Clarke can spare you?"

"She's taking a bath, and that always means at least an hour."

Cecilia sighed. Then there would surely be no hot water left for anyone else! Danby had plumbing, put in when her mother became countess, but it was not the latest and was rather finicky. "Well, I promise it won't take an hour to get *me* ready."

Jane smiled and cautiously opened the wardrobe doors. Cecilia was sure that after the splendor of Miss Clarke's lost trunks, her own garments must look rather meager and dowdy. But Jane's smile softened as she touched the dark-blue velvet of a riding habit, the creamy lace trim of a tea gown.

"So pretty," she whispered. "Which one do you want to wear, then? Oh—wear then, *my lady*? I was told I have to remember to call you that."

Cecilia laughed. "You don't have to! And maybe I'll wear that pink one. It's from my Season last year, but I do like the color so much." She would save her newer dresses for the upcoming parties. As she turned away from the window, she glimpsed a flash of color in the gathering blue twilight. Curious, she peered closer, and to her shock she saw it was Miss Clarke. She was wrapped in a dark cloak, but her height and that auburn hair was unmistakable as she dashed across the lawn. So Annabel wasn't taking a bath after all? Whatever was she doing outside?

Cecilia started to ask Jane why her mistress was racing around the gardens, but the maid was busy laying out the dress and looking for matching shoes. When Cecilia glanced back, Annabel was gone, the garden empty.

"Maybe it was the Blue Lady," she muttered.

"Beg your pardon?" Jane said.

"Oh, nothing." Cecilia shook her head and went to sit at her dressing table, fiddling with her brushes. "I thought I saw something outside. But it was probably just the Blue Lady."

Jane took the silver-backed brush from her and started untangling the long, red-blond strands. "Who is that, then? My lady."

"She's the family ghost."

Jane's eyes widened in the mirror. "A family ghost? Jeepers."

"My great-great-something-grandmother. They say she hid the king, Charles II, when he was running from the Roundheads. Her husband, who wanted to keep peace with Cromwell, locked her up in the old tower as punishment, and she went mad. Now she runs in the woods at night, trying to escape."

"Oh, you're lucky to have a ghost, my lady." Jane sighed. "I've heard such thrilling tales. I used to read the penny papers at home, when I could afford them."

"Me, too!" Cecilia cried. "My favorite is *The Vanishing Mist*, where Lady Eleanor is captured by the demon monk in the haunted woods. It made me think of the Blue Lady. Have you read it?"

"I don't think so. Our stories in New Jersey are a little different."

"I will loan it to you, then." She was happy to find someone who shared her taste for such stories on a stormy night. Patrick only read scientific tomes, her father the sporting pages and some of the news, and her mother read *The Lady*. "What sort of ghost stories do you have in America?"

Jane bit her lip in thought as she pinned Cecilia's hair into elaborate whorls. "Well, where I grew up, everyone knew about the Jersey Devil."

"A devil. Truly?" Cecilia breathed.

"No one is sure *what* it is, really. They say it can fly, with bat-like wings, but it has hooves, and a head like a goat. It screams and lashes out with its claws. They say some people saw it a few years ago; it even attacked a trolley car! But I don't think I've ever seen a real spirit, though."

"I don't think I have, either. Usually, the Blue Lady is only supposed to appear at a full moon. I used to try and stay up to catch her when I was child, but I always fell asleep."

Cecilia thought of what she had just seen, the woman running across the lawn. She was sure it was Miss Clarke, but she didn't say so to Jane. The girl had enough to worry about, working in a new house. She wasn't her employer's nanny. "I don't know why she would be out today."

Jane helped Cecilia out of her dressing gown and into her corset, tightening the laces with careful, practiced movements. She held out a lace-trimmed petticoat. "Maybe she just wanted a look at the party, my lady?"

Cecilia laughed and stepped into the frothy underskirt. "Maybe so. It's been a while since Danby has seen so much activity."

"It's a really beautiful house. I've never seen anything like it in real life."

"I like it, too." Cecilia thought of all the corridors and staterooms, how confusing it could all be, and she hoped Jane didn't find it so strange anymore. "How is your cat faring? Jack, wasn't it? How does he like Danby?"

Jane helped her into her pink taffeta gown, smoothing the pin-tucked and lace-trimmed sleeves and starting to fasten up the pearl buttons at the back. "Oh, he loves it. He was meant to stay in my room, but he's been sneaking out and getting treats from some of the other servants. He'll be a porker in no time!"

"A porker?"

"Fat, my lady. But he's so funny and sweet, no one can tell him no. And so smart."

Cecilia laughed, picturing a cat growing fatter and fatter by Mrs. Frazer's stove. "I must meet him, then. I do adore cats." She stepped into the pink satin shoes Jane held out. "And your employer? What does she think of Danby?"

A frown flickered over Jane's face, quickly erased as she reached for the strand of pearls Cecilia had laid out on the dressing table. "She doesn't really say much, my lady, not to me," she answered, fastening the necklace. "I don't think it's quite what she's used to, even though I haven't been with her for long. I haven't even been a lady's maid very long. But I know she thinks it's all very beautiful. Who could help but think that?"

"Hmm." Maybe, now that she was here, Miss Clarke didn't care for Danby? Maybe she would leave soon, and they wouldn't have to worry about her after all. But if she did not marry Patrick, what would they do?

"Do you have earrings to match the necklace, my lady?"

"Oh yes, in here someplace." Cecilia found her pearl drops in her mostly empty jewel case and handed them to Jane. The maid carefully slipped them on, then smoothed the gown's rustling skirt. She retied the white satin sash at a jauntier angle.

Cecilia examined herself in the mirror. Her hair looked prettier than she could ever remember it, its waves tamed into a smooth swirl, her gown straight and crisp. "I say, Jane, you are certainly very good at all that. Are you sure you haven't been a lady's maid very long?"

Jane's cheeks glowed pink at the compliment. "Not long, my lady, no. I was a maid at a hotel, and before that for an elderly lady who didn't entertain much. But I used to help the lady guests at the hotel when they needed it. And a few who weren't *really* ladies." She giggled, making Cecilia laugh, too. How she would love to hear more about the "not lady" guests! "I liked the clothes, and figuring out how to do the hair to make everyone look their best. Much better than making beds and scrubbing floors."

"I would imagine so." Cecilia gave a little twirl. "Well, you have made me look better than I ever have! So clever of you." The little porcelain clock on the mantel chimed, sending tiny paste cherubs spinning around. "Surely, you should see to Miss Clarke, though? I've stolen you for too long."

"Of course, my lady." Jane bobbed an awkward curtsy. It was obvious she wasn't quite used to English country house ways, but she was trying hard, and Cecilia very much liked her for it.

After the maid left, Cecilia reached for her gloves. She glanced out the window, half hoping, half fearing she would see some spectral figure racing across the lawn. But no one was there.

Almost everyone was gathered in the White Drawing Room when Cecilia made her way downstairs. Redvers and the footmen handed around trays with small glasses filled with a strange, pale-green liquid, almost opalescent and glowing in the firelight. Redvers did not look as if he approved.

"They're called cocktails," Aunt Maggie said, waving her glass aloft. Her bronze satin gown and beaded turban gleamed. "They serve them at Delmonico's in New York, and I also had them at Shepheard's Hotel in Cairo. So refreshing. I asked Redvers here to help me mix them up, so you can all try them."

"Always happy to be of assistance, Mrs. Solent," Redvers muttered.

"They are certainly—interesting, Maggie dear." Lady Avebury gasped as she took a sip.

"I quite like them," Lord Avebury said cheerfully, taking another from the tray.

"May I have one?" Cecilia asked, terribly eager to try it.

"Just a small one, darling, and sip slowly," her mother warned, and Cecilia could see why when she took a drink. It quite burned as it went down, but not in a terrible way. In fact, it was rather nice.

"Where is the guest of honor, then?" Lord St. John asked. His voice was slightly blurry, as if he had tried one too many of the green drinks. "Surely, Americans love cocktails."

Cecilia glanced around and saw that Annabel wasn't there yet. Nor was Patrick, or Mr. Hayes. The Byswaters chatted with Mrs. Rainsley by the fire, while Maud frowned as if she was deep in her own thoughts, twitching at the sleeve of her lavender chiffon gown.

"Her maid helped me dress," Cecilia said, feeling a bit guilty for keeping Jane so long. But the girl was so nice to talk to, so interesting. "Miss Clarke might be running a little late."

Lady Avebury glanced at the gilded clock and pursed her lips. "Redvers, can you ask Mrs. Frazer to hold dinner just a bit longer?"

"Of course, my lady," Redvers answered stoically, but Cecilia knew Mrs. Frazer would be unhappy about her carefully calibrated crab bisque.

Maud came up to Cecilia and took her arm so they could steal away from the rest of the group. Patrick appeared in the doorway then, looking rather puzzled, his tie crooked as usual, his hair mussed. Cecilia smiled at him and waved for him to join them, but he shook his head.

"Shocking," Maud whispered. "When do you suppose dinner was last late at Danby?"

Cecilia giggled with her. "Well, Miss Clarke *is* American. Maybe she doesn't know about the tyranny of the dinner gong."

"She is certainly an interesting sort. At luncheon, she kept talking about a place called the Poconos. Where do you suppose that could be? It sounds like Brighton."

They paused next to the case holding the collection of snuffboxes. Maud glanced at them and frowned. "Is this quite right, Cec? It seemed like the rows were much straighter before."

Cecilia studied the boxes and saw that Maud was right. The neat five-by-five lines were all jumbled and uneven, the Marie Antoinette box turned on its side.

And the one in the middle, her favorite with the emerald, was gone altogether.

"That's not right." She gasped, startled. She studied the lock and found some tiny scratches on the metal. "Redvers?"

"Yes, my lady?" he asked, coming closer with his now-empty tray.

"Were the servants cleaning in here earlier? It seems like the emerald box is not in its place."

"Surely not, my lady. The servants were setting up for charades this afternoon, but no one was cleaning over here. This case is never opened." They exchanged a puzzled glance. "I will see to it, my lady. Perhaps his lordship was showing someone the collection."

"Yes, of course." She nodded. She knew if there was anything at all amiss, Redvers would be the first to set it to rights. But she still felt disconcerted as she glanced back at the empty spot in the case. Perhaps the box had been sold, like other items had been recently? But it was there just yesterday.

"I'm so sorry I'm late!" Miss Clarke sang out, making her entrance at last. She wore a stunning gown of dark-blue velvet spangled with beaded stars, her hair piled high and twined with pearls. Cecilia wondered where she had found such a creation. Surely not the village dressmaker.

"It is quite worth the wait, Miss Clarke. You look stunning," Lord St. John said, taking her hand and kissing it. She frowned at him. "I do hope we're sitting next to each other at dinner. I do adore Americans."

"Miss Clarke is next to Mr. Hayes, Cousin Timothy," Lady Avebury said, her smile tight.

Cecilia turned to see that Mr. Hayes had entered the drawing room without her noticing. He offered his arm to Annabel, and she seemed to hesitate before she took it.

"How lovely, Miss Clarke," he said smoothly. "It has certainly been an age since I visited San Francisco. Is that not where your father is from? I am quite aching to hear how it has been recovering since the earthquake. One does hear miraculous things."

"And I can't wait to tell you all about it," Annabel said with a little laugh. "Such fun!"

Chapter Eight

"Are you alone, my lady?"

Cecilia glanced up from her book to see Jane hovering in the chamber doorway, whispering. Cecilia had been enjoying the quiet of her room following all the activities of the day after the late dinner the night before, an afternoon of tennis and tea, but she was quite excited to see the nice American. "Yes, of course. Is something amiss?"

"Not at all." Jane slipped into the room, closing the door carefully behind her, and Cecilia saw she had a covered wicker basket with her. A soft "mrrww" sounded from inside.

"Oh!" Cecilia gasped. "Is that your Jack?"

"He wanted to say hello."

Cecilia dashed over eagerly as Jane opened the basket, and a little red-gold head popped up. He looked around cautiously with wide greenish eyes and sniffed Cecilia's hand as she held it out to him. His fur was like velvet under her touch.

"He is adorable," she exclaimed.

"I think he's the same color as your hair," Jane said.

Cecilia was delighted at the idea. She ran her fingertips over his tufted ears. "Do you think so?"

"Just look at him! If you were a cat, my lady, you would be Jack. Except for him being a boy, that is. He's very smart, too. I'm almost afraid he's going to learn how to open the door to my room and go out exploring when I'm not there. Your Mrs. Caffey wouldn't like that."

"I would imagine not." Cecilia knew, from long experience, that Mrs. Caffey liked her rules and routine. She was fair and friendly, but strict. A cat roaming the servants' hall wouldn't be in her plans.

"She says she's fine with him staying with me, as long as he's kept in my room."

"I hope they're all treating you well, Jane, you and Jack. Even if he has to stay inside for now."

"Oh yes, my lady. I admit I was a little afraid of Mr. Redvers at first, he looks so stern, but he's been so thoughtful about what Miss Clarke has been through. I think they know very well how to keep their guests happy."

Cecilia was sure that was true. Annabel's happiness at Danby was paramount to her mother. "Redvers has been here since I was a child, before that even, and he scares *me* sometimes! He's so particular about how the house is run, I'm sure I always forget the correct way to do things and he despairs of me. But he's a softy, really."

"You, my lady? Forget the correct way of doing things?" Jane looked doubtful.

Cecilia laughed. Jack leaped out of his basket and went to sniff under the dressing table. "I had a wonderful governess, but I admit I loved her so much because she would often let me run wild. I would always rather read a novel or climb a tree in the park than practice my music or French verbs. I was the most unaccomplished debutante last year."

Jane sighed and leaned back on her palms, watching Jack explore with a wistful expression on her face. "There weren't very many trees where I grew up, but I did love to read whenever I could. Our neighbor worked as an assistant in a library at one of the grand houses in Manhattan, and she would sometimes lend me things."

Cecilia was intrigued at this peek into a life so different from her own. "What was it like, where you grew up?"

Jane laughed. "Not like here. It was an apartment building; we had nine other families as neighbors, and four little rooms for the six of us. My parents, my three brothers, and me. But it wasn't so bad. We had windows for fresh air, and my mother kept it clean and tidy all the time. She had a mania for cleaning. I'm not sure how I'm her daughter, really! I hate cleaning."

Cecilia knew the feeling. She sometimes wondered what kind of daughter she should be, to gain her mother's approval. "And your father?"

"My dad works at a greengrocer's, so we always had plenty of fresh food to eat. Especially once I got the work at Mrs. Heseltine's house, and then the hotel."

"Four rooms." Cecilia tried to envision it. She thought of all the twisting corridors and hidden stairs of Danby, all the chambers she had never even seen. "Did you meet lots of people working in a hotel? I've never even eaten dinner at one in London, though my mother has taken us to some in Paris and Berlin."

"Oh yes, ever so interesting! We weren't the grandest of hotels, but nice and respectable, so there were lots of tourist families, and businesspeople having meetings and dinners and such. I got to practice doing ladies' hair, there, too. It was never the same way twice, not like at Mrs. Heseltine's house. She was old and awfully set in her ways. There were people of all ages at the hotel." A sudden cloud seemed to pass over Jane's face, and she fidgeted with the skirt of her black dress. "And then sometimes there were people you would have to avoid like the plague, my lady. Men who thought maids were no better than they should be and tried to grab us, even though we were just paid to carry towels and such. No more of that for me here."

Cecilia gasped in horror. She remembered Lord St. John and his pinching fingers, his leering smiles. He seemed just the sort to stay in that hotel. "Were you often—bothered, then, Jane?"

"Not after I figured things out. And lots of the other girls had been working there for a long time; they knew the regulars to watch out for."

Jack suddenly leaped out from under the table, growling and hissing as he snatched at a stray ribbon. It was as if he was declaring he was a fierce jungle cat who would protect them from all villains. Cecilia and Jane laughed at him.

Cecilia slid the ribbon across the carpet for him to pounce on. "Is that how you met Miss Clarke? At the hotel?" She broke off, suddenly realizing this was a moment Redvers would *not* approve of her manners. The servants were entitled to their own lives at times. Everyone had their place. "I'm sorry, I'm being terribly nosy."

Jane smiled shyly. "It's nice to talk to someone for a while, my lady. And I did meet Miss Clarke at the hotel. She was staying there while she waited for her ship to England."

Cecilia felt a twinge of sympathy. "Is it lonely for you, Jane? Being away from your family."

Jane bounced the ribbon for Jack, who grabbed it between his paws. "I do miss them, it's true. But I'm so lucky, really! I get to see England. Not many girls from my neighborhood can say that. It's like seeing things in real life I thought I could only see in books. I'll have so many stories to tell them when I go back. So many memories. Most of the girls I know at home work in shops or factories, or they've already married."

"And you get to do it all on your own!" Cecilia sighed. She thought of her months in London last year, all the dances and teas and theaters that were supposed to be such fun, the portal to adult life, yet she was chaperoned every minute. "I'm never really alone. Someone is always watching." Jack batted at the sash of her skirt, softly, as if he sympathized.

"I'm never alone now, either, my lady! Not with Jack. He's always waiting on my pillow when I go to my room. He's a good friend, not too noisy, and he never steals my things like my brothers did."

Cecilia giggled. "Miss Clarke didn't mind you taking him with you?"

"She didn't notice at first. I made friends with him during the voyage. Then there was so much confusion when we had to get in the lifeboats, and poor Jack was just following me around. I scooped him up and wrapped him in my coat. Miss Clarke did yell a fair bit at first, it's true, but once we were on land she was a lot like your Mrs. Caffey. Fair. Said he could stay if he was quiet and didn't make a mess outside his sandbox." She paused, a shadow of sadness in her eyes. "I know she seems a bit—well, loud. And bossy. And she is. She's very particular about things, and has a terrible tantrum sometimes. But she can be nice, too, in her way."

Loud and bossy. Cecilia worried about Patrick, her

quiet, sweet, distracted brother. What would his future be like with Miss Clarke? "It must have been hard, just the two of you, being shipwrecked like that."

Jane grinned. "Well, I did say I wanted adventure, my lady, just not quite of that sort. I don't mind admitting I was scared out of my wits, though Miss Clarke wasn't. Not that night. She just rowed and kept yelling at us all to keep going forward. Your Danby Hall is like heaven after that."

"I quite like it. But I'm not sure it's heavenly." She thought of her home, the portraits, the old carpets, Ralph the armor, all the things that had always been there. The things she had assumed would *always* be there. A sudden reverberating sound startled her. "Oh, there's the first gong already! Where has the time gone?"

Jane pushed herself to her feet and reached out to help Cecilia. Jack caught at her hem. "We should get you dressed for dinner, my lady. I'll have to go see to Miss Clarke soon."

"Of course. I'm afraid we've made rather a lot of work for you here."

"It's good to keep busy." Jane opened the wardrobe and sorted through the dresses. "What would you like to wear tonight?"

Cecilia sat down at her dressing table and started brushing out her hair. Jack sat back and watched her as he groomed his paw. "Why don't you choose, Jane?"

Jane took out one of the new gowns, white silk beaded with tiny pearls and sequins in a lily-of-the-valley pattern.

She laid it out and smoothed the delicate fabric, then found a pair of matching white shoes, gloves, even a white lace fan. She deftly fixed Cecilia's hair in a stylish upsweep, finding some pearl combs to fasten it in place, and told her stories about her brothers' pranks back in New Jersey that made them both laugh helplessly. Cecilia was very glad Miss Clarke had found Jane and brought her to Danby; she and Jack brightened up the house party very much.

But as Jane helped her fasten the tiny pearl buttons at the back of the white gown, there was a sudden shout in the corridor.

"Jane!" someone shrieked, so loudly Cecilia could hear it through the door. "Jane! Where are you? I need you right *now*!"

Cecilia and Jane exchanged a startled glance, and Jack ducked under the bed. The blue satin quilt swayed behind him. "Is that—Miss Clarke?" Cecilia whispered.

"It must be," Jane answered, her face a bit pale. "But she was napping when I left her. I do remember some of the other girls at the hotel called her 'her nibs' sometimes."

"Her nibs?" Cecilia whispered. How interesting slang words were.

"*Jane*!"

"You should go to her," Cecilia said. "I'll make sure Jack stays in here."

Jane nodded hastily and ran out of the room. Cecilia followed on her stockinged feet, peeking out into the corridor to see Miss Clarke, looking a bit like the wraith of the Blue Lady. Her auburn hair fell in waves over the shoulders of her sky-blue satin dressing gown. She looked very different from the confident lady who played lawn tennis so fiercely that afternoon.

"I've been waiting for you for *ages*, you stupid girl," Annabel snapped. "I need to look my very best for dinner. Do you hear me? My best!"

Cecilia was appalled. Jane had said Annabel was really quite nice, but it was hard to believe at that moment, as she grabbed Jane's hand and pulled her down the corridor.

"I am so sorry, Miss Clarke, but Jane was kindly assisting me, and I kept her too long," Cecilia said. "You only had to ring the bell, and someone would have been with you in a moment."

Annabel whirled toward Cecilia. Her cheeks were bright red, her eyes bright. "A bell? Are you still in the Middle Ages in this place? There are telephones in every room of my father's house! And servants in every hallway!" She suddenly seemed to realize who she was talking to—her possible future sister-in-law. Her face quickly smoothed out, and she sniffed. "But if she was helping *you*, Lady Cecilia, that is quite all right."

"She was most kind. I won't detain her so long again," Cecilia said firmly.

Annabel nodded and left as quickly as she had appeared.

Jane ran after her, and Cecilia closed her chamber door behind her again. Jack was peeking out from under the bed, his green eyes jewel bright in the shadows.

"Is she always like that, Jack?" Cecilia asked. He sighed and put his chin down on his paws. "Poor Jane . . ."

Chapter Nine

"And how are you enjoying the invasion of your lovely house, Lady Cecilia?" Mr. Hayes said as everyone turned to speak to their second dinner partners after the fish course of salmon mousseline. "I hope we're not interrupting you *too* terribly."

Cecilia laughed and shook her head. "I've been enjoying it very much. It's nice to be shaken out of our routine for a while." And it was true; she certainly *was* coming to enjoy the gathering, despite the strange disappearance of the emerald box, and the Blue Lady in the garden. There had been a lively game of lawn tennis that afternoon, which she and Maud finally won against Patrick and Lady Byswater, despite the fact that Lady Byswater was a fierce player. Miss Clarke kept score, sometimes calling out encouragement even though she seemed strangely quiet before that. Barely even a word about the splendors of her lost trunks, which she liked to talk about so much.

Indeed, she was talking about it at that very moment. On the other side of Mr. Hayes, Cecilia heard her say, "I can't believe the incompetence of some people! I was sure they would send my luggage after me; there was plenty of time . . ."

But Cecilia did like having other new people to talk with for a while. Maud's stories of Girton almost made Cecilia think she might go there herself, and Lady Byswater was surprisingly amusing with tales of the misadventures of house renovations. Her mother seemed to be relaxing a bit. Cecilia glanced at Lady Avebury at the end of the table, chatting with Lord Byswater. She even smiled.

On the other side of Mr. Hayes sat Annabel, laughing with Patrick after her complaints of the lost luggage. How quickly she did change! She tapped on his sleeve, making him blush. The frantic lady who shouted for her maid earlier was gone, leaving a chattering, confident, sparkling Annabel in her place.

The dining room even seemed to look more splendid than usual. The red silk walls gleamed, such a contrast from the icy whites and blues in the foyer just beyond the doors, the amber-colored velvet upholstery looked richly medieval, the lights from the Venetian glass chandelier glittered on the ladies' jewels, and the silver on the Elizabethan buffet sparkled. It all seemed to be coming alive again.

But Cecilia's grandmother didn't seem to look terribly happy about it all for some reason. Maybe it was not a party in the vein of the ones *she* had given during her time at Danby. Her lips pursed as she took a sip of her wine and slipped a morsel to Sebastian under the table. He was the only dog who dared come into the Danby dining room under Redvers's nose.

"I am having a lovely time, Mr. Hayes, and I hope you are, too," Cecilia said. She took a drink of her own wine, which she found was one of her father's finest clarets, and gave Maud a quick smile across the table. Poor Maud sat next to Lord St. John and looked rather desperate as he chattered on to her, leaning much too close.

"Certainly, I'm enjoying myself," Mr. Hayes answered with a small smile. "Nothing like a real English country house in the springtime, is there?"

"I'm afraid we must be very dull after all your travels."

"Lady Cecilia, I promise you, *dull* is the last thing I would call my time here at Danby."

Cecilia was rather puzzled by his words. The tennis and teas were fun in their own way, of course, but surely nothing next to trekking across deserts and through Persian palaces. "I confess I was very happy to hear I was sitting next to you at dinner tonight. I've been aching to ask you more about your adventures. I think Mrs. Solent said you were planning on writing a book about it all?"

"Ah yes, the intrepid Mrs. Solent. What an unusual lady

she is! I always enjoy it when we run into each other in some far-flung hostel."

"I believe she said she is going to India later this year."

"Everyone should see India at least once. I was at the Durbar last year. It is astonishing. The brilliant colors, the music, the smell of spices in the humid air. Mrs. Solent is wise to travel there now." He swept a long glance over the table, the chatter, the sparkle of the jewels, and gave a small half smile. "Of course, she is far from the only adventurous lady I know these days. Many of them have much more astonishing tales to tell than I do. Perhaps you have thought of traveling yourself, Lady Cecilia?"

Cecilia saw shimmering white Indian palaces in her mind, endless desert sands, camels passing in front of the pyramids. But she knew her parents would never let her go there, just as they wouldn't let her go to Girton like Maud. "I think I would enjoy that very much. I read all the time about distant lands, amazing people. But I doubt my parents would agree."

"Times are changing, Lady Cecilia, more rapidly all the time. Surely, you even see it here in Yorkshire. Life is brief. We must seize it while we can." Redvers refilled their wineglasses, and Mr. Hayes took a long sip. He gave a satisfied nod. "But in the meantime, perhaps you can read my book. It is true I've been approached by a few publishers, and one has made me an acceptable offer. I plan to travel to Switzerland soon, find some peace and quiet in order to write it. It will be full of many stories I have encountered in my travels."

"How splendid!" Cecilia exclaimed. "I can't wait to read it. What do you think your favorite adventure has been? India? Somewhere in Africa, perhaps? Or those lapis Persian palaces?"

"It is true that my safari in Kenya was most memorable. We were nearly devoured by lions in our camp one night! And, as I am sure Mrs. Solent would agree, Egypt has a special magic. It's in the light, you know." He glanced down the table. "But I recently had a most interesting voyage indeed. All the way across Canada."

"Canada?" Cecilia pictured endless expanses of snow. "But surely, it's quite enormous."

He laughed. "Indeed. And so varied, it's hard to imagine. Forests, cities, mountains. All of it fascinating. And I ended by traveling down the West Coast of the United States. From great evergreen woods to the ocean."

"How fascinating," Cecilia said. "And did you see San Francisco? That's where Miss Clarke is from, I believe." She studied Annabel for a moment, as Miss Clarke smiled at Patrick and nodded at something he was saying. She reached out and fiddled with some of the large row of silver next to her plate.

"I did see it. A most interesting place. It was quite destroyed, you know, in the earthquake a few years ago. Now it has risen, very phoenixlike, from the ashes, and is splendid. Surprisingly foggy, even more than London, but with its own society in place. Opera houses, restaurants, music halls, and always that gorgeous ocean just beyond."

"I am surprised anyone would want to leave it, then, and come to stuffy Danby." Cecilia felt rather sorry for Annabel, departing a vibrant new city with an ocean view. Maybe she was just homesick and that made her shout at Jane.

Mr. Hayes leaned closer, and in the light of the candelabra on the table, Cecilia noticed a very strange thing. There was a large bruise beneath one of his eyes, half-covered by powder a shade paler than his sun-bronzed skin. Where had he got such a thing? And he smelled of wine and some lemony-green cologne. The wine smelled fruity, strong on his breath, and he sat his glass down unsteadily. "Never underestimate the glamour of ye olde England to Americans, Lady Cecilia, especially Americans who find their coffers suddenly overflowing. They will do anything to possess history to go with their new riches. The tales I could tell you . . ." He reached for his glass for another long drink.

"I would like to propose a toast!" Annabel suddenly cried merrily. She leaped to her feet, her pale-gold silk and lace gown gleaming, the topaz and diamond necklace at her throat flashing. As Cecilia peered closer, she saw to her surprise that it was her mother's necklace. Part of the topaz parure that had once been a wedding gift. Had her mother actually given it to Annabel? Before any announcement? Annabel waved one of those heavy pieces of silver in the air, as if she would give a toast with her fish fork. Was it an American thing, then?

Lady Avebury studied Annabel with wide, startled eyes, her hand frozen on her own fork. Ladies did not give toasts at dinner parties! But then again, the best wine from the Danby cellars *had* been flowing freely all evening, the chatter growing steadily louder. Lady Avebury quickly gave a fixed smile, as if this sort of thing happened all the time.

"Is this an American custom?" Cecilia's grandmother snapped. "No wonder New York dinners are interminable."

"How charming," Lady Avebury murmured. Patrick just looked confused, and Lord Avebury barely turned from the talk he was having with Lady Byswater about the best clarets.

"You've all just been so very kind, so marvelous to me, after my terrible, terrible ordeal," Annabel declared with a bright smile. "I absolutely must thank you all, thank beautiful Danby, my darling refuge. I could never have hoped to find a better harbor!"

Redvers and the footmen came in with the entrée course, and the butler froze at seeing the unprecedented scene in his dining room. He glanced at Lady Avebury, who gave him a subtle little wave. He had Paul go ahead to the dowager countess with his silver serving tray of lamb cutlets, and the new footman behind him with the mint sauce. Cecilia saw it was Jesse from the village, and he winked at her behind Redvers's back. *The cheek!* She turned away, her face warm.

At least no one had seen him do that. Redvers would surely have had an apoplexy with a winking footman added to a lady giving a toast. The butler's low murmur seemed to tell them to take their time serving Annabel, the guest of honor, as she talked on.

Suddenly, Paul seemed to trip. He stumbled against the table, spilling some of the tray onto Lady Byswater's lap. She cried out, leaping to her feet, while Lady Avebury hurried over to try and placate her and Redvers pulled Paul back. Sebastian growled under the table, and the dowager laughed in delight at the silly scene before her.

"I don't feel at all well," Mr. Hayes gasped. Cecilia swung back around to face him and saw he had turned quite gray. He half rose to his feet, grasping the damask tablecloth in his fist. Cecilia, most alarmed, reached for his arm to try and steady him. But he fell sideways, taking the cloth, plates, and silver with him. He was ill all over the mess, a greenish, foamy sort of sick tinged with red blood, and seemed to tense into a convulsion.

"Oh, help, please!" Cecilia screamed. She knelt down by Mr. Hayes, trying frantically to pull him onto his back, but he went very still.

"Here, let me," Jesse said. He knelt down beside her, taking off his livery jacket as he frowned down at Mr. Hayes. He lifted him, steadying his stiff neck. "What happened? Did this come on suddenly?"

Cecilia was amazed at his calm demeanor, the way he

seemed to know what he was doing. “Very. We were talking, he took a drink of the wine, then poor Paul tripped . . .”

“That was *my* wine!” Annabel screamed. Cecilia looked up to see her gesturing toward the spilled glass next to Mr. Hayes’s curled fingers. The red wine was dribbling out onto the carpet.

“I hardly think that matters right now,” Patrick said, trying to draw Annabel away. “Let’s go over here, give him some air.”

“Redvers, call the doctor at once!” Lady Avebury cried.

“I think it’s too late,” Jesse said grimly. “He seems to be dead.”

Chapter Ten

Jane heard a very wild commotion outside Miss Clarke's door as she sat by the fire, sewing a lose button on a satin glove, Jack curled up at her feet, grooming his paw. Footsteps ran past the door, and someone called out muffled, frantic words. It was very strange, since the first thing she had noticed about Danby Hall was that, at least upstairs, it was always quiet. The servants' hall was always bustle and movement, but the awe-inspiring, plush-lined house was quieter than anything she had ever known.

But not tonight. Jack gave her an inquiring glance, his paw still held up. Jane shrugged and laid the glove aside to go peek out the window. The Green Chamber looked out onto the back lawn and the rose garden, and everything was dark and still outside.

Someone else ran past the door, and Jane knew something had to be up. No one *ever* ran upstairs at Danby.

"Come on, Jack," she said, scooping him up in her arms. "You're an old pro at being an upstairs gentleman now, after staying with Lady Cecilia. Let's go see what's happening."

Jack gave a "rrrww," and Jane made her way through the gallery to the grand staircase. She knew her way now, too, careful to learn all the twists and turns of the house. No proper lady's maid would ever get lost, and Jane had found that she really enjoyed being a proper lady's maid—or at least a starter lady's maid. Everyone else in the servants' hall still gave her curious glances, asked cautious questions, and she was sure Mrs. Caffey and Mr. Redvers were still doubtful about a young American servant. But they all treated her with respect and courtesy and gave her a place of honor at the belowstairs dining table.

Just like now. She found a knot of people gathered at the landing, crouched down behind the carved balustrades. She saw James, one of the footmen; Pearl, the kitchen maid; Sumter, who was Lady Avebury's own maid; and Rose and Bridget, the housemaids. Rose gestured to Jane to sit beside her and slid over to make room for her. The maid gave Jack a scratch between the ears, but she didn't look away from the foyer below.

The doors to the dining room were thrown open, golden light spilling out onto the chilly white marble floor. People were racing back and forth, apparently without reason or purpose, and there was much shouting and sobbing. It was like a theater.

"What's happening?" Jane whispered to Rose.

"No one really knows yet. Redvers went to the telephone earlier, and Mrs. Sumter thought she heard him asking for the doctor and then Colonel Havelock. He's the local magistrate." Jane must have looked confused, for Rose explained, "The neighborhood justice; he investigates local crimes and such."

"Is someone hurt, then?" Jane cried, shocked that anything bad could happen in a place like Danby.

"It must be. But we don't dare go in the dining room. Maybe Paul will come out soon. He was serving with that new footman. He can tell us."

Jane remembered that Paul and Rose were courting, on the quiet-like. He seemed like a nice sort who wouldn't keep secrets from Rose, even about the Bates family, but in the meantime it appeared they just had to sit tight and wait.

But waiting was so hard to do!

After a few minutes, Redvers came out of the dining room and hurried toward the front doors. He admitted a man in a somber black overcoat and homburg hat, a leather case in his hands. They made their way quietly across the foyer. Redvers must have known all the servants were watching, and even Jane knew they should certainly not be there. But he didn't even glance up at them.

"That's Dr. Mitchell," Rose whispered.

As if the doctor's arrival was a signal, everyone poured out of the dining room then. They all rushed toward the front doors, as if escaping a haunted house. Jane couldn't see Lord Avebury, who must have stayed with the doctor and Redvers, seeing to whoever was ill.

The Dowager Lady Avebury came behind the rest, her walking stick in one hand and her black terrier dog under her other arm. The beast caught sight of Jack and wriggled and barked and snapped, almost toppling his owner. Jack arched and hissed.

Lady Avebury turned back and took her mother-in-law's arm. She looked drawn and frantic but struggling to stay calm. "Mama, why don't you come sit in the music room? It's quiet in there."

"Quiet? Why on earth would I want *quiet*, Emmaline? This is the most interesting Danby has been in ages! Help me outside with the others."

As they left, Jane heard a piercing scream. She turned back to the dining room and saw that Miss Clarke had finally emerged, clinging to Viscount Bellham's arm. Her hair was falling from the pins Jane had placed so carefully, and she looked utterly terrified, as did the viscount. Lady Cecilia trailed behind them, looking worried, her face as white as her silk gown, except for a stain near the beaded hem.

Jane half rose, wondering frantically what she should do. Lady Cecilia glanced up and saw her and hurried up the stairs. Around her, the other servants ducked down, but Lady Cecilia was certainly not the type to reprimand them.

"Oh, Jane, I'm so glad to see you!" she cried. "Will you look after Miss Clarke? I'm afraid she's had quite a shock. The gentleman sitting next to her at dinner has died."

"Died?" Jane whispered.

"Yes, and in quite a nasty way," Lady Cecilia said with a grimace. She rubbed wearily at her eyes.

"Wh—who was it, my lady?" Rose asked timidly.

"It was Mr. Hayes," Cecilia answered.

"But surely, Miss Clarke didn't know him well," Jane said. She knew Mr. Hayes was well-known in England, some kind of explorer or writer, but she had only seen him from a distance. He seemed sunburned, but well-dressed.

"I'm not sure anyone here knew him, except maybe Aunt Maggie, but it was quite shocking," Cecilia said. Miss Clarke gave another scream. "It's all right, Jane; you must go to her now. I'll take care of Jack. We're old friends now."

Jane nodded quickly and handed Jack over to Lady Cecilia. He nestled into her arms with a purr, the fickle beast, and Jane dashed down the stairs to Miss Clarke's side.

She was sobbing, her face starkly pale, her hair tangled, the cap sleeve of her gold silk gown torn. Lord Bellham patted her arm awkwardly, muttering softly, glancing around him with a most panicked expression.

"Annabel, we should go outside with the others," he

said, flailing one hand toward the open door. "Some fresh air would do you good."

"I can't go out there with *them*," Miss Clarke sobbed. "Someone tried to kill me! Don't you understand? I can't trust anyone now."

Jane gently took her other arm. She was shaking like a branch in the winter wind. "You can trust me, Miss Clarke."

"Jane?" Annabel gave her an unfocused stare. "What are you doing here?"

"I heard you needed my help, Miss Clarke. His lordship is right. A breath of fresh air would do you some good. We should give the doctor some room to work in here, right?"

"Quite right," Lord Bellham said.

Annabel finally nodded and let them lead her outside. She only went as far as the cold stone front steps and sat down heavily with a sob. Jane sat down next to her and helplessly patted her hand.

"Should I—should I fetch some wine?" Lord Bellham said, waving his hands as if he didn't know what to do with them, or himself.

"That would be very kind, my lord," Jane answered. "And maybe a shawl for Miss Clarke?"

He hurried off, seemingly grateful for the errand, and Jane studied the gravel driveway as she murmured softly to Miss Clarke, as she would have to one of her siblings after a nightmare. Lady Cecilia sat perched on the stone ledge of the fountain in the center of the drive, Jack sitting beside her, while the dowager hobbled back and forth, followed by Lady Avebury who kept trying to get the older lady to sit down. A man on a bicycle appeared out of the darkness and stopped to talk to Lady Cecilia, who was still sitting on the edge of the fountain with Jack by her.

"Why would someone want to do away with me? Why now?" Miss Clarke gasped. "When everything is finally coming together!"

Jane had no answer for her at all.

The marble fountain seat was starting to get cold beneath Cecilia's silk dress when things finally began to quiet down outside Danby. Colonel Havelock had vanished inside what felt like ages ago but was probably only a half hour. Grandmama had gone home with Sebastian, which was good since Jack seemed itchy to run after the snappy canine. Lady Avebury had taken the confused guests to the music room for tea and brandy, and Jane led Miss Clarke away to the Green Chamber. Only Cecilia and Jack were still outside.

Cecilia shivered and tilted back her head to study the night sky. It was clear and bright, like tiny diamonds scattered on black velvet, and the moon cast its silvery glow over the house and gardens as if nothing had happened at all. As if a man hadn't just collapsed dead at her feet. It was all so strange, like a dream fading away in the mists of daybreak.

Redvers appeared on the front steps, one of Cecilia's

cashmere shawls in his hands. "There you are, my lady," he said sternly, coming to her side. He tucked the warm, soft wool over her shoulders. "You should come inside before you catch a cold and Dr. Mitchell has another patient on his hands. He is already seeing to Miss Clarke."

Cecilia smiled up at him, remembering all the times he had looked after her ever since she was a toddler. "You are so kind, Redvers. I'll be inside in just a moment. I need to clear my head a bit."

"Perfectly understandable, my lady. Nothing of that sort has ever happened at a Danby dinner before."

"I should hope not." She shuddered, remembering poor Mr. Hayes and his gray face, his blank eyes. "That new footman. Jesse, is it? He was a very quick thinker. I wonder if he has had some medical training."

Redvers frowned. "I couldn't say, my lady. He was very coolheaded in a crisis, I will give him that. Always a very useful thing in a footman."

And he was dreadfully handsome, too, though Cecilia didn't dare say that. "What is happening in there now, Redvers?"

"Dr. Mitchell is nearly finished, I think, my lady, and will have the, er, Mr. Hayes removed shortly. Colonel Havelock is being set up in the library. He wants to ask everyone a few questions while the evening is fresh in their minds."

Cecilia hopped down from the fountain, and Jack jumped

beside her. He padded confidently up the front steps, as if he had always lived at Danby. "I should be one of the first, then."

Redvers looked most concerned. "Oh, I am sure he wouldn't want to disturb you tonight, my lady."

"Redvers, I am already quite *disturbed*. I'm happy to be of help to Colonel Havelock, if I can."

"Perhaps you would want to join the others in the music room for now, my lady. Tea has been sent in."

"Good idea, Redvers. I'll do that." Cecilia hurried into the house and found Jack waiting for her next to one of the large Chinese vases. She hesitated for a moment, but she didn't turn toward the music room. She went instead to the library, where she knew the perfect cozy spot for a bit of eavesdropping. Jack followed her confidently.

She had learned all the best hidey-holes of Danby long ago, the spots where a girl could hide to read a book in peace. One of her favorites was the gallery of the library. Even when her father was working in there, he had never known his daughter was up above him.

Cecilia's grandparents had long ago transformed the Danby library into a medieval Gothic style that was the height of fashion in Queen Victoria's heyday. It was a fantastical space, with a soaring, carved-beam ceiling, stained dark to pretend it had been there for centuries. Wine-red velvet draperies displayed stained glass windows, darkened now but jewel bright with red, gold, emerald green, and sapphire blue in the daylight. Matching red velvet and tufted leather chairs were scattered about on the red-and-blue carpet, cozy spots to peruse the floor-to-ceiling shelves of volumes.

At one end of the room was a massive fireplace with an elaborately carved oak chimneypiece, modeled on one at Hampton Court, large enough to roast some medieval oxen. And at the other end, reached by a spiral staircase, was a minstrels' gallery. It ran the breadth of the room, hidden by a pierced wooden wall meant to resemble a rood screen, backed by more bookshelves.

Cecilia knew that if she tucked herself down in the corner, she could peek through the screen to see the whole library, and no one could see her in return.

She settled down for a good listen and wished she had brought a blanket, and maybe a small snack after the interrupted dinner. But Colonel Havelock was already settled at a desk near the fire, a few velvet chairs drawn up before him, and Cecilia dared not move. Jack curled up on her lap, a silent, steady, most welcome companion.

Her parents sat with the colonel, and Cecilia saw that her mother looked distraught, crying softly into a handkerchief. No such disarray and scandal had ever been let into Danby under her watch. Cecilia's father patted her arm awkwardly.

"I won't keep you or your guests very long tonight, Lord and Lady Avebury," Colonel Havelock said gently. "I know it must be a terribly upsetting event. I just want to get a picture of what may have happened when it is fresh in everyone's mind, for the inquest."

"Anything we can do to be of help," Lord Avebury said, and his wife nodded, clearly a bit reassured by the colonel's quiet ease and confidence.

Cecilia did like Colonel Havelock very much. An old army veteran who had last fought against the Boers, he seemed to enjoy his quiet life at Mattingly Farm now, growing prize-winning begonias, seeing to the small matters that cropped up now and then in the neighborhood in his position as magistrate. Cecilia, her mother, and her grandmother all served on various charitable committees with Mrs. Havelock, who was a kind, cheerful, helpful lady. Surely, if anyone could get to the bottom of that strange scene in the dining room, and not ruffle any feathers while doing so, it was Colonel Havelock.

Yet as she watched her parents glance at each other uncertainly, Cecilia couldn't help but feel a little nervous herself. Someone had died, possibly been killed, right in their own home. She remembered how Mr. Hayes looked as he collapsed beside her, the blood and the sickness, her world suddenly exploding, and she shivered.

Colonel Havelock smiled at Lady Avebury, who smiled back nervously. "Lady Avebury, as hostess of this gathering, what can you tell me about Mr. Hayes?"

"Not very much, I'm afraid, Colonel," Lady Avebury answered. "I only met him maybe once before, briefly, at a party in London two years ago. I think he was on his way to Iceland then. Or Siberia? But he is very well-known as a traveler and explorer, you know. He is in all the papers. I thought he might be a very interesting guest."

And so he was, Cecilia thought. Much too interesting.

Colonel Havelock gave Lady Avebury a doubtful look. "So you just wrote to him on the basis of your meeting two years ago in London?"

Lady Avebury laughed. "Oh no, Colonel! The Bates name *is* sometimes a draw, I admit. Danby has so much history, it is of much interest. But I doubt Mr. Hayes would have thought so, after all his adventures. My friend, Mrs. Margaret Solent, saw him in Egypt and suggested he might like to visit. Or maybe he asked her? I am not sure."

"And does Mrs. Solent know him well?"

Lady Avebury bit her lip. Cecilia knew her mother never liked to gossip about her friends, and Aunt Maggie was as close as a sister. "I shouldn't think so. She does meet so many people on her travels."

"I see." Colonel Havelock scribbled something in his notebook. "Does Mr. Hayes have family? A wife, maybe, that should be contacted?"

"No, he is a well-known bachelor," Lady Avebury said. Cecilia remembered rumors of several ladies' names connected to Mr. Hayes in the papers, but such things never came to much.

Lord Avebury coughed loudly, and Colonel Havelock

arched his brow at him in question. "Lord Avebury? Do you know of someone we should perhaps contact?"

Lord Avebury looked uncertainly at his wife, and she snapped, "Oh, Clifford, for heaven's sake! We have been married for decades, and I've been out in Society for a long time. You can speak in front of me. I won't wilt."

Cecilia knew they would *not* speak if they saw her there, which made her even happier for her hiding places. Otherwise she would never learn anything. She sat up straighter in interest.

"I don't know, of course," Lord Avebury said, "but I did hear at my club that Hayes had a—a special friend for a rather long time. It seems this friend was not shy about pressing him to marry her. Perhaps she got tired of his refusals and decided to do away with him?"

"Here at Danby?" Lady Avebury cried, aghast.

"I suppose it is rather like a penny dreadful, but not impossible," Colonel Havelock said. "Love and anger joined can be like gunpowder. Do you know this friend's name, Lord Avebury?"

"I'm afraid I don't. I might ask people I know who are in the Travellers Club, as was Mr. Hayes."

"That might be a good idea," Colonel Havelock said, writing in his notebook again. "Tell me, Lady Avebury, do you have any new members of staff?"

Lady Avebury frowned in thought, twisting her handkerchief between her beringed fingers. "No new maids, except Miss Clarke's lady's maid, and she is American. One new footman. He just started yesterday, as a matter of fact. Jesse—hmm. Fellows is his last name, I think. But he is the nephew of Mrs. Mabry from the greengrocer's shop. Surely, he could mean no mischief."

"He was most helpful when Mr. Hayes was taken ill," Lord Avebury said. "Seemed to know just what to do."

"Hmm," Colonel Havelock murmured. He made another note. "You noticed no arguments between Mr. Hayes and anyone else, then?"

"Not at all," Lady Avebury said. "He seemed quite friendly, and everyone enjoyed his tales of his travels."

Cecilia remembered seeing that bruise on Mr. Hayes's face. Someone hadn't found him so very friendly.

"Thank you, Lord and Lady Avebury, you have been very helpful," Colonel Havelock said. "Perhaps you might ask Mrs. Solent to come in?"

"Are we finished, then, Colonel?" Lord Avebury asked.

"For now, yes." Colonel Havelock paused. "I must tell you, though, that in light of Dr. Mitchell's preliminary report on how Mr. Hayes died, and what I observed myself in the dining room, the chief inspector of Leeds, as the largest nearby city, and his team will probably be called in to make inquiries. I am sure he will not want anyone to leave soon."

"Oh, I say," Cecilia's father growled. "Must people come trampling in on Danby and our guests like that? Surely, Hayes had a heart attack or food poisoning or some such thing. A gentleman like you coming here is one thing, but . . ." He jumped to his feet, his wife following.

But a real policeman was quite another. Cecilia sighed. She knew from her reading that the world was changing rapidly, daily almost. The days when old families and aristocratic houses were left alone to mind their own affairs were coming to an end. But her father seemed ready to fight that with all he had. Not that he would ever win against the twentieth century.

"I am afraid it's quite clear Mr. Hayes did not die of natural causes," the colonel said gently. "And more people could possibly be in danger."

"Are you saying one of our own guests is a killer?" Lady Avebury cried. "Someone under my own roof? That cannot be!" She swayed on her velvet shoes, her face white, and Cecilia's father held her upright. She leaned heavily onto his shoulder with a groan. "The scandal!"

"I should take my wife upstairs, Colonel Havelock," Lord Avebury said. "I can send Mrs. Solent in to see you."

"Thank you, Lord Avebury. You have been very helpful."

Cecilia's parents left the library, her mother's sobs echoing in the Gothic rafters, and in a few moments Aunt Maggie appeared. She still looked quite composed, her deep green satin and chiffon perfect, the feathers in her aigrette waving. She did not look as if she had ever swooned in her life.

"Colonel Havelock," she said briskly. She sat down in

Lady Avebury's abandoned chair and took off her green silk gloves, folding them in her lap as if she was about to dine. Or maybe bare-knuckle box. One was never sure with Aunt Maggie. "How can I help you? Such a ghastly business."

"Indeed. It must have been difficult to see your friend in such a state, Mrs. Solent."

A frown flickered over Aunt Maggie's face. "I wouldn't say he was a *friend*, Colonel Havelock. An interesting acquaintance I sometimes saw on my travels. And I have seen many shocking things in the desert, I'm afraid."

"Lady Avebury says you recommended he be invited to Danby."

"Yes. The last time I saw him he mentioned how much he missed the English country life. Foxhunting, birds chirping in hedgerows shrouded in morning mist, that sort of thing. Emmaline needed another man for her party, preferably someone amusing, and it seemed a good idea." She glanced down at her gloves and shivered. "I am sorry for that now."

"As you know Mr. Hayes, Mrs. Solent, I must ask you—do you know of any, er, friendships the gentleman might have had? Particular friendships?"

Aunt Maggie smiled wryly. "I am a widow, Colonel Havelock, and a world traveler, though not quite as intrepid as Mr. Hayes. You can ask me. Did he have an amour? I believe so. That is the gossip, anyway. A long-standing liaison, if rumor is correct, though I don't think I ever heard her name. It didn't seem to stop him from flirtations abroad." She laughed at Colonel Havelock's doubtful expression. "Oh no, not me! My interests lie quite elsewhere."

"And you have no idea where this—long-standing amour might be found?"

"None at all."

"Did Mr. Hayes have any enemies?"

Aunt Maggie fidgeted a bit with her gloves. "I'm sure he must have. He was no green youth, and he was famous for his adventures abroad where he met many people. I'm certain he inspired envy. Maybe even hatred in someone who wanted such fame for themselves, or one of the husbands of his little romances." Her eyes widened, and she leaned toward the colonel. "Could he even have been doing government work on those travels? *Secret* government work? Perhaps a spy had to silence him?"

Cecilia wondered if Aunt Maggie had been reading some of the same novels she herself devoured. Mr. Hayes a spy—it sounded most intriguing, and dangerous.

"I—er, anything is possible, I suppose, Mrs. Solent," Colonel Havelock muttered. He sounded doubtful, as an old military man surely would be, but Cecilia noticed he was scribbling swiftly in his notebook. "As far as you know, though, Mr. Hayes had no connections to anyone else in this party?"

Aunt Maggie tapped her finger to her chin in thought. "I shouldn't think so. Miss Clarke only just arrived in England,

and the Byswaters are aspiring country gentry. Not the sort to interest Richard Hayes much."

Colonel Havelock glanced at the list in his book. "Mrs. Mary Rainsley has a young daughter. Could Mr. Hayes have been looking for a new—flirtation?"

"Not with Maud Rainsley. She's a young girl, unmarried, and a respectable bluestocking. She's at Girton, you know. Mr. Hayes knew the rules of romance very well."

"And Lord Avebury's cousin? Lord St. John? Could he have some quarrel with Mr. Hayes?"

Aunt Maggie laughed. "Only if he climbed out of a bottle long enough."

"Bit of a tippler, is he?"

"You could say that. I suppose he could have irritated Mr. Hayes with his inane conversation, or maybe they fancied the same woman. But that hardly seems a reason for murder. And Miss Clarke said something about Mr. Hayes drinking from her own glass. Perhaps someone tried to do away with her?"

"One never knows, Mrs. Solent. I think that's all I need at the moment. If you happen to remember anything else . . ."

"I will give it a great deal of thought, Colonel Havelock, I promise you that."

"Thank you. Perhaps you could send in Viscount Bellham? Lord St. John, the Byswaters, and the Rainsleys are free to retire tonight."

After Aunt Maggie left, Patrick appeared. He looked

quite petrified, his eyes wide, his mouth frozen in a straight line. His hair stood straight up, as if he had run his hands through it repeatedly. Cecilia crossed her fingers for him and silently willed him to stay strong.

"I won't keep you long, Lord Bellham," Colonel Havelock said softly, as if he sensed Patrick's vulnerability. "I know it's been a very trying evening."

"The worst," Patrick said. "I'm not sure how I can help. I barely knew Mr. Hayes and had little interest in this party."

"You are an idea man, I understand, Lord Bellham. A man of science, yes?"

Patrick relaxed a bit. "I like to think so."

"Then I'm sure you are quite observant," Colonel Havelock said. Cecilia wasn't so sure about that. Patrick so often seemed to be in his own world. "Tell me, how has the party been spending its time?"

Patrick frowned in thought for a long moment, the only sound in the vast room the slow, steady baritone ticktock of the old German grandfather clock. "Well, Miss Clarke arrived. Her ship had been wrecked, you know."

"A terrible thing indeed."

"Yes, but she does seem so plucky about it all. She even wanted to see my laboratory."

Colonel Havelock arched his brow. "Your laboratory?"

"Yes, it's behind the old stables. I don't often let anyone in there; the experiments can be quite delicate, you see. But Mama was most insistent I be very welcoming to Miss

Clarke, after her long journey, and she wanted to see every part of Danby."

"Your particular interest is botany, I think, Lord Bellham."

Patrick brightened. "Oh yes. I am interested in the use of plants to cure human disease. There is so much we don't know about the natural world, of course."

"Using natural plants to heal?"

"Yes. Digitalis, for example, can be quite dangerous, but also a great help in heart conditions and things of that sort."

Cecilia grew tense. Where was the colonel leading Patrick with such questions? Dr. Mitchell said Hayes had been poisoned, and Patrick was around dangerous plants all the time in his work. Cecilia had no doubt Patrick *could* poison someone if he wanted to, but her sweet brother would never do such a thing. Not unless it was to protect someone else. And he hardly knew Miss Clarke! Surely, Colonel Havelock could not suspect Patrick.

Cecilia shook her head and hugged Jack tightly. It was quite absurd. Surely, Mr. Hayes had died because of something with this mysterious mistress? Or Aunt Maggie's spy idea? Or even a quarrel with another guest, unknown to everyone else. The Byswaters were quite ambitious, after all. Maybe he had insulted Maud? Or the vicar? Mr. Brown was a most proper gentleman. Easily insulted?

Cecilia pictured Philip Brown cold-bloodedly poisoning someone's drink and realized she was just being silly. He was kind and gentle, dedicated to his profession. But it seemed that *someone* had done away with Hayes, and Colonel Havelock was still asking Patrick about his botanical experiments.

And Patrick was starting to squirm in his seat.

Colonel Havelock finally took pity on him. "Thank you, Lord Bellham, you have been very helpful. That should be all for this evening."

Patrick looked hopeful. "I—I can go?"

"Of course, and everyone else is free to retire. Perhaps I may use your telephone before I depart? I must inform Inspector Hennesy of what has happened."

Patrick nodded and practically fled the room. Cecilia hurried from her own hiding place, limping a bit as her legs had cramped from sitting there so long. She caught up with her brother in the foyer, Jack trailing behind her. Patrick looked quite stunned and exhausted, just as she felt.

She looped her arm through his and led him toward the staircase. "It's been a very strange evening, Patrick darling. Like a nightmare. You should get some sleep."

"Oh, Cec," Patrick said, taking her hand and swinging it as he had when they were children. "I'm quite sure the colonel thinks *I* did this."

"How could he think that? You didn't even know Mr. Hayes."

"He asked all these questions about my experiments. It's true I do *have* some plants that could be lethal, but they can also heal when used properly, in the right amounts. That's the only reason those plants interest me at all. I would never use them to hurt anyone."

"I know you wouldn't. Everyone who knows you cannot help but understand that." Cecilia realized she had never seen Patrick's laboratory at all, though he had shown it to Miss Clarke. "What *do* you do in that lab of yours, Patrick?"

"My experiments, of course. Keep my equipment there, my slides, things of that nature."

"You never let anyone see them. Except Miss Clarke."

Patrick blushed. "She did seem to be so interested. She's really very nice, Cec. I didn't expect that."

Cecilia had her doubts about that, after seeing Annabel shout at her servant and get upset about the bathroom, but Jane and Patrick said she had hidden depths. "I am glad you like her, Patrick." They paused at the entrance to the Elizabethan gallery, where Cecilia would turn toward her room and Patrick the opposite corridor to his. "Good night, my dear. Do get some sleep, and don't worry about the colonel. He's just trying to find out what really happened. It's his duty as magistrate."

"I know. Good night, Cec." He kissed her cheek and shuffled away, his shoulders slumped.

To Cecilia's surprise, Jane was waiting for her in her bedchamber, and Jack went to groom himself by the fire. Cecilia was suddenly glad not to be alone with her feelings and fears, with the dark night outside that seemed like it would never end. Jane was always such a cheerful, sensible presence.

"Does Miss Clarke not need you, Jane?" she asked, kicking off her shoes. She wriggled her aching toes in the soft carpet.

"The doctor gave her a draft to help her sleep. She was very upset." Jane started to unfasten the pearl buttons of Cecilia's gown, all quiet efficiency. "I thought you might need some help."

"Thank you, Jane. You are very thoughtful." She suddenly remembered what Annabel had screamed as she stumbled out of the dining room, that she herself was the intended victim. "Is Miss Clarke still afraid *she* was the target?"

"She was saying it was her glass that Mr. Hayes took. Do you think that's true, my lady?"

Cecilia sighed as Jane loosened her stays, and she tried to remember exactly what happened at the dinner table. It had all occurred so quickly, in a terrible blur. The screams, the plates and glasses crashing down. Mr. Hayes on the floor at her feet. "It might have been her glass he drank from, as she was giving a toast and it was rather confused, but I can't remember for sure. Does she have any idea of who might want to hurt her?"

Jane shook her head and handed Cecilia her muslin nightdress. "She isn't really making very much sense tonight. Maybe she'll feel better tomorrow."

"I do hope so. Colonel Havelock is calling in an actual inspector. I'm sure this man will want to question everyone."

Jane looked puzzled. "An inspector? Like—a policeman?"

"Is that what they're called in America? A policeman. Fascinating."

"Well, you would never want one coming around your place in New Jersey, my lady, I promise you that." She took up Cecilia's silver-backed brush and started untangling Cecilia's red-gold hair.

Cecilia dangled the ribbon for Jack, who pounced on it and made her smile at last. "I'm sure this inspector won't be too mean. He'll just ask his questions, put together the inquest." She did hope she was right. She couldn't imagine her home being disrupted any further. Danby had always been a haven of peace.

She hoped that was true—at least for poor Patrick's sake.

Chapter Eleven

The next morning, Cecilia sat with her mother and their guests in the White Drawing Room, all of them trying desperately to pretend everything was quite normal. Rain pattered against the windows, trapping them inside and adding a strange, sad rhythm to the Chopin nocturne Aunt Maggie played at the piano. Lady Avebury played whist with Mrs. Rainsley, Lady Byswater, and the vicar, their voices low, indistinguishable murmurs over the shuffle of the cards.

Lord Byswater and Lord Avebury read the newspapers by the fire, while the dogs slept at their feet. Patrick, Miss Clarke, and Lord St. John hadn't yet appeared, even for breakfast. Maud had gone to the library to find some books for her studies.

Cecilia sat by the window, trying to read her own book,

but her thoughts kept interrupting. Poor Patrick, afraid he was the main suspect. Mr. Hayes and his scandalous secret life. Annabel in hysterics. Danby all in chaos and uproar, so unlike its usual life of routines and rhythms.

She put down her books and stared out the window, trying to make some sense out of a scene that could only be—senseless. Not even the gardeners were out today, and the flower beds were a blur.

Out of the corner of her eye, she saw a flash of color, movement, and she half wondered if it was the Blue Lady, come to warn them of disaster. She turned and saw it was Rose and Paul, the footman. Cecilia couldn't imagine how they escaped the sharp eye of Mrs. Caffey, but they seemed intent only on each other. Paul held Rose's hands tightly, his head bent close to hers as he whispered in her ear. Rose shook her head, her face tearstained under her white ruffled cap.

Paul kissed her cheek, and she cried even harder. Was Paul the one Rose said she shared an understanding with, then? Cecilia could see why Rose wanted it a secret for now, as Redvers was awfully old-fashioned about servants' romances and would never approve. But Rose and Paul seemed like they would be so sweet together! Cecilia couldn't help but feel for them.

Why, though, were they so upset today? Were they arguing? Then again, the tension through the whole house after what happened to Mr. Hayes was so taut. Like it could all snap at any moment. Surely, everyone was affected.

Redvers came into the drawing room and whispered discreetly into Lady Avebury's ear. Cecilia's mother nodded slowly, keeping the smile on her lips, but Cecilia saw that she turned rather gray.

"Maggie, darling, would you take my place for a few moments?" Lady Avebury said. She laid down her cards and rose to her feet, smoothing the pale-yellow silk of her skirt.

"Of course," Aunt Maggie said. She left the piano and came to the card table as Lady Avebury followed Redvers to the door.

"Clifford, could you join us?" she called, and Lord Avebury reluctantly put aside his papers. Cecilia, curious, followed them at a careful distance.

Two men stood in the pale, chilly morning light of the foyer. One was a uniformed sergeant, very tall and broad shouldered, with a broken, half-healed nose, pockmarked skin, but with a kind expression on his otherwise rather fearsome face. The other was an equally tall but ascetically lean man, thinning dark hair brushed back from his harshly carved face, wearing a nicely tailored gray tweed suit.

"Lord and Lady Avebury?" he asked, his voice with the rough edges of a cigar smoker. Utterly no-nonsense. "I am Chief Inspector Hennesy of Leeds, and this is my sergeant,

DS Dunn. Colonel Havelock called us in about the—unpleasantness here at Danby Hall last night."

"Of course," Lord Avebury said. "Good of you to come at such short notice."

"I'm sure we all want this resolved as quickly as possible. The newspapers will soon be greatly interested in such a man's demise," Inspector Hennesy said. He glanced quickly around the foyer, the carved white plasterwork, the ancient battle flags and weapons captured in long-ago battles. He did not look impressed. "I have Colonel Havelock's notes from last night, and Dr. Mitchell's preliminary report. He is doing a complete autopsy today. I assume he has taken the body?"

Lord Avebury glanced at his wife, who bit her lip. "Er—yes. He took it to his surgery for the—er, required . . ."

"Postmortem, yes," Inspector Hennesy said. Not a man to tiptoe around, then, Cecilia thought. Most people at Danby would not care for *that*. "I will call in to see the doctor this afternoon. In the meantime, Lord Avebury, do you have a place where I can conduct my interviews? My sergeant will question your servants."

"I'm quite sure they could not have seen anything of interest," Lady Avebury protested. "And their work will be interrupted!"

"I'm afraid I must insist, Lady Avebury," the inspector said firmly. "In my experience, those belowstairs are often far more informed than anyone else."

Cecilia knew he was right about *that*. She was often

quite astonished at how much the maids and footmen knew that she never even noticed.

"I can show you to the library," Lord Avebury said. "And Redvers will take your sergeant to the servants' hall and find him an appropriate spot."

"I'm sure he can use the butler's pantry, my lord," Redvers said sternly. "If you will come this way, Sergeant Dunn."

As Redvers and the burly sergeant left, Lord Avebury asked, "Where would you like to start, then, Inspector Hennesy? Most of our guests are gathered in the drawing room."

Inspector Hennesy glanced down at a sheaf of documents in his hands, which Cecilia noticed seemed to come from Colonel Havelock's notes. "It seems no one has spoken to Miss Annabel Clarke yet. I would like to start with her."

"I'm afraid Miss Clarke is still in her chamber," Lady Avebury said disapprovingly. "She was most upset last night. Dr. Mitchell gave her a draft."

"I can imagine it must have been a shocking sight," the inspector said. "She was afraid she might have been the intended victim?"

"She was upset. And I would be happy to answer any of your questions, Inspector, while Miss Clarke is fetched," Lord Avebury said quickly. "If you will just come this way?"

Once they were out of earshot, the library door closing behind them, Lady Avebury hissed, "The nerve of that man!"

"Mama?" Cecilia asked.

Her mother whirled around to face her. She looked

furious, frightened, but she quickly covered it with her usual social smile. "Cecilia. A man like that, coming in here and disturbing us all. Asking whatever questions he desires. When I was young, no one would have been so disrespectful, so disrupted the peace of a house like Danby."

Cecilia nodded. But she knew how things had changed in the last few years. The old ways, when families at Danby ruled their fiefdoms and were not questioned, were allowed to run their own affairs as they saw fit, were gone. She wasn't sure her parents would ever see that.

"The sooner he finds out what really happened to Mr. Hayes, the sooner everything will return to normal," Cecilia said.

"Will it?" Lady Avebury blinked hard, her eyes surprisingly bright, as if she was about to cry. "Mr. Hayes. Why did I ever invite him here? What does anyone know about him, really? Look what he has brought down on us!"

"I'm sure he didn't *know* he was going to be killed over dinner, Mama."

Lady Avebury took a deep breath. "I must return to the drawing room. Cecilia, will you go and inform Miss Clarke she is needed in the library? Oh, it is all too bad. She will never want to stay at Danby now, and we will be ruined."

"I wouldn't be too sure about that." Patrick did seem to like Miss Clarke, strangely enough—and there was still the earldom. Cecilia suspected Annabel was made of sterner stuff than it seemed. "I will go see to her."

Lady Avebury nodded and made her way back to the drawing room. Cecilia hurried up the stairs to Annabel's Green Chamber. Everything seemed quiet there as she knocked at the door.

Jane peeked out. Her cap was straight on her wispy blond hair, her black dress impeccable, but her cheeks were pale. "Yes, my lady?"

"I'm afraid the inspector has arrived," Cecilia said. "He says he must speak with Miss Clarke."

"She's in the bath. I was just arranging her morning dress."

Cecilia remembered how upset Annabel had been after the ill-fated dinner. "How is she this morning?"

"Quiet. Tired. But she did stop crying, and ate a bit of breakfast."

"That's good. I have the feeling this new inspector is very no-nonsense. It may be like rowing the lifeboats again."

Jane gave a wry smile. "I will warn her, my lady."

Cecilia glanced at Jack, who was sitting at the foot of the unmade bed, studying her with his green eyes. "Do you think we could talk later, Jane?" she whispered. "I have so much running through my mind today, I feel like I will scream if I can't share it with someone."

Jane looked intrigued. "Of course, my lady. This afternoon? I think Miss Clarke said something about going to see the dressmaker, but I'm sure she'll want to stay in now."

"That sounds good." Cecilia started to turn away but

then glanced back and said, "There's a sergeant, as well, asking questions in the servants' hall. I'm sure he will want to talk to you, too, Jane."

"Me?" Jane gasped. "But I don't know anything at all about this Mr. Hayes."

"Me neither. He seems to be quite the man of mystery. But forewarned is forearmed, right, Jane?"

Back in the foyer, Cecilia found Aunt Maggie hurrying toward the front doors, pinning on her hat. "Oh, Cecilia, dearest! I just handed my cards over to your mother, and I was going for a walk in the gardens now that the rain has stopped. I need to get away from this gloomy old place for a moment. Care to join me?"

"Oh yes, please!" If anyone could raise her spirits—or answer a few questions about Mr. Hayes—it was surely Aunt Maggie. Cecilia hurried to take her arm, and they made their way out into the cloudy, damp day.

Even in the gray light, the gardens were lovely, the flowers shimmering with raindrops, the fountains overflowing, the little teahouse shrouded in mist. It all looked so eternal, so unchanging, even as the ground shook underneath them.

"You must be terribly upset, Aunt Maggie," Cecilia said. "Since you knew Mr. Hayes."

Aunt Maggie looked solemn but not at all tearful. "Of course I'm most devastated, my dear. It's not every day a man drops dead in the middle of a respectable dinner party.

But, though Mr. Hayes was quite amusing whenever we met, I didn't know him particularly well."

Just enough to know the gossip about his mistress. "But you saw him in Egypt?"

"Yes. And once in Morocco, and Ceylon." Aunt Maggie laughed. "Oh, Cecilia, you can't imagine what these far-flung outposts of the Empire are like! One does tend to see the same people wherever one goes. It's like a Mayfair drawing room dropped into a Baghdad souk sometimes. I do think I should try someplace more remote. Tibet, perhaps?"

They sat down on a granite bench at the rise of a crest, looking down at the house. It all looked so quiet, so tranquil, no hint of the turmoil behind its stone walls and blank windows. "So you had no—no romantic interests in him?"

Aunt Maggie laughed. "My dear, after Mr. Solent died I realized I have no interest in romantic entanglements. Why should I? I'm free to do what I like for the first time in my life. The wandering existence suits me. And I have—well, *other* interests in that direction. And Richard Hayes, for all his wandering eye, would have no interest in an old widow like me."

"Did he really have a wandering eye, then?"

"Oh yes. Rather notorious for it. But never as clumsy about it as Lord St. John. Richard was not, shall we say, especially picky, but he had his own tastes, and was not shy about pursuing them."

Cecilia thought of the talk of Mr. Hayes's long-standing mistress. "So he had no strong connections to anyone at all."

Aunt Maggie frowned. "I'm not sure if your mama would approve of me talking about such things to you, Cecilia darling."

Cecilia nudged her with a grin. "Then I definitely want to hear all about it."

Aunt Maggie laughed. "Very well, then. Richard did have a mistress of rather a long connection, in London, I think. He never did speak of her much, and I don't know who she was. An actress or dancer, I would imagine. He would sometimes ask opinions on gifts to send back to her. We all just assumed they had an understanding, and he was free to pursue who he liked while she had her own life. So many people do live like that, thanks to the example of our dear late king."

Cecilia wondered what might have happened if the mistress's "understanding" was that Mr. Hayes was faithful to her, and then she found out he was not. What if she heard of it and was furious? But who was she? And would she have pursued him all the way to Danby?

"Do you think he was involved with anyone here?" Cecilia asked.

Her mother would have been scandalized she wanted to talk about such things, but Aunt Maggie just tilted her head in thought. "If he was, there was no talk of it in London.

Who could it have been? Not your mother, of course, and Mrs. Rainsley is too old, Maud Rainsley too young, not to mention too brainy. Richard did prefer his women to be far less intellectual than himself. Lady Byswater is pretty, and very rich, but also not in the first bloom of youth. Miss Clarke is a beauty, but I doubt even Richard Hayes could work so fast."

Cecilia sighed. Could the romance angle, so often a culprit in the novels she read, be a dead end already? Then she remembered the bruise on Mr. Hayes's face at dinner. "Maybe an angry rival? Lord St. John also has an eye—and a grabby hand—for the ladies. He might have been in a fight."

"Ah yes. Timothy is terribly tiresome. But he would have to sober up enough to so much as land a lucky punch on a rival, let alone kill him. And Richard was quite fit from all that mountain climbing and such." She shot Cecilia a puzzled glance. "You seem awfully curious about it all, my dear."

Cecilia shook her head. She didn't want to give away too many of her thoughts, not yet. "Mama is worried that the scandal may cost Patrick his engagement to Miss Clarke. Well, his possible engagement."

"Emmaline is most intent on the match, I know. But Patrick is a nice boy, and the earldom a great prize. I can't imagine one unfortunate evening would end it all. Eligible peers are not thick on the ground at the moment."

"But Miss Clarke seemed sure someone was trying to kill *her*. If she's scared, she might flee." And Cecilia found she didn't want to lose Jane and Jack. Their company was too enjoyable and made Danby far less lonely.

"Then we must do all in our power to save your mother's party," Aunt Maggie said. They sat in silence for a long moment, watching the vista of the house below them, a mellow gold in the sudden sunlight. "But what of you, Cec, my dear?"

"Me?"

"Yes. What do *you* want to do with your life? Your brother will marry Miss Clarke and run Danby, which of course is not as enviable a prospect as it sounds. What of you?"

Cecilia kicked her feet against the grass, thinking of the world of Danby, and the world outside. "Mama says I should marry as quickly as possible."

"Has she any candidates in mind?"

Cecilia laughed. "Anyone at all, I suppose. It's too bad the Byswaters have no sons of the right age; maybe they would have been content to marry a Bates when they couldn't buy our land."

"And take it as your dowry? How medieval." Aunt Maggie frowned in thought. "I wouldn't be so sure they have given up their acquisitive ambitions, though. I was talking to them earlier, and they are quite full of plans to expand their park."

"Perhaps they are doubtful the Clarke marriage will come off and think Papa will soon be more desperate." Everyone knew the Byswaters would love to be the most important landowners in the neighborhood. But would they really wreak such havoc as murder to bring Danby down?

"I don't think the Byswaters' ambition ought to worry you, my dear. Nor should marriage, unless there is someone you really love."

Cecilia remembered the new footman, the handsome, coolheaded, competent Jesse Fellows with his golden hair and bright-blue eyes. But that would never do. If only there was a duke's son so handsome out there! "Not at all, I'm afraid."

"What about university, like your friend Maud Rainsley? Or maybe travel? I know of a party of young people going to Greece in the autumn that would be happy to include you in their number."

"I should dearly love to see Greece! But I doubt Mama and Papa would agree."

"I can talk to them, if you like." As they watched the house, a figure appeared on the terrace. It was the vicar, Philip Brown. He shielded his eyes from the glare of the sun and scanned the gardens. Aunt Maggie gave Cecilia a sly smile. "Or perhaps you have a suitor closer than you think?"

Cecilia looked at her in shock. "Mr. Brown?"

"Certainly. He watched you all through dinner, you know,

couldn't take his eyes off you. He seems like a nice fellow. The nephew of a viscount, I hear. And quite beloved of all the ladies of his congregation. I can certainly see why."

Cecilia thought of the past few Sundays, the way he would seek out their family after the service, and sit beside her when he came to Danby for tea or dinner. He did seem nice, and had lovely eyes, but . . . "He is nice, true. But I fear I would be a terrible vicar's wife."

Aunt Maggie shrugged. "It can be an important job, I'm sure, depending on what you make of it. Rather fulfilling, if one wants a duty to perform. But do remember what I said about Greece. Ah, here comes the handsome parson now. I must walk on, my dear."

"Aunt Maggie . . ." Before Cecilia could stop her, Maggie had hurried away toward the teahouse on the rise of the hill, leaving Cecilia alone as Mr. Brown strode toward her from the house.

He gave her a shy smile, his hair shimmering in the light like topaz. He *was* very handsome, Cecilia realized, and had a certain gentle demeanor that seemed reassuring after all that had happened at Danby. How had she never really noticed that before? "Lady Cecilia. I was quite worried about you, out here for so long. Are you not chilled?"

"Not at all, Mr. Brown. I just needed a moment of quiet, that's all."

"Of course. These terrible events. You must be quite shaken by it, a young, sheltered lady such as yourself."

Sheltered lady. Cecilia sighed. How very tired she was of being that! But for the moment, she had no choice but to give Mr. Brown a wan smile, take his arm, and let him lead her back to the house.

❧

The servants' hall was like a beehive that morning, buzzing with the hum of gossip and chatter. Jane tried to stay quiet in her corner, her head bent over the torn lace of one of Miss Clarke's petticoats. The tear was a small one, stained at the edge with some strange greenish smears, but she pretended to be very busy sewing in order to listen.

"I heard Mr. Redvers tell Mrs. Caffey that a sergeant will be here soon to question us," James the footman told Pearl the kitchen maid as she chopped vegetables for luncheon. "What on earth will they ask us, I wonder? Maybe one of us is in trouble."

"Well, it won't be me," Pearl declared. "I was down here all night, working my fingers to the bone. I never see anything exciting!"

"I didn't, either," James said regretfully. "I was just carrying up the potatoes dauphinoise. Only Paul and that new fellow were in the dining room."

"I heard he collapsed screaming in a pool of blood," Pearl gasped, her eyes wide. "That it sprayed everywhere!"

"That's not true," Bridget the housemaid said, as she walked past with a basket of linen for the laundry room.

"Rose and I had to clean in there this morning, once the inspector said it was all right. It was a right mess, but not much blood. Mostly sick and spilled wine, a few bits of blood mixed in. That tablecloth is ruined, though. I thought poor Rose was going to be ill, herself."

"Paul said he fell right over. Mr. Hayes, that is," James said. "No warning. But that new footman knew just what to do, as if he was a medic or something."

Pearl leaned closer to him over the table, and Jane had to strain to hear her. "Where do you think he really came from? He seems strange, knowing things like that."

"He's the nephew of Mrs. Mabry at the greengrocer's shop," Bridget said.

"But what does that mean?" James muttered. "He shows up, and right away a murder happens. Nothing like that usually happens at Danby."

"I don't like it," Bridget said, shaking her head so the ribbons on her cap trembled. "Danby Hall is the best house in the neighborhood. What if there's a big scandal? None of us could get such good work again. I'll be back in my uncle's bakery, ugh."

"I think he's handsome," Pearl said dreamily, the knife dangling forgotten in her hand over the carrots.

"My uncle?" Bridget cried.

"No, silly," Pearl said. "That new footman."

Bridget sighed. "He is that."

"But where did he come from?" James said irritably. "Who knows who he really is? And why did he get put on serving sauces right away, when I had to bring the potatoes? All I know is that trouble followed him here. What if he had something to do with it?"

"Who had something to do with what?" Paul asked, hurrying into the kitchen. He looked rather harried, his dark hair mussed, his buttons awry again. He still wore his gloves, too.

"The new footman," Bridget said. "James thinks he's trouble."

"Jesse?" Paul said. "He's a good 'un. Certainly knows what he's about in the dining room. And we can use the help, with all the extra guests in the house now."

"And who knows when they'll be leaving." Bridget sighed.

"Why do you still have your gloves on, then?" James asked Paul.

Paul glanced down at his hands, as if he had quite forgotten the gloves were there. "Er—Mr. Redvers asked me to polish some silver. I was just going to the silver room now."

Mrs. Caffey appeared in the doorway and frowned as she saw everyone standing about talking. Everyone went quiet. Even Jane knew Mrs. Caffey's rule—no gossip about the family, especially with guests and their servants roaming around.

"Where is everyone, then?" she snapped.

"Um—Mrs. Frazer is fetching more castor sugar from the larder, Mrs. Caffey," Pearl said timidly.

"I was just taking this to the laundry, Mrs. Caffey, while Paul is to polish some silver for Mr. Redvers," Bridget said. "The guests' maids and valets went to see to everyone's afternoon clothes."

Mrs. Caffey's lips pursed, and she turned her steely gaze onto Jane. "And you, Miss Hughes?"

Jane swallowed hard, her voice vanishing. "Er—Miss Clarke is still bathing, Mrs. Caffey, and hasn't rung for me yet. I was just mending this petticoat now."

"Very good. All of you, get back to your duties as quickly as possible. There is still luncheon to prepare, and the sergeant will be calling for you at any moment. I believe he has gone to fetch some papers from the inspector's car. And where on earth is Rose?"

"Dusting in the music room, the last time I saw her, Mrs. Caffey," Bridget said.

"Then take that to the laundress, and fetch Rose at once. Lady Cecilia will need to be seen to when she returns from her walk."

"I can do that, Mrs. Caffey," Jane said, wondering how Lady Cecilia was faring with all the interrogations that day. "If Miss Clarke doesn't yet need me."

"That is kind of you, Miss Hughes." Mrs. Caffey cast a

harried glance around the servants' hall. "I don't know how we will manage it all. And Lady Avebury is still insisting on having her garden party and masked ball! Even more guests to see to." A knock sounded at the outside door, and Mrs. Caffey hurried to answer it, her black silk gown rustling, the keys at her belt jangling. She opened the door, and Sergeant Dunn stepped in, respectfully removing his helmet. A file of papers was tucked under his arm.

Jane peeked at him over her mending, trying to stay inconspicuous. That was what everyone back in her neighborhood did when the police came around, and this man looked very intimidating. Very tall, burly in his dark-blue uniform, his hair roughly cut and falling over his brow, pockmarks on his cheeks and a nose broken once or twice and healed wrong. But he also looked strangely shy as he shuffled his booted feet and gave Mrs. Caffey a little half bow.

"I'm Sergeant Dunn, ma'am," he said, his voice soft for such a tough-looking fellow.

"Oh yes, of course," Mrs. Caffey answered briskly. "Her ladyship said you need to ask the servants a few questions. I'm Mrs. Caffey, housekeeper here at Danby Hall. Mr. Redvers has put his butler's pantry at your disposal. I hope that will be satisfactory?"

"Very much, thank you. I'll try to stay out of your way. My mother was a cook. I know how busy a large house can be."

Mrs. Caffey seemed to soften a bit. She nodded and led him down the corridor toward Mr. Redvers's pantry. Paul and Bridget had vanished.

"He doesn't seem so bad," Pearl whispered to James.

James glared suspiciously after the sergeant. "He should pay more attention to them upstairs than get in our way. The things that go on up there . . ."

"Like what?" Pearl asked, goggle-eyed.

James looked over his shoulder to make sure Mrs. Caffey or Mr. Redvers was nowhere near. He didn't seem to notice Jane. "I saw that Mr. Hayes arguing with Miss Clarke before dinner. On the terrace."

"Miss Clarke?" Pearl said. "That doesn't make any sense. She just got here all the way from America."

Jane agreed—that made *no* sense. Miss Clarke didn't even know anyone at Danby! Annabel was a picky sort of lady to be sure, and demanding, but surely, even she couldn't already have a quarrel with another Danby guest. Could she?

"Clear as day," James said. "She was waving her hands while he shook his head, and then he gave her a little push, like this." He nudged Pearl's shoulder. "They were talking loudly, but the window muffled their words so I couldn't hear them. Then Lord Bellham came along and took her away. She was all smiles then."

"What did Mr. Hayes do?" Pearl asked.

"Laughed and lit up a cigar. He was an odd one. Maybe everything that happened wasn't so unexpected after all."

Mrs. Frazer burst into the kitchen with the bag of sugar in her hands, her cap askew on her frizzy curls. "Pearl! Those vegetables won't chop themselves."

Pearl immediately went back to her task, and James vanished. Mrs. Frazer turned to the stove. Jane was left in her corner, trying to puzzle out why Miss Clarke would be arguing with Mr. Hayes, of all people. What could it possibly mean for his death?

Mrs. Caffey came back, smoothing her hands over her black silk skirt. "Miss Hughes, the sergeant would like to speak with your first."

Jane felt a jolt of nervous fear. "Me, Mrs. Caffey?"

"I'm afraid so. I told him you have two ladies to see to, but as Mr. Hayes brought no valet with him, and your Miss Clarke sat beside him at dinner, he needs to speak with you. Don't worry, I will stay with you. Remember—no one need volunteer any information unless he asks you a direct question."

Jane wasn't sure what "information" she could offer the sergeant. Annabel had been most upset since the whole thing happened and had said very little of coherence. And Jane had seen nothing at all. She certainly wasn't going to pass on hearsay about any quarrels.

But as she looked at Mrs. Caffey, her kind but implacable expression, Jane knew she couldn't run away. She had to face up to what was happening there at Danby Hall. She had wanted to be there, hadn't she? Come what may.

It was either that or return to New Jersey. And, after seeing some of the world that was out there, she wasn't going back there. Not yet.

She laid aside her mending, stood up, and smoothed her black muslin skirt. "Of course, Mrs. Caffey. Lead the way."

Chapter Twelve

"I beg your pardon, Lady Cecilia, but I believe you are needed in the library," Redvers said quietly, speaking into Cecilia's ear as she played chess with Maud Rainsley.

Cecilia glanced up at him in surprise. He looked most solemn, his bushy brows drawn together. It had been a very quiet, almost dull afternoon, the rain moving back in after the brief sunny reprieve. Everyone sat around the White Drawing Room, playing cards, reading, sewing, as they were called one by one into the library. "Are you sure it's me, Redvers? Not my mother? I think she is in the music room at the moment, going over the garden party arrangements with Mrs. Caffey." Her mother still insisted on going ahead with the garden party, inviting the whole neighborhood despite what had happened. All must appear normal at all costs.

"I am afraid so, Lady Cecilia. Inspector Hennesy has just spoken with the vicar and now wishes to see you and Lord Bellham."

Patrick? What sort of questions could the inspector have for her brother? Would the inspector want to know more about his knowledge of poisons, like the colonel? Cecilia found herself quite worried.

"Don't worry, Cec, I will use the time to plot my next move. Your knight does look quite vulnerable," Maud said, though she, too, looked concerned about Patrick. She leaned closer and whispered, "And you can warn me about what sort of questions the fearsome inspector might have! I'm sure he will want to question Mother and me soon enough. Do you suppose someone will be led out in leg irons this afternoon?"

Cecilia laughed, but she feared she might actually burst into tears. *Someone* hated Mr. Hayes enough to do away with him, and it must have been someone close to him. Someone at Danby.

Or maybe Annabel was right, and she was the intended victim. If that was true, would the killer strike again? Someone who now played cards or read or tinkled at the piano in Cecilia's own familiar drawing room?

She shivered, drew her Indian cashmere shawl closer around her shoulders, and followed Redvers to the door of the library. It was closed, but Patrick paced the carpet outside. He looked like he had just come from his laboratory, his old tan coat stained with some green plant matter, a streak on his cheek.

He smiled when he saw her, and Cecilia ran up to give him a hug. "I'm sure all will be well, Patrick darling," she said. "They'll find Mr. Hayes had a terrible accident, a heart attack maybe, and everyone will leave Danby and you can go on with your work." Except that he would have to marry Annabel Clarke, or there might be no more laboratory for work at all.

Or Miss Clarke might be poisoned, too. Along with anyone else who might get in the way.

"I hope so, Cec," Patrick said wanly. "I'm no good at this sort of thing at all. I just want a quiet life."

"I know." The library door opened, and Inspector Hennesy waved them in without even glancing at them. Cecilia took Patrick's hand and led him inside.

Inspector Hennesy had utterly taken over her father's library. The desk was cleared of estate ledgers and sporting papers and was tidy except for two stacks of notebooks. Two straight-backed wooden chairs had taken the place of the velvet armchairs, and Cecilia and Patrick sat down there carefully. She didn't even feel as if the usually cozy stained glass and wine-red settees she had always known and loved were there at all. She looked up to the minstrels' gallery and wished she was there instead, curled up with Jack and a book.

"It's like being sent to the headmaster at Eton," Patrick whispered. Cecilia bit her lip to hold back a nervous giggle.

"Now, then, Lady Cecilia, Lord Bellham," the inspector said, tapping at the papers in front of him. "I understand you had not met Mr. Hayes before this week."

"I had read about him in the newspapers, of course, but debs like me don't usually meet famous explorers," Cecilia said.

"Hmm, yes." Inspector Hennesy frowned as he looked to Patrick. "And you, Lord Bellham?"

Patrick swallowed hard. "I'm too busy with my work here to mix much in Society. Though I understand Mr. Hayes *did* send back some very unusual plant specimens from Congo to Kew. I was looking forward to asking him about it. But I didn't have the chance."

Inspector Hennesy glanced between them. He looked so stern, so unreadable, he made Cecilia want to wriggle. He was certainly good at his job. "But you do know the other guests?"

"Yes, of course," Cecilia answered.

"And, as far as you know, none of them had a quarrel with Mr. Hayes?"

Cecilia remembered the bruise on Mr. Hayes's face at dinner. "Not as far as I know. Perhaps Mr. Brown? He does get rather passionate about raising funds for the new roof at St. Swithin's. Perhaps he importuned Mr. Hayes for money."

Inspector Hennesy's scowl showed what he thought of levity. Though there was a suspiciously bright glint to his eyes. "We know Mrs. Solent met the deceased before, and it seems Mrs. Rainsley sat next to him at a dinner in Belgravia once. She told him about her recent voyage to Ramsgate, and says he was insufficiently impressed, having just returned from Ceylon."

Cecilia wondered if the inspector had a sense of humor after all, and she respected him even more. "I would imagine the pleasures of Ramsgate and its fine English seaside, complete with regimental bands and rock candy, might be lost on such a man."

"It also seems Lord Byswater invested in a journey to explore Canadian railroads, recommended to him by Mr. Hayes, but which came to nothing. Did you know about that? Or perhaps know of anyone else who made such an investment?" the inspector asked.

"Of course not," Cecilia said, puzzled why he would think they would tell her, a young debutante, anything about railroad investments at all. Would Lord Byswater be angry enough about losing money thanks to Mr. Hayes that he would do away with him? Or, horror of horrors, could her own father have used such an investment to try and escape from some of Danby's financial woes?

Inspector Hennesy turned his hard gaze onto Patrick, who fidgeted. "What about you, Lord Bellham? Perhaps you also require investments for your—plant experiments. Maybe you asked Mr. Hayes to bring you those specimens from the Congo, rather than to Kew, and he disappointed you."

Patrick loosened his tie, his face reddening. "I wouldn't even know how to begin such a thing. I am strictly an amateur."

"I am not a scientist myself, Lord Bellham, but I would imagine such things do not come cheaply." Inspector Hennesy looked down at his notes. "I understand you are engaged to Miss Annabel Clarke."

Cecilia glanced at Patrick, who was turning even redder.

"We are getting to know each other," Patrick said tightly.

"You seem well acquainted enough to show her your laboratory," the inspector said. "My sergeant tells me the servants are not even allowed to clean in there."

Patrick shook his head hard. "That is because my work is very delicate. Nothing can be moved."

"Yet you were eager to show it to Miss Clarke." The inspector folded his hands atop his papers and leaned toward Patrick. He smiled, and somehow that seemed even worse than the scowl. "What is it exactly that you have in that laboratory, Lord Bellham? Dangerous substances, maybe? Ones that could be fatal to people you do not care for?"

Patrick looked as if he would jump up and run away. Cecilia longed to reach out for him but forced herself to sit still. "Well—I—No! Some of the samples could be of some danger, I suppose, if properly synthesized. But that is not my aim at all!"

Inspector Hennesy sat back in his chair. "I understand Mr. Hayes had something of an eye for the ladies. And Miss Clarke is very beautiful. If he pestered her—well, I would also be quite angry if anyone insulted Mrs. Hennesy. Most understandable."

Patrick's face darkened to an alarming amethyst color, and Cecilia laid her hand gently on his. "Mr. Hayes hardly had time to speak to Miss Clarke, Inspector, let alone proposition her, I'm sure."

He turned to Cecilia with an inquiring smile. "And what about you, Lady Cecilia? Any troubles with Mr. Hayes? Unwanted attentions?"

No one had ever spoken so bluntly to her before. She knew she should be insulted, but really she was a bit—relieved. It was hard sometimes to live in the hieroglyphic world of the English aristocracy, where everything had to be guessed at or known since birth.

"Not at all," she answered. "And I have heard no gossip about his visit to Danby." Though she did wonder if Hayes had maybe argued with Lord St. John, if they had fancied the same lady. But Cousin Timothy would have been too drunk to be subtle about poisoning.

Inspector Hennesy stared at them for a long moment. Cecilia was about to start fidgeting, maybe even blab that *she* was the murderer to get that basilisk stare off of her, when he nodded and looked away.

"Very well," he said. "I'm sure I will have more questions very soon. You can go. Lady Cecilia, perhaps you would ask the butler to send Miss Clarke to the library? If she is quite finished with her ablutions. And tell everyone else they will need to stay here at Danby Hall for at least another several days."

Cecilia knew no one would like *that*. They had other house parties to go to, or London houses to open for the upcoming Season. Aunt Maggie probably had another voyage to plan. She nodded and grabbed Patrick's hand to pull him out of the library behind her.

"The nerve of that man!" Patrick choked out when they were out of earshot in the empty foyer. "How dare he imply *I* might have killed Hayes? I don't even stay for the end of a foxhunt. I hate all blood and violence." He stormed out of the front doors into the gray daylight.

Cecilia quickly told Redvers to send for Miss Clarke, and she ran after Patrick. He was halfway across the driveway, near the fountain. A soft, steady drizzle was beginning to fall from the sky. She ignored the threatening rain and ran to grab Patrick's arm. She had never seen her gentle, distracted brother quite like that before, so angry, so frustrated.

"Oh, Patrick, I'm sure he does not think that," she said. "It's just his job to treat everyone as a suspect. How else does one become a chief inspector?"

"But I would never kill someone, Cec! You know that. Not even for their rare plant specimens."

Or for a woman he cared for? "I know that, darling." She thought of his experiments, the work that seemed to consume him. Would he ever try an experiment on a human? "What is it you really do in that laboratory? You did show it to Miss Clarke, but I've never seen it."

Patrick kicked at the gravel. "She said she had read Aiton's *Hortus Kewensis* and was interested to see it."

Cecilia would not have pegged Annabel as the sort to read obscure eighteenth-century botanical treatises, but people were always surprising. "And was she? Interested, that is."

Patrick's face brightened. "Oh yes, very. She had lots of questions about the properties of many of my samples. You know, Cec, I was so worried about Mama's plans for Miss Clarke's visit. And she really is much too pretty for the likes of me. But she's easy to talk to, really. She asks so many questions and really listens to me. She's not such a bad sort."

"Oh, Patrick. I am glad you like her." Cecilia remembered Annabel shouting at Jane, but Jane and now Patrick said she was nice, really. Cecilia hardly knew what to think. "But what *do* you work on in your laboratory, then? Is it really something to do with poisons?"

Patrick seemed to stand up straighter, his eyes narrowing. On the rare occasions he did talk about his work, he almost seemed like a different person. Confident, assured.

"Some of my specimens are, of course. *Abrus precatorius* or *Aconitum*, or something like *Caltha palustris*, which could possibly cause some of the symptoms Mr. Hayes exhibited, such as convulsions and vomiting. But I promise, I am only hoping to do good with them, Cec. Digitalis can be used to relieve heart conditions, or nettle for gout. You remember how our grandfather suffered."

"Yes," Cecilia said, thinking of how their grandmother had spent hours trying to soothe their grandfather as he shouted in pain, his legs swollen like an elephant.

"I only want to help people, you see. And I'm sure Mr. Hayes did, too, in his own way, if he was collecting new specimens on his travels." He glanced toward the chimney of his laboratory, just visible beyond the old stables. "I should go look in on my experiments now, before Mama finds me."

And where he could hide from the inspector's questions? Cecilia would rather like to do that herself—but she knew she couldn't hide from worry about her family and friends now. Inspector Hennesy had them in his beady sights. "Of course, darling. Just be back for tea. Grandmama is coming."

Patrick grimaced. "Ugh. All the more reason to stay with my plants. They never tell me what to do."

Cecilia nodded and made her way back inside. The library door was closed, and no one was in the foyer. Danby seemed quiet and at peace for the moment, but she knew very well it wouldn't last long.

❧

"Miss Clarke," Jane whispered. She tiptoed closer to the bed, where Annabel huddled under the green brocade coverlet. The heavy satin draperies shutting out the drizzly daylight, her pale-gold evening gown crumpled on the floor. She had seemed to feel a bit better earlier, but now Jane feared a relapse.

Miss Clarke groaned and rolled over, but she didn't even peek over the lace-edged sheet.

"I'm so sorry, Miss Clarke, but Mr. Redvers says that the inspector wants to speak to you most urgently," Jane said. She picked up the gown and shook out the delicate silk, but it looked hopeless. She put aside the stockings that were tossed on the chaise for darning later.

"I don't have anything to tell him. Why would he want to talk to me?" Annabel said hoarsely. She shoved down the blankets with a huff. Her skin, usually so rosy and ivory, was blotchy, and reddened from the hot bathwater. Jane knew she would have to mix up a milk and rosewater mask.

"I think he has to talk to everyone, Miss Clarke," Jane said. She poured a cup of tea from the breakfast tray. It was long cold but luckily dark and strong. She handed it to Annabel, who gulped it down. "Just a routine."

"Did he talk to you, then, Jane?"

Jane put away the satin evening shoes in their muslin bags and looked for a hairbrush in the tangle of pots, bottles, ribbons, and jewelry on the dressing table. She saw that Lady Avebury's diamond and topaz necklace had a broken clasp, and she tucked it into a drawer for safekeeping. She noticed some of the notepaper with the Danby crest and green edges in that drawer, crumpled with a bit of cork and more half-empty pots of powder and scent. It seemed Annabel had quickly replenished her supplies of toiletries. Underneath there was a photograph, faded to a dull amber brown, of two girls. One was Miss Clarke, her hand on the shoulder of a smaller, blond girly.

"His sergeant is talking to the servants, Miss Clarke," she said.

Annabel's face darkened. "And what did you tell him?" she snapped. "I hope you won't be gossiping!"

Jane was hurt. Surely, she had never given anyone, let alone Annabel, a reason to doubt her? "Never, Miss Clarke. He must be aware you barely even knew Mr. Hayes, and we've only been here at Danby for a short time."

Annabel relaxed back onto her lacy pillows. "Good. I can't stand being gossiped about. And this inspector is going to get a piece of my mind, I can tell you! I am the one that was meant to be killed. I hope he has a plan for my protection."

Jane nodded, still feeling nervous. "Should I dress your hair, Miss Clarke? Mr. Redvers said the inspector was in a hurry. Soonest begun soonest ended, my mother always says."

Annabel stared thoughtfully down into her empty teacup. "My grandmother always said things like that, too. But I'll just wear something simple. That blue suit, maybe. No need to impress some stupid policeman."

Chapter Thirteen

My lady? Can I help you dress for dinner? Miss Clarke is in the bath again."

Cecilia looked up from the selection of dresses she was perusing in her wardrobe, grateful to see Jane at the chamber door. She had been staring at the frocks for fully fifteen minutes without even seeing them. She kept remembering the scene in the library with Inspector Hennesy and worrying about Patrick seeming to be the main suspect.

"Oh yes, thank you, Jane," she said. "I wanted to find you anyway, to see if you might like to borrow this." She took out her well-thumbed copy of *Lady Arabella's Abduction*. "It's one of my favorites, very chilling."

"My lady! How kind of you." Jane took the book eagerly, studying the image on the cover of a young lady in her nightdress, her long hair streaming, as she swooned on a windswept cliff. "I'll start it tonight."

"You'll have to tell me what you think about it all. I've had no one to discuss it with, and I'm quite longing to see if I'm right about what happens in the haunted woods." She sat down at her dressing table and started brushing her hair as Jane took over studying the gowns. She held up a pale-lavender silk embroidered with darker purple violets, and Cecilia nodded.

"How have you been faring, Jane?" she asked. "I'm afraid Miss Clarke has seemed terribly upset by everything."

Jane shook her head sadly. "She is that, my lady. She keeps saying she's sure that she was the intended victim. She seemed quiet after talking to the inspector."

"Do you think that's possible, that she was the real victim? No one here knows Miss Clarke very well, or Mr. Hayes, either, of course."

"I couldn't really say. I only met Miss Clarke in New York right before we came here. She was sometimes a little haughty with the people on the ship. But lots of people are a bit rude, aren't they? They don't go getting killed for it." She paused in searching for a pair of shoes. "It does remind me of *An Inspector Investigates*."

"By Mrs. Hawes?" Cecilia said eagerly.

"You've read it, my lady?"

"Of course. It was very popular last year. Terribly thrilling, I couldn't figure out the culprit at all. Do you mean in the way that inspector discovered that it was really the gardener all along?"

"Yes. And everyone thought it was the sister-in-law who was the killer, because she imagined she saw spirits who told her to do the murders."

Cecilia's mind was racing. "Do you know, Jane, I thought I saw the Blue Lady on the lawn not long ago." She remembered the figure dashing across the lawn. She had thought maybe it was Annabel, out alone before dinner, but Aunt Maggie and Mrs. Rainsley had fair hair, and her own mother also had dark hair. "Isn't that silly?"

Jane shook her head solemnly. She didn't seem to think it was silly. "You mean your family ghost?"

"Yes. They say she comes around to predict danger for the Bates family."

"Do you think someone else is going to get hurt, my lady?"

Cecilia very much hoped not. But with someone who was willing to use poison in their midst, it was impossible to know. What was the motive? What if they had made a mistake and really would strike again? "You are worried about Miss Clarke, aren't you?"

"Yes, I suppose I am."

"Well, I am worried about my brother." Cecilia spun around on her satin bench, studying Jane carefully. She had liked the maid from the first moment she met her, liked her openness, her kindness. Surely, she could trust her, at least to some extent? They both wanted to see people they cared about safe. "When Inspector Hennesy questioned us today, I had the distinct sense he suspects Patrick."

"Lord Bellham?" Jane cried. "But why?"

"His botanical experiments, mostly. Patrick does have some knowledge of poisons, though he would never use it to hurt anyone. The inspector also mentioned jealousy." Cecilia remembered seeing Rose and Paul arguing in the garden. Even people in love could be driven to anger sometimes, it was true. But surely not Patrick.

"Jealousy, my lady?"

"Yes. He thought maybe Mr. Hayes was bothering Miss Clarke."

Jane sat down on the edge of the bed, her face thoughtful, one silk shoe in her hand. "Sergeant Dunn has been asking some questions in the servants' hall, too. And also . . ."

"Also what?"

"I do hate to gossip, my lady, but it seems important. James said he did see Miss Clarke arguing with Mr. Hayes one night, though he couldn't overhear them."

"Oh dear." Cecilia sighed. It seemed no one liked Mr. Hayes at all, and quarrels were an epidemic at Danby. "Jane, I am sure that if we put our heads together, we could make sense of a few things. I can't talk to the sergeant, and you can't talk to the inspector. But I know we can both learn things that will help Patrick and Miss Clarke."

Jane nodded resolutely. "I'll do anything I can to help, my lady. Maybe then we can all sleep in peace again!"

Cecilia went to her little writing desk by the window and gathered up some paper and pencils before she sat next to Jane on the bed. "What do you remember of the dinner, Jane? What was the sergeant asking everyone?"

Jane swung her feet in silence for a long moment. "I'm afraid I don't know much about the dinner. Everyone was in such a rush, I just tried to stay out of the way until I heard the commotion. Later I heard that James wasn't very happy that the new footman, Jesse, was sent out ahead of him."

"Would that be a reason to poison someone? Make them ill, maybe, if James was in a play and wanted revenge on someone who had taken unfair precedence over him." Cecilia remembered how Paul had tripped just before Mr. Hayes became ill. "I remember Paul stumbled just as it all happened. He dropped his tray, which is most unlike him."

Jane nodded. "And Paul has been wearing gloves all day, even when he went in to see the sergeant. Mr. Redvers wasn't happy about that."

"Gloves? Why?"

"He said he had been polishing silver and his hands got stained. But I noticed that the table in the silver room still had candlesticks and such on it, rather tarnished."

"Hmm. Just like *An Inspector Investigates* again. The gardener was allergic to the poisonous mushrooms he harvested," Cecilia murmured. Had Rose found out and confronted Paul, and that was why they argued? Was Paul indeed Rose's mysterious fiancé?

"Oh yes! You should write that down, my lady."

Cecilia jotted down, *Paul, gloves, fell at dinner. Allergies, mushrooms.* She did have a hard time envisioning the footman as a poisoner, but then again, as the books told her, love and anger could be a potent combination. And Rose *had* been crying.

She wrote down, *Rose?*

"What of this new footman? Jesse Fellows?" she said, remembering how handsome he was, how he made her want to blush and giggle like a schoolgirl. That made her feel silly, but didn't make him a killer. Did it?

"It sounds like most of the others aren't too sure of him yet. He's so new, and Redvers has given him lots of responsibilities. But Paul says his aunt lives in the village, so he's not a stranger, and he seems good at the work."

"That is true." Cecilia remembered how Jesse seemed to know just what to do when Mr. Hayes was taken ill, was quick and calm. *Jesse—medical training?* she wrote. Maybe Jesse Fellows knew Mr. Hayes from somewhere else. She would have to search her mother's desk for his references, or maybe talk to Mrs. Mabry in the village.

"There was the snuffbox going missing, too," she murmured, remembering the bare spot in the drawing room case.

"Snuffbox, my lady?"

Cecilia told her about the collection, the pretty emerald box, and the way it vanished. "I'll have to ask Redvers if he ever found it, though it hasn't reappeared in the case."

Jane frowned. "I haven't noticed anyone suddenly flush with money belowstairs, but I can look around."

"That would be very helpful, Jane. And then, of course, there is Mr. Hayes arguing with Miss Clarke, if that's what was happening," Cecilia said, though she couldn't imagine a woman like Annabel, with a countess title in her sights, taking up with someone like Hayes. "Surely, they barely knew each other. What could have gone wrong?"

Jane shrugged, an unhappy look on her face. "I suppose I can see what Miss Clarke might tell me, though I'm not sure she would."

"I suppose I could imagine it if he was in a quarrel with Lord Byswater or something."

"Your neighbor, my lady?"

"It seems Lord Byswater got involved in some Canadian railway investment Hayes told him about, and it went wrong. The Byswaters are very rich, but still I can't imagine he would be happy about losing that money." And there was also the fact that the Byswaters were keen to get the Danby land. Would they murder someone just to cause a scandal for the Bates family? And then there was the most intriguing insinuation that Hayes had been some sort of spy on his travels.

She jotted down, *Byswaters—money. Spying?* "I will see what I can find out about it all."

"What about the other guests? The Rainsleys, or Lord St. John?" Jane shuddered. "What a grabber he is!"

"Indeed," Cecilia agreed. "I don't know which method is worse—St. John's drunken pinches or Hayes's seductions. Maybe they disagreed about a woman?" She remembered the bruise on Mr. Hayes's face at dinner. Who gave it to him? "It wouldn't have been Maud, though. She would have slapped them both into next week if they tried anything." Maud would be more likely to be jealous about Patrick than any other man, too.

"I suppose Mrs. Frazer or Pearl would have the best chance to poison someone," Jane said. "They put the last touches on the food just before it goes upstairs."

"They have the means, yes. And Mrs. Frazer *does* have a temper. But I can't see why they would."

Jane sighed. "Me, neither. What about anyone in the village? I don't know them at all."

Cecilia thought of everyone she knew in town. Mrs. Mabry, Jesse's aunt; Dr. Mitchell, who had declared Hayes to have been poisoned; Mr. Smithfield at the florist; her dear Mr. Hatcher; the Misses Moffat who ran the tea shop; Mr. Jermyn, the attorney. As far as she was aware, none of them would even know Mr. Hayes, except maybe Mr. Jermyn, who was sometimes known to dabble in investments.

Then she remembered what she had heard at the greengrocer's shop. "Oh! There has been a stranger seen about lately."

"A stranger?"

"Yes. Most odd around here; everyone does tend to

know everyone else. I have no idea who he is or what his business could be. I would imagine he's gone by now, especially if he had something to do with Mr. Hayes."

Jane smiled. "So you see, my lady? It was just a lurking stranger!"

That would certainly make things much easier, Cecilia thought. A random madman, striking in the night and then vanishing. Nothing to do with her family or friends at all. It would be such a relief. Yet she had doubts. "How did he get into Danby? And strike at Mr. Hayes specifically, when there was a dining room full of people?"

Jane shrugged. "It's such a huge place, so many hiding places."

"Very true." Cecilia shivered to think of a villainous stranger lurking in her favorite quiet spots. She wrote down, *Stranger—village.* "It looks like we have our work cut out for us, Jane. Arguing lovers, investments gone awry, jealousy, strangers lurking about."

"What if . . ." Jane broke off, looking quite worried.

"What if what, Jane? If we are to be detecting partners, which I hope we are, you can tell me anything."

"It's just—what if Miss Clarke is right? What if *she* is the intended victim?"

"Then that complicates matters even more." Cecilia looked down at her list. She wouldn't even know where to start with Miss Clarke's enemies. "We do know so little of her here. Even you just met her a few weeks ago. As far as we all know, she could have scores of enemies and disappointed suitors who followed her across the Atlantic."

Jane shook her head. "We *do* have work to do, my lady."

"Especially if I want to protect my brother." The first gong sounded, and Cecilia realized how late it was getting. "I should dress quickly, Jane, so you can see to Miss Clarke."

"Of course, my lady. I'll start trying to find out more about her life in America, too; see if she might suspect anyone in particular of wishing her harm."

"A good idea." Cecilia held up her arms for Jane to slip on the lavender gown. "Maybe tomorrow Rose could see to Miss Clarke for a few hours in the morning? I think we should go to the village. Maybe that stranger is still hanging about somewhere."

She suddenly felt quite filled with a new energy. She had something to do, something important! Something that could help her family and get them all out of that mess. Life at Danby was certainly no longer dull.

Dinner that night was a rather desultory affair, despite the fact that Mrs. Frazer had produced a delicious, fashionable turtle soup, and Aunt Maggie told amusing stories about the people she met on her travels. Patrick said little at all, just stared down at his plate, and Annabel, though dressed in a stunning creation of deep purple satin with a spangled net tunic overlay, was also rather silent. Cecilia couldn't stop worrying about her brother, and she almost wished Annabel would start shouting about the soup being cold or something, just to break the tension.

She herself tried not to stare at the spot on the floor where Mr. Hayes had collapsed. It had been cleaned up this morning, as if nothing had ever happened.

She took a sip of wine and tried to avoid Lord St. John's hand as it searched for her knee under the edge of the damask tablecloth. At least *someone* seemed unaffected by the horrid events. She wondered again if maybe Hayes and St. John really had quarreled over a woman's affections, but she had no idea how to broach the subject. All her governess's lessons about how to seat guests at dinner and introduce polite conversations had been of no help when it came to murder.

A platter of asparagus in béarnaise sauce appeared beside her, to go with the lamb tournedos James had served, and she glanced up to see Paul holding the tray very carefully in his gloved hands. He looked impassive, and Cecilia wondered why he had argued with Rose, if they were in love. She also wondered how she could get a peek under those mysteriously constant gloves. Again, those useless governess's lessons. Why had she never been taught how to investigate crimes?

She took a small portion of the asparagus. "Where is the new man, Paul? Jesse, right?" she whispered.

"Mr. Redvers is letting him help decant the dessert wine, my lady," Paul whispered back.

"Really?" Now that was most unusual. Possibly even stranger than Mr. Hayes being poisoned. Redvers never let anyone touch his wine.

Paul nodded and started to move to the next guest, but Cecilia held him back. "Is your hand quite all right, Paul?"

He looked surprised, as well he would. Guests didn't converse with the footmen at meals. It interrupted the delicate dance of the dinner. Her mother shot her a stern glance. "Of course, my lady. Why do you ask?"

"You are just holding that tray so carefully. And James brought the lamb."

Paul bit his lip. "Just a touch of a rash, my lady, nothing serious."

Cecilia saw Redvers looking concerned, and she didn't want to get Paul into trouble on top of everything else. She nodded, and he moved to Lord Byswater on her other side. Cecilia turned to Lord St. John with a polite smile. He smiled back, a wolfish flash of teeth, and he smelled strongly of wine. Cecilia tried not to lean away.

"Lord St. John," she said.

"Cousin Timothy, my dear. We are family, are we not?"

"Yes, of course—Cousin." Cecilia carefully cut her lamb into tiny bits. She had no appetite that night, but she had to do *something* to keep from slapping him silly. "I do hope these awful events have not affected your enjoyment of Danby."

His smile widened. "Not in the least. I always look forward

to time in the country. And Cousin Emmaline is an exquisite hostess." His smile flickered into a frown. "I know this may be a shock to you, my sweet cousin, but it's no surprise when certain people come to a sticky end."

"Did you know Mr. Hayes well, then?" Maybe this was her chance to find out if the two men had a romantic rivalry.

"Not well. I am a London man, you know, and he was always off to such desolate spots. Why would an Englishman want to see such heathen places, when there are such beauties right here? But when he was in Town . . ." His words trailed off.

"You would sometimes meet in London?"

Lord St. John took a gulp of wine, which Redvers then refilled. "Here and there, once in a while. Shocking places, my dear little cousin, you would never know."

She could imagine, though. A man like Lord St. John probably frequented gambling dens and houses of ill repute. "So you had—friends in common?"

"I doubt we shared similar tastes. But there was one little opera dancer. Gorgeous red hair . . ."

"Cousin Timothy," Lady Avebury said loudly. She was watching them sternly down the table. "I am sure Cecilia is not interested in such things as London matters."

Now, there her mother was quite wrong. Cecilia was very interested indeed. Could the red-haired opera dancer be the source of a murderous, jealous feud? But she had no choice but to turn to Lord Byswater on her other side.

She knew very well that the Byswaters coveted Danby land. Would they want it enough to cause a great scandal for their rivals? But his smile was kind, and he was something of a relief after Lord St. John. Lord and Lady Byswater were known to be quite devoted to each other, and Cecilia couldn't imagine him quarreling with Mr. Hayes about loose women. Yet there was that rumor of an investment gone awry . . .

Dishes of lemon sorbet were served. After some chatter about the best places to ride around the neighborhood, and a new mare Lady Byswater had just bought to use for the hunt, Cecilia said, "I did want to ask your advice about something, Lord Byswater?"

He smiled. "My advice, Lady Cecilia? I am most flattered."

"I know that you have so much knowledge of the financial markets. My grandfather left me a small legacy." That was true enough. She had begun wondering if it was enough to go to Girton, like Maud, but that was a question for another day. She had to be a bold-faced liar at the moment. "I have no idea what to do with it. I know nothing of such things. I did hear poor Mr. Hayes, before his sad demise, was talking about a Canadian railway . . ."

Lord Byswater frowned. "My dear Lady Cecilia, I have no wish to speak ill of the dead, but I fear Mr. Hayes did not know what he was speaking of. He seemed to make a specialty of specious schemes lately. But I am afraid such terrible things can be easy to fall into, unless one is constantly wary."

"As you are always wary?"

His smile turned gentle. "I do try to be. But even I am sometimes vulnerable to wild, romantic schemes. Just ask my long-suffering wife." He gave his wife a tender glance across the arrangement of lilies on the table. "I am usually able to recover. Luck sadly runs out for all of us at times."

Cecilia thought of the Byswaters' fine house, with its new roof, its Italian marble floors, Lady Byswater's new mare. It seemed their luck was quite fine, even if there had been bad investments on Mr. Hayes's advice. "So Mr. Hayes's idea was not sound. He must have been taken in as well."

Lord Byswater shook his head. "Some people specialize in taking others in, Lady Cecilia. Put your money in the five percents. Safe, regular. It will give you a nice nest egg."

"Or there is always borrowing," Lord St. John interrupted, his voice slurred.

Lord Byswater looked at him pityingly. "That is a fool's method, Lord St. John."

"Then I cannot turn to you for such a thing, Lord Byswater?" Lord St. John laughed.

Cecilia felt her face turning hot at his rudeness, and she wondered if he, too, was desperate for funds. Desperate enough to kill someone for it?

The next course was luckily brought in then, an assortment of savory tarts, and Lord St. John fell silent.

"I thought we could play charades after dinner," Lady Avebury said brightly. "The stage is still set up in the drawing room. And maybe tomorrow tea on the lawn? That horrid inspector still has some questions, I believe, but that shouldn't ruin our fun. The neighbors are looking forward to our usual garden party, as well. The roses are blooming quite early this year. It should be very lovely."

"Not as lovely as *my* roses," the dowager muttered, giving Sebastian a tidbit of fruit.

"I must take the train to Leeds tomorrow," Lord Avebury said. "I should be back by the evening, though."

Lady Avebury looked dismayed. "You must leave now, my dear?"

"Unavoidable business, I'm afraid, which can't wait."

Cecilia's mother didn't look happy, but she went back to toying with her plate and talking to the vicar, who had earnest questions about the altar flowers. Lady Avebury always organized the blooms for Sunday services.

Cecilia saw Aunt Maggie turn toward Lord Avebury with an inquiring glance, and he whispered to her, "I will send a message to Mr. Clarke while I am there. He deserves to know all that has been happening to his daughter. She seems too upset to contact him herself."

Aunt Maggie nodded. Cecilia wondered what poor

Mr. Clarke would think, his daughter shipwrecked and then marooned far from home at a house where there was murder and uproar. Would he come to fetch Annabel back to America? Was Patrick's marriage, and the salvation of Danby, over before it began?

Even worse—would a cold-blooded killer never be caught at all?

Chapter Fourteen

The next day, Lady Avebury's outdoor tea was canceled due to a chilly drizzle of rain, and Cecilia was able to beg off duties of playing whist and torturing everyone with her harp playing. Instead, she offered to run errands to the village, and Jane was able to go with her, as Miss Clarke took yet another bath and returned to her bed with a headache.

Collins drove them, as walking was impossible in the gray day, and Cecilia insisted Jane break the rules and sit with her in the back seat so she could tell Jane what she had heard at dinner, about bad investments, red-haired opera dancers, and Mr. Clarke in America.

"If Lord St. John needs to borrow money, my lady, could he have stolen the snuffbox from the case?" Jane whispered back.

"Oh, I didn't think of that!" Cecilia gasped. "Jane, you *are* clever. I wouldn't put it past him if he was desperate, though I think someone would have had to be sneaky to open that case."

Jane giggled. "Drunkenness doesn't always lend itself to sneakiness."

"No. But neediness does. And other things have gone missing recently at Danby, though I don't know what has been sold and what possibly stolen. How can we find out who might have taken the box?"

"I beg your pardon, my lady," Collins said. Surprised, Cecilia glanced up to find him watching them in his rear-view mirror. "I know it's not my place, but I couldn't help but overhear. I may be able to help."

"Really, Collins?" Cecilia said. She hadn't known Collins long; he had only come to Danby after her father decided to give up the carriages in favor of a motorcar, much to her mother's dismay. Collins was handsome, quiet, a good driver, and that was almost all she knew. "Please, do tell us!"

"I have a cousin who has a new, small shop in the village," Collins said. "He sells antiques, mostly, but he also buys a lot of items people bring him. He will even pawn them, if someone is really desperate."

"Pawn?" Cecilia asked.

"Like a loan, my lady," Jane said. "Someone brings in something like jewelry, the shopkeeper gives them money, and if they pay it back in time they get the object back. If not, it's sold."

"Oh, I see," Cecilia said. Had the snuffbox been pawned, then?

"I can take you to his shop, if you like, my lady," Collins said. "He might know if someone tried to sell an item like that recently, or if not to him he can ask about. He used to work in Leeds and knows lots of antiques experts."

"How kind of you, Collins," Cecilia said. "That would be very helpful."

"Looking into what happened to that Mr. Hayes, then?" Collins asked, rather cheekily.

Cecilia and Jane exchanged a long, wary glance. "In a way, yes," Cecilia said carefully. "I hate for scandal to affect my own home."

Collins nodded. "I used to work for a man in London, a member of the Travellers Club. He was never best pleased when Mr. Hayes came back to England, which luckily didn't seem to happen that often."

"What did he not like about Mr. Hayes?" Cecilia asked. Such curious tales seemed to come from every quarter— and none of them flattering to Richard Hayes.

"I couldn't say, really. Just that Mr. Hayes caused an uproar among the other members of the club. They were often amateur archaeologists, you know, my lady, and very jealous of their own projects in Mesopotamia or Egypt or such. Mr.

Hayes liked to pip them at the post sometimes, on tombs or temples they just discovered. It was all very strange, grown men getting so upset about things that have been dead for thousands of years."

"It does sound like it," Cecilia agreed. She didn't know anyone at Danby excavating temples at the moment, but could someone else have come in without them realizing it?

"I hear he was also one for the ladies," Jane said boldly. "If one of those explorers was off in the desert, and his poor wife was lonely . . ."

Collins laughed. "I wouldn't be surprised."

"Jane, you are a minx," Cecilia said admiringly.

They turned onto the main lane into the village. It was a busy day, people hurrying in and out of the shops, the display windows bright as if to greet the guests at Danby.

"That's my cousin's shop. It hasn't been open long, my lady," Collins said, pointing out a thatched-roof place near Mr. Hatcher's bookshop. The bow window showcased a sparkling array of china and crystal, silver candelabra, swaths of scarlet brocade. It seemed very enticing, very luxurious, and Cecilia couldn't imagine how she hadn't noticed it before.

"Oh, let's stop there first, Collins," she said. "It does look terribly intriguing."

Collins found a place to leave the car, and they made their way to the new shop. Inside, it was just as charming as the window promised, small but filled to the brim with towering shelves of sparkling, mysterious treasures. Like a jewel box or a fairy-tale pirate's cave. There were gilded settees, Louis XIV commodes, engraved silver, paintings, porcelain figurines.

"Oh, my lady, look at this," Jane whispered, pointing carefully at a small Limoges figurine of a shepherdess with delicate waves of red-gold hair under her straw hat, looped skirts of pink-and-yellow stripes. "It looks like you!"

At the sound of the tinkling doorbell, a man emerged from an office door at the back. He looked rather like Collins, with sharp, handsome features and smooth, dark hair, but graying and somewhat stooped, as if he spent much time examining details of antiques under magnifying glasses. "Matthew, my boy! What a surprise. I didn't expect to see you today."

"Lady Cecilia, Miss Hughes, this is my cousin, Mr. Talbot," Collins said, tucking his peaked chauffeur's cap under his arm. "Cousin Harry, this is Lady Cecilia Bates and her maid Miss Hughes."

Mr. Talbot beamed. "Oh, wonderful, wonderful! What can I help you with, Lady Cecilia? I have a lovely seventeenth-century toilette set."

"What *can't* you help me with, Mr. Talbot?" Cecilia said, goggling at a sapphire-hilted sword that could have belonged to Ralph, the suit of armor. "Your store is amazing. I can't believe I haven't been here before."

"I only just opened, Lady Cecilia," Mr. Talbot said. "I did have a shop in Leeds, but health concerns made me look for a quieter situation. Matthew was kind enough to seek out a placement nearby to help me."

Cecilia studied Collins curiously, realizing how little she knew about him. He had not worked at Danby long. "How kind of him."

"Cousin Harry practically raised me," Collins said with a fond smile. "Lady Cecilia is looking for something specific today, I think."

Mr. Talbot clasped his hands eagerly, as if looking forward to a challenge. "Oh yes? Some earrings, perhaps? Or that toilette set? It's a pretty thing, still in its original case."

Cecilia laughed. "Yes to both, Mr. Talbot. But today I do have a question. Collins says sometimes you accept, er, pawn items from customers."

"It is not my main line of work, but if something is fine enough, I do consider it."

"Have you perhaps seen a snuffbox recently? Eighteenth century, Russian, chased silver and gilt with a cabochon emerald?"

Mr. Talbot tapped his foot in thought. "I don't believe so. Let us see . . ." He unlocked a small glass case filled with pendants and enameled boxes, tiny Limoges figurines of dogs and horses. "Are any of these what you're looking for, Lady Cecilia?"

She studied the sparkling array. "No, I'm afraid not," she said, disappointed.

"I do know many people with shops in other cities, Lady

Cecilia, even in London. I can make inquiries, if you like, see if any of them have seen such an item. It does sound unusual."

"That would be most kind of you, Mr. Talbot." Cecilia glanced at Jane, who was laughing with Collins as they studied an antique marionette dressed in Elizabethan clothes. "I'm afraid I have a few errands to attend to, but why don't you stay here for a while, Jane? Have a good browse."

"I could make tea," Mr. Talbot said. "I quite want to know how you are faring at Danby, Matthew."

Cecilia left them in that magical little shop and made her way to the bank in the next lane. It was a branch of Coutts in London, where her father did all his financial transactions, and Cecilia had never been in there alone before. She had to admit, she was rather intimidated by all the cold stone floors, the gilded tellers' counters, the curious stares she attracted, but she made herself hold her head up and march ahead. She needed to learn more about the small legacy her grandfather had left her, the one Lord Byswater said to invest safely. If matters at Danby continued to be as they had been of late, she might need it.

Half an hour later, after charming the manager and declaring sad tales of her pin money not covering all the hats she needed to buy, she marched out again in possession of her own bankbook. Contingent on her father's signature, it was a tidy sum. She made her way to Mrs. Mabry's greengrocer's shop to place an order for Mrs. Frazer.

"Oh yes, Lady Cecilia, we did hear of the sad events up at Danby," Mrs. Mabry clucked as she studied the list. "Do they know how long the guests will be staying?"

"Not yet, Mrs. Mabry, and Mrs. Frazer is quite worried about feeding them all, as well as the usual extras for the garden party and masquerade."

"Not to worry, my lady, we'll be able to deliver this by the evening." She peered closer at Cecilia. "So, the garden party is going ahead, is it?"

"Indeed. Mama feels we could all use a bit of cheer right now."

"Very wise of her ladyship. We all do look forward to it every year." The garden party was the only time the gates of Danby were open to the public. It had always been a great tradition.

Cecilia studied an array of tinned fruit on the shelves and wondered about the mystery of Mrs. Mabry's nephew, the new footman. Where had he really come from? "I must thank you for sending your nephew to us. He has been of such help."

Mrs. Mabry smiled. "I'm glad, my lady. I'm sure he enjoys working in a big house again."

"Has he worked in large houses before, then?" Cecilia asked. Her mother had taught her how to hire proper servants, in expectation that she would one day run her own household, but Cecilia was never shown references now.

Mrs. Mabry's smile turned cautious. "He has had a few

positions, my lady. He's a smart lad, always has been; he just needs to find his correct place in life. I'm sure Danby is it."

Cecilia remembered that terrible dinner, Jesse's reassuring, calm presence. "Has he perhaps worked in a hospital, then?"

Mrs. Mabry frowned. "Why would you think that, my lady?"

"Oh, he was just very helpful when—well, when the unpleasantness happened. Very calm in a crisis."

"I'm happy to hear it, my lady." Mrs. Mabry looked down at the list. "Now, are you sure this is all that's needed? I did get in some lovely pineapple just this morning . . ."

And Cecilia knew she would discover nothing more about the mystery of Jesse Fellows from his aunt. She would have to find a way to read his reference letters kept in Mama's desk. She thanked Mrs. Mabry and left the shop, straightening her gray felt and velvet hat. She wondered about the other servants. Everyone belowstairs always seemed to know far more about what was happening locally than anyone else. She knew Bridget the housemaid was the niece of a local baker, but Rose, Paul, and James were from other places, and it seemed Collins had worked in London. And no one would tell *her* anything, anyway. That was Jane's job now.

She decided to let Jane stay with Collins at the antique shop for a while and turned toward the bookshop to see if Mr. Hatcher had anything new. As she passed the Misses

Moffat's tea shop, she glanced inside, tempted to stop for one of their cinnamon cakes. It was a lovely, cozy space, the windows swagged in pink gingham, the little round tables draped in the same with pale-green cushions on the white chairs. Glass cases displayed dainty, pastel pastries, and pink-aproned servers hurried past with tiered trays of little sandwiches and scones. Even through the window, she could smell the sugars and spices.

As she studied the tempting cakes, she caught a glimpse of something most strange—a single gentleman. He sat alone at a table in the back corner, a pot of tea in front of him along with an open notebook. He was quite nondescript, not fat or thin, tall or short, old or young, with brown hair and spectacles, and a plain dark-brown suit.

Was this the stranger she had heard about, the one seen lurking around the village before Annabel arrived? What was he still doing there?

Cecilia hurried inside, her heart pounding at the thought that she might be close to an answer at last. But as soon as she stepped through the door, the man rose from his table, tucked his notebook into a small leather valise, put on his hat, and walked out. He gave her a small nod as he passed.

"Would you like a table, Lady Cecilia?" one of the pink-aproned waitresses asked.

"Oh—no, thank you, Nancy. Just some cinnamon cakes to take with me, I think." She craned her neck to look out the window, but she only had a glimpse at the back of the man's brown suit. "Nancy, do you happen to know who that gentleman is?"

"The one who just left, Lady Cecilia? No, but he has come in here a few times in the last several days." She leaned closer and whispered, "We all wonder if maybe he's royalty in disguise! Or maybe a famous writer."

"A writer?"

"Because he always has a notebook with him. And he never says much. He's polite enough, but doesn't really answer questions. He won't even sign his name to a bill! He likes the raspberry tarts, though."

A writer / secret royal who liked raspberry tarts and paid in cash. Cecilia sighed. That wasn't much help. But then she recalled the theory that maybe Mr. Hayes had engaged in some espionage on his travels. Maybe the stranger was a spy.

By the time she made her way back to the street, the mystery man was nowhere to be seen. But she did still have a few minutes before she should find Jane again, so she went on to the bookstore.

Mr. Hatcher was atop one of his rickety ladders, shelving books. "Lady Cecilia!" he said. "I didn't expect to see you today."

"I'm only stopping for a moment, Mr. Hatcher. I was wondering—do you have any foreign newspapers? America,

Canada, maybe Germany?" She thought of Annabel Clarke, an American, all Mr. Hayes's travels, and the ill-fated Canadian railroad. Maybe it would help if she could learn more about them.

"Not many, but I can certainly order some from London for you. They may be somewhat out-of-date. Is there anything in particular you require?"

"Oh, San Francisco, I think. And New York, Montreal. Maybe Berlin? Vienna? Whatever you can find would be of help."

Mr. Hatcher climbed down from the ladder, a pile of volumes in his arms. He looked most curious, but he said nothing. He was too accustomed to her changing interests. "I'll order them today. In the meantime, I just got this book I thought Lord Bellham might enjoy."

He handed Cecilia a heavy, leather-bound volume—*Healing Plants of the World.* Patrick said he wanted only to heal, to use plants that could also harm if used in the wrong way. Maybe she should glance through it before she gave it to Patrick.

"Thank you, Mr. Hatcher," she said. "You have been very helpful."

As she left the bookshop, Cecilia realized she would have to practice something she was not at all good at—patience. She had to wait to look at Jesse Fellows's reference letters, to find the stranger, to research the newspapers, to learn about poisons.

But then again—good things were said to come to those who could wait. And those who could ask questions.

❧

"Do you think you will be staying at Danby for some time, then, Miss Hughes?" Collins asked as he drove the car toward the garage, after they left Lady Cecilia at the front door.

Jane peeked at him shyly from under the brim of her hat. He was certainly a good-looking young man, this chauffeur, with his honest brown eyes, his dark hair, and kind smile, and it had been fun to look around his cousin's shop with him. He hadn't even thought her immature for being fascinated by the children's marionettes, but instead put on a silly show for her with them, making her cry with laughter. He was nothing like the boys back in New Jersey.

"I—well, that's up to Miss Clarke, of course," she said. "But I've been enjoying my time here very much."

He gave her a wry smile. "Despite our rather overly dramatic welcome? I promise it's not always like a penny dreadful novel."

"Oh, do you read those, too? They are ridiculous, but I enjoy the thrill of the tales," Jane said happily. "Lady Cecilia just loaned me one about a lady who escapes from an evil monk by running along the cliffs in a storm. It's quite chilling. I doubt what happened to poor Mr. Hayes had anything to do with demon monks, though. Unless it's the Blue Lady . . ."

Collins laughed, a delighted sound. "You see, Miss Hughes, you are right at home here already. You know about the local ghosts, and Lady Cecilia is loaning you books."

Jane studied the outline of the grand house just before the car slid into the garage behind the old stables. The garage was dim and smelled of oil and metal, but very tidy. She was sure Mr. Collins was quite particular about that, just like his own appearance in his neat gray uniform and perfectly cut hair. "It's not like anywhere I've ever been before. I think I *would* like to stay for a while, learn more about it."

"Especially as lady's maid to a future countess?"

"I . . ." Jane found she didn't know how to answer. When she pictured Danby, it was hard to see Miss Clarke there for years to come, part of that history. "I hadn't thought about it that way. Miss Clarke might want an English maid to help her settle in."

"Someone like Mrs. Sumter?"

How would Mrs. Sumter deal with Miss Clarke's tempers? Better than Jane did, probably. Mrs. Sumter seemed a very no-nonsense sort of woman. "Probably. She knows so much more about the job than I do."

"But you're much nicer to look at over the dining table, Miss Hughes," he said with a teasing smile.

Was he *flirting* with her? Jane felt her cheeks turn hot, but before she could answer he left the driver's seat and came to open her door and help her out. As if she was a proper lady. His hand lingered on hers for a second, but he didn't try anything. Not like the boys at home at all, true.

"I did enjoy seeing your cousin's shop, Mr. Collins," she said. She knew she should go inside to see if Miss Clarke needed her, but she was strangely reluctant to leave just yet. It was nice there in that garage, warm and quiet and oddly homelike. "Such amazing things he has to sell!"

Collins took off his hat and ran his hand through his dark hair, mussing the perfect strands. It made Jane want to smooth it down again for him. "When I was a boy, my parents died and I went to live with Cousin Harry. He would take me to auctions and sales with him. It was much more fun than going to school, or working in a cobbler's shop as my father did before he died. Harry knows every historical event you could imagine, from the Battle of Hastings to the Boer War, and he would always tell me tales of kings and knights and battles."

"How fascinating." Jane sighed, remembering how she had to hide her books at home. How all the girls in her neighborhood talked about getting married and having babies to get away from the factories, and the boys just wanted to sneak a feel where they shouldn't. No stories of histories or kings or romances. "How did you end up a chauffeur? Did you not want to sell antiques, too?"

He looked away, his expression seeming to close down. "I have to make a living, don't I? I found out I was good with mechanical things."

"Have you been here at Danby long?"

"Not very long. I was in London, with the gentleman from the Travellers Club, until he went to Persia." He gave her another smile, as if that shadow had never been. "Maybe we could learn more about the house together?"

Jane could feel her blush come roaring back, as hot as a summer's day on the beach. "If I end up staying. I should go, as Miss Clarke will be looking for me. Thank you again, Mr. Collins."

Jane ran across the gravel drive, past the old stables and Lord Bellham's laboratory, into the entrance to the servants' hall. To her surprise, it was quiet, though Mrs. Sumter's workbox was on the long, scrubbed pine table, and she could hear Mrs. Frazer shouting at Pearl about the béarnaise sauce from the kitchen. Only Rose was there, huddled in the corner with her apron pressed to her face. Jane heard a soft, muffled sob.

Terrified someone else might have died, Jane ran to kneel beside Rose and reach for her hand. "Rose, what on earth has happened? Are you ill?"

Rose shook her head. Her hair was straggling from under her lace-edged cap. She slowly lowered her apron, and Jane saw that her face was all red and splotchy. "It's Paul, Jane."

"Paul? The footman?" Jane remembered how Rose and Paul were said to be courting. "Never say he's thrown you over! That louse."

"Oh no, it's not like that. At least I don't think it is." She glanced around nervously. "It's just—I found out something. Something awful."

Jane sat back on her heels, her hand tight on Rose's. "You can tell me. I promise, I'm awfully good at keeping secrets, when they won't hurt someone else, and not much shocks me. Not with as many brothers as I have."

Rose sniffled. "I saw Paul without his gloves."

Jane was startled. Was this some strange English impropriety? "No gloves?"

Rose nodded. "He's been wearing them all the time lately. But I saw his hand, and it was all bruised and scraped up. I asked him what happened."

"And what was it?"

Rose whispered in Jane's ear, "He—he *hit* Mr. Hayes. On the day he died. Right in the face!"

Jane was shocked. "He fought with Mr. Hayes? But why?"

Rose buried her face in her apron again. "Because Mr. Hayes made a pass at me, and Paul found out. He saw Mr. Hayes had cornered me in the music room, and Paul was so furious. I've never seen him like that."

"Oh, Rose. You poor thing." Jane patted Rose's shaking back, trying to push down her own rush of hot anger and sadness. "Paul was quite right to deck him one!"

"But he could have lost his position! And then what would we have done? We haven't saved enough to marry yet." Rose shuddered. "Mr. Hayes was awful. His hot breath, the way he seemed to—to like how scared I was. But I knew how to get away from him. I've done it before. Not here, of course. Everyone at Danby is nice. But my last place."

Jane remembered some of the men at the hotel, their pinching hands in the corridor. "That doesn't mean it's right."

"No, it's not." Rose sat up straight, and she suddenly looked so much older, weary. "But it's our world, isn't it, Jane? That's why I want to marry, have my own house, my own family. No one lurking around."

Jane could see that. The thought of a quiet space where there was safety and belonging was tempting. Why did she so often long for something—more? She had no idea. "Does Sergeant Dunn know? That Paul punched Mr. Hayes?"

Rose looked horrified. "Of course not!"

"Well, I think Paul should tell him. He'll find out anyway, and it will look bad if Paul wasn't the one to tell him. Believe me, Paul won't be the only man upset that Mr. Hayes bothered his lady."

Rose shook her head doubtfully. "I will tell Paul what you said, Jane. You're so smart."

Jane didn't feel smart at all. She felt confused and sad and angry. It had ruined her lovely day with Mr. Collins. She squeezed Rose's hand. "Don't worry. They'll find who really did this, and everything will go back to normal soon. We'll be dancing at your wedding in no time."

Rose gave her a watery smile. "I hope so."

Mrs. Sumter appeared in the doorway, looking quite

stern in her black silk and tight chignon. She scowled at them sitting there in the corner. "Miss Hughes. The first gong will be soon. Miss Clarke will need you."

"Of course." Jane hated to leave Rose just then, but she knew she had to. She gave the poor girl one more reassuring smile and hurried out of the servants' hall.

Only to run right into Sergeant Dunn in the corridor.

"Oh!" She gasped, falling back a step. "You startled me, Sergeant."

"I'm sorry, Miss Hughes. Didn't mean to," he said, an apologetic look on his pockmarked face. "Is everything all right, then?"

"Yes, of course. Well—as all right as it *can* be, with a murderer around."

"It must be worrying, I'm sure. But the inspector is a good 'un, he'll catch his man fast, and there are constables keeping watch."

"I do hope so. That he'll catch them soon, that is."

"You haven't been here long, have you, Miss Hughes?"

Jane shifted on her feet, wondering if she really stuck out that much. She did so want to learn to fit in. "Not long at all."

"Well, I promise England isn't usually like this. I hope you'll give us a chance."

He looked so earnest, so hopeful, that Jane had to smile at him. "Aside from that nasty business, I'm liking England very much. I'd always dreamed of visiting here."

"I'm glad to hear it." He glanced around carefully. "And your employer? How is she faring?"

"She is very upset, of course."

Sergeant Dunn nodded. "Knew the victim, did she?"

"I don't think she knew him at all. Or anyone here," Jane said carefully.

"But she *was* seen talking with him most heatedly before—before the events. Do you happen to know what that was about, then?" the sergeant asked.

The bell to the Green Chamber rang. "I'm sorry, but I must go." Jane gasped, feeling rather frightened that word of that argument had spread. And how did the sergeant know? Had James told him? And what would it all mean for Miss Clarke?

"Of course, Miss Hughes," Sergeant Dunn said with a stern glance. "Just be careful, right? These big houses—they're like a world of their own."

Jane was beginning to learn that. She nodded and ran up the stairs that led to the opulent upstairs corridors.

Annabel was pacing the green, cream, and gold carpet of her bedchamber, her ecru lace dressing gown floating around her. Her hair fell free over her shoulders, tangled, and her arms were crossed. She seemed very far away in her thoughts, almost sad, but at least she wasn't angry and throwing things.

"I hope you had a good rest, Miss Clarke," Jane said

carefully. She picked up a pair of shoes tossed on the floor and tucked them away.

"I could barely close my eyes. All this stuff is giving me the frights." Annabel waved her hand at the elaborate Green Chamber, the paintings and bibelots and gilding. "Once I'm countess, there's going to be some redecorating, I promise you that."

"So you're planning to stay, Miss Clarke?" Jane said, thinking of Collins and his questions about whether she would be at Danby later. "Despite everything that's happened?"

Annabel paused in her pacing to stare at Jane in astonishment. "Of course. Isn't that why we came here? Unpleasantness happens everywhere. Believe me, I know. But I'm not giving up now that I'm so close. Are you with me, Jane?"

"Of course, Miss Clarke," Jane answered. She *would* like to stay at Danby, she realized. It was a whole new world she wanted to explore.

"Good." Annabel sat down at the dressing table, and Jane reached for the hairbrush to try to get the tangles out of Annabel's auburn hair. She noticed it was a new brush, gold, monogrammed with an A and a circlet of tiny diamonds. Had it been a gift? Maybe from Lord Bellham, and that was what preoccupied her employer today. An imminent engagement.

"One of the maids said you went into the village with

Lady Cecilia," Annabel said, opening and closing a small pot of rouge.

"Yes, to help with some errands for the garden party. I hope you didn't need me while I was gone."

"Not at all. I'm glad you were helpful to her. I need to make friends with these people if they're going to stand by me. They're going to be my family, after all." She dropped the pot, and an expression of uncharacteristic doubt flickered over her face. "Do they—have they said anything about me, Jane?"

"Not really, Miss Clarke. Only that they seem most eager to impress you."

Annabel gave a twisted smile. "I would think so. Look at how shabby this place is! They do need my help." She looked down at her fingers tapping on the table, the lack of a ring on her finger yet. "Lord Bellham isn't quite what I expected."

Jane twisted the smoothed curls atop Annabel's head. "Is he not?"

"No. I thought English men were supposed to be dashing and outdoorsy, always riding to foxes and all that." Annabel sighed. "He just seems interested in plants. And not even pretty flowers, but weird samples and slides with slimy greenery! So dull. But he'll do."

Jane remembered that Annabel had already gone with Lord Bellham to his laboratory. Was she going to give up sharing his interests once she had that ring? "Will he, then?"

"He's a viscount, isn't he? And I doubt he would ever say boo to a goose. He'll let me do what I want. I'll be safe then."

"Safe, Miss Clarke?" Jane asked, puzzled. Annabel was rich and beautiful. How much safer could she be? Maybe she was thinking of the fright of the shipwreck.

"Yes. Just look at this place! It needs some polishing up, true, but it's been here hundreds of years. And it can be mine."

Jane tied a ribbon through Annabel's hair, trying to think how she could tactfully bring up Mr. Hayes. "And how do you find the other guests, then, Miss Clarke?"

Annabel shrugged. "They're all right, I guess. A little boring, maybe. And that Maud Rainsley—I'm sure she's after Lord Bellham, even though everyone knows now that he's mine. Everyone will see that after Lady Avebury's ball. And Lord St. John! What a creeper. Can you believe he was once the heir? He tried to touch my leg in the drawing room. I told him off right away."

"And Mr. Hayes?" Jane said, as casually as she could. She reached for a strand of pearls and fastened it around Annabel's neck. "Did you have any problem with him?"

Annabel spun around on the bench, a scowl on her face. "Why? What have you heard, Jane?"

Jane took a deep breath, reminding herself to be careful. "He had a reputation downstairs for, er, bothering some of the maids."

"I'm not surprised. I saw him following one of the girls one night. She looked scared. I told him off."

Jane sighed in relief. *That* must have been the quarrel James saw. Annabel was trying to help Rose. "But he didn't bother *you*, Miss Clarke?"

Annabel snorted. "He wouldn't dare! Now, should I wear that new coral and black lace dress? I am so glad some of my new things have arrived!"

Chapter Fifteen

Cecilia was still sitting at her little desk by her bedroom window, scribbling notes about everything she had heard in the village, when Jane appeared to help her dress for dinner. She looked up at the clock, surprised.

"Is that the time already?" She gasped. "I didn't even hear the first gong."

Jane laughed. "That gong seems to rule the world here."

Cecilia sighed. "Indeed it does." She laid aside her notes reluctantly but clapped her hands in delight as Jack emerged from behind Jane's skirts. She fetched his ribbon from the drawer and dragged it over the carpet to make him pounce and roll.

"Just wait until you hear what I've heard downstairs, my

lady," Jane said, taking a pale-blue corded silk dinner gown from the wardrobe.

"What is it?" Cecilia asked eagerly, tugging the hem of her skirt away from Jack's paw.

"This is in strict confidence, my lady."

"Of course."

"You know that Paul and Rose are courting?"

"Yes, but it has to be kept rather quiet for now." Jack jumped up into Cecilia's lap, and she cuddled him close.

"Well, Mr. Hayes tried to get fresh with poor Rose. She was very upset about it."

"Oh no!" Cecilia cried, anger and dismay burning through her for sweet Rose. Jack made an angry little "rrrww."

"So Paul found out and hit Mr. Hayes right in the face. That's why he's been wearing gloves all this time. His knuckles were scraped."

"And the bruise on Mr. Hayes's face," Cecilia murmured. "Did you see that, Jane? On the day he died."

Jane nodded. "And Miss Clarke said that's why she quarreled with Mr. Hayes, too. She saw him following Rose and told him to knock it off."

Cecilia sighed. "It does make sense, I suppose. I have to admit, Jane, I feel less terrible about Mr. Hayes's fate all the time. Isn't that awful?" Jack settled into a steady purr.

"Not at all. I feel that way, too. Horrible man. What do you suppose Mr. Hayes's mistress thought of it all?"

Cecilia shrugged. She gave Jack a kiss on the top of his

head and put him down on the floor to chase his ribbon. "Either she didn't care at all—so many couples seem that way, though it sounds like a sad way to live to me. Or maybe she was furious. I wish we knew who she really is."

As Jane helped her out of her shirtwaist and skirt and into the silk dress, Cecilia told her what she had learned in the village. Jack batted at his ribbon under the bed and emerged with a bracelet Cecilia had thought she lost long ago. "Oh, very clever, Jack! How good you are at finding lost things."

She scooped up the bauble, patted Jack's head—and a thought popped into her mind.

"Jane, how long do we have before dinner?" she asked.

Jane glanced at the clock. "About half an hour, my lady."

Cecilia clapped her hands. "Just enough time, then."

"Time for what?"

"To search Mr. Hayes's room!"

Jane looked doubtful. "Haven't the police done that?"

"I'm sure they have. But they don't know all the hidey-holes like I do. Come along! There's not much time." She grabbed Jane's hand and pulled her along down the corridor, with Jack trailing behind them.

Mr. Hayes had been put in the Chinese Room, next door to the Byswaters. The whole corridor was quiet, and the door was unlocked when Cecilia tried it. She and Jane slipped inside, both of them seeming to hold their breath until they were closed inside.

Inside a dead man's room.

For an instant, Cecilia thought of the Blue Lady, and how this would surely be the best place in the whole house for her to flit around. "Don't be silly," she muttered, and forced herself to march farther into the room, Jane close behind her, Jack at their heels. Jane's stalwart, quiet company reassured her. If there was a ghost, they would see it together.

Jane drew back the brocade draperies a bit, giving them enough of the fading daylight to see but not enough that anyone walking outside might notice. It was obvious the place had been searched once; the wardrobe doors were ajar, a few drawers open, the green-and-gold rug askew, the gold brocade coverlet tousled. It all seemed musty and disused, even though it had only been empty a few short days. Mr. Hayes's cases were stacked by the wall, ready to be packed and sent to his London lodgings when Inspector Hennesy was done with them. Jack ducked under the bed, hopefully in search of more lost objects.

"You search the desk, Jane. There might be something there they missed," Cecilia whispered. "And then maybe a glance at those cases. In the books, they sometimes have false bottoms."

"Where will you look, my lady?" Jane whispered back, even though there was no one to hear them except Jack and the Blue Lady.

"I know a place." When she was a little girl and her

grandparents had been the earl and countess at Danby, she had often visited them and escaped from her governess when her parents were sequestered with her grandfather in the library to talk boring estate business. She had been a small girl, able to wriggle into the most interesting spots. The attics were her favorite, and full of the dusty relics of past Bateses, but the guestchambers were also endlessly fascinating. No two were alike.

And the Chinese Room, like its Chinese box namesake, was something of a puzzle, rooms in rooms. There was a small dressing room through a door just past the bed and the carved, lacquered wardrobe. Only a few coats hung there now, and the combs and brushes on the dressing table. Cecilia took a quick look through the pockets, finding only some handkerchiefs, and then went to where she really wanted to be—a small door in the corner, behind the coats.

When clothes were stored there, it would be mostly hidden, the seams of the wood fitting perfectly into the paneling. When she was a child, she wondered if it was some Tudor priest hole, like in ghost stories. The Bates family had never been very religious, and had been favored by Queen Elizabeth, but it was a rather romantic notion. Whatever it was, she had once quite thrilled at the discovery of it.

But she hadn't been back to that door in years. There was no handle, just a spot to push, and it stuck under her hand so she had to throw her whole weight against it. Surely, that was a good sign—maybe the inspector had not been there yet. But had Mr. Hayes found it? He was an explorer; surely, he wanted to find all the nooks and crannies of old houses. Or maybe his killer had been there?

Once Cecilia got inside, it was just as she remembered, a tiny, dark space that smelled of dust and mold. She went back for the candles kept in the dressing room in case the new and slightly unreliable electricity went out, and she lit one before she headed into the secret closet.

It was just a small, windowless box, no carpet on the plank floor, which seemed to have been recently swept clean. She knelt down, praying her mother wouldn't catch her later with a dirty skirt, and pried at the loose panel she knew was at the back of the space. It was very loose, though, and came right off.

When she was a child, she had stored books there. Now it was just one of those interesting little legends the servants sometimes told guests, that strange, useless, maybe priest hole. She did hope someone had told Mr. Hayes about it.

"Don't let there be mice," she whispered, and by the light of her candle she reached inside the tiny, shelflike space. Cobwebs stuck to her fingers, but it was worth it. Her grasp actually closed on a packet of papers.

"Oh, hurray!" she cried. She pulled them out and saw they were a small bundle of letters, tied with string. She glanced over them quickly, with no time to settle in for a long read just at that moment. They weren't crackling old parchment, but fresh sheets of stationery, pale cream, not the thickest but not cheap, either.

She checked to make sure nothing else was there, but it was empty. She ran back to the bedchamber with her prize.

"Look, Jane!" she exclaimed. "I found letters in the secret closet. Did you come across anything?"

"Just Mr. Hayes's address book, in one of the trunks. It's mostly just initials, though. And Jack found a cravat under the bed. He does enjoy digging things out." Jack sat back on his haunches, the strip of green silk held proudly in his sharp little teeth.

"I think I've seen that before." Cecilia gasped. "Lord St. John was wearing it one evening. Why would Mr. Hayes have it here?"

"Maybe Lord St. John tried to strangle Hayes?" Jane whispered, her eyes wide.

"Very clever, Jack," Cecilia said, untangling the strip of fabric from his tiny teeth and tucking it in with the letters.

They heard a cough and footsteps in the corridor. Time was running out. "Come on, let's get back to my room, where we can take a proper look at it all. We have a little time left before the gong."

Once safely locked in Cecilia's chamber, they sat down in front of the fire with Jack on Jane's lap to read the purloined missives.

"It looks like only the last was delivered here at Danby,"

Cecilia said, sorting through them. She carefully laid the cravat aside. "The rest are addressed to the apartments at the Albany. Mr. Hayes must have had his London lodgings there, very swank."

"Who are they from?"

"They're all just signed *Alice* or A. Maybe that's his mistress?" Cecilia found the one with the earliest date, and read that one to Jane. They certainly began as rather standard love letters, expressing the need to "feel his sweet kisses" again, planning rendezvous, asking how Marrakesh or Moscow was treating him, and when he would return.

Then, a few months ago, the messages seemed to take a turn. "Good heavens, Jane, listen to this," Cecilia said.

> *If I am not paid immediately, who knows what steps I may have to take? Remember all I gave up for you! Now I implore you not to forget what is owed. I cannot be evicted.*

"I suppose Mr. Hayes paid for her house even when he was abroad."

"And then he stopped? Did he break it off with her?"

"I'm not sure." Cecilia turned to the next letter, the last one delivered to Danby. It was even more frantic and angry, declaring the immediate need for funds, demanding to know when he would finish his book.

"Surely, Mr. Hayes was a wealthy man," Jane said. "He's in all the papers and such. What happened?"

Cecilia thought of Danby's own downfall, the falling rents and missing paintings on the walls. "Who knows? Too many bad investments? Too many mistresses to support?"

Jane absently stroked Jack's ears as he batted at his ribbon toy. "What about the last letter, then?"

Cecilia unfolded the last note, the one delivered by post to Danby after Hayes arrived. There was no preamble, as there was in the others, no "My darling" or "Richie-Richardest." Even the handwriting had changed, going from bubbling and even to jagged.

> *If I don't have the rent by the end of the month, I will be tossed out and bailiffs will come to seize my furniture. Surely, you don't want that for your Alice-kitty? After all the time we've been together, all I've given up for your sake. All the patience I've shown you, the understanding. Not to mention all those itty-bitty secrets we share. Like that silly Canadian railway. You were a clever-wever boy to make all that up. But where has the money gone? Are you hiding it from your kitty? Unless I'm paid this week, I know my conscience will force me to tell someone. I would never* want *to do such a thing to my Richie, but how can I starve on the street? I'll*

look for your bank draft, my dearest-weerest. Or shall I come to Danby Hall for it?

Your little Alice

Cecilia dropped the letter, utterly shocked. "He was making up that Canadian railway scheme out of whole cloth. That weasel. I wonder what else he had lied about?"

"What does that mean, my lady?"

"It means Lord Byswater would have been awfully angry with Mr. Hayes if he found out. The Byswaters seem to have lost quite a tidy sum in that scheme."

"Do you think this Alice had already spilled the beans about it all, then?"

Cecilia tapped her fingers thoughtfully against the letter. "It was only delivered right before Mr. Hayes died. If she was expecting him to pay up, I'm sure she would hold this secret in reserve for a while. If only we knew who Alice is! And who else Hayes owed money. Maybe St. John, and that was how the cravat came to be there?" She wondered if maybe the stranger seen in town was one of his creditors, or someone else he hoodwinked. Why on earth had Hayes kept these, instead of tossing them in the fire? He didn't seem a sentimental sort.

The gong sounded, and Cecilia bundled the letters back together with a sigh. "You should go to Miss Clarke, Jane. I can tidy myself up. We'll have to be down to dinner soon, and I want to take a peek in my mother's desk before she can catch me." She thought that, while she was on her snooping game, she might as well look for Jesse Fellows's reference letters. It did seem a little odd that he had appeared at Danby at almost the same time as Mr. Hayes.

Jane eased Jack off her lap and stood, brushing his hair off her black dress. "I'll help you straighten your hair first, my lady. It looks a bit like a bird's nest! But do you think . . ." She suddenly broke off and looked away.

"Think what, Jane?"

"That we should show these letters to Inspector Hennesy?"

Cecilia considered this. It was certainly sensible, and what they *should* do, if only she was sure that they could trust the inspector. "Not just yet. Soon. Let's see what we can find out about this Alice first."

❧

Cecilia was downstairs before anyone else, thanks to Jane's quick help with her impossible hair, and made her way to the music room, where her mother kept her desk. A small, delicate, white-painted and gilded Louis XV piece, Lady Avebury ran the whole house from its fragile-looking space.

Cecilia opened the top drawer and found menus, several of her mother's famous lists, and plans for the garden party. The next drawer was dedicated to the masquerade ball, meant to be the grand finale of the party and hopefully the moment to announce Patrick's engagement. Cecilia wasn't sure how *that* plan was going at all.

In the bottom drawer, she found the files for the newest staff. Jesse Fellows's was at the front, as he was the most recently hired, but the letters were disappointingly uninformative. Honest, clean, smart, a fine worker.

She glanced at Paul's file, since he was the one who gave Hayes that bruise. Nothing in his previous employment seemed to indicate he was a habitual brawler, though. She closed the drawer with a sigh.

Just in time, too, as she heard the echo of her parents' voices coming along the corridor. She quickly ducked behind the Japanese painted screen in the corner, not wanting to explain why she was in the music room rather than waiting for everyone in the White Drawing Room.

". . . Mr. Brown next to Cecilia at dinner," her mother was saying as they came into the room. Cecilia heard the rustle of satin, the click of crystal as her father reached for the brandy decanter.

"A drink, my dear?" he asked.

"Yes, please, Clifford. I must admit these last few days have been quite harrowing to my nerves. I may need to go off to Baden-Baden once it's all over. Maybe I could persuade Maggie to go with me."

"Quite understandable you should feel that way." One of the settees creaked as Lord Avebury sat down. "But why Mr. Brown for Cecilia?"

"He's rather nice, don't you think?" Lady Avebury said. "And his uncle is a viscount. He could be a bishop one day. Maybe even Archbishop of Canterbury! And he does seem fond of Cecilia."

Cecilia pressed her fingers to her lips to hold back a gasp. Her mother was trying to matchmake again—with the vicar!

"She's only had one Season," her father said. "Surely, there's no hurry."

"One Season where she refused every offer! She's become quite impossible. I blame the bad influence of girls like Maud Rainsley."

Cecilia had refused because they were all terrible offers! Boys who never read, never thought, just talked on and on about cricket. But surely, she was not an old maid just yet. Philip Brown, while handsome and nice, just as her mother said, *was* a vicar. Maybe Cecilia wasn't entirely sure what she wanted from her future, but years of arranging altar flowers and village fetes didn't seem like it.

"What about her happiness?" her father said. Her sweet, sweet father.

"I know such a match wouldn't exactly make her a duchess, but eligible dukes are thin on the ground, and it's not so very bad. He comes from good families," Lady Avebury answered. "She could be a bishop's wife!"

"Eventually."

"Yes, eventually. She needs security. What if Patrick's

match with Miss Clarke doesn't happen? It seemed promising at first. He even showed her his botany laboratory. But now she seems so upset, so—so distant. She's always napping or moping in the bathroom." The heavy brandy snifters clinked. "What did you find in Leeds, then, Clifford?"

"Oh, it was quite interesting. After I sent the telegram to Mr. Clarke, I had luncheon at the Headingly and met some Americans."

"Americans?"

"Yes, a charming couple, just arrived for their honeymoon on a European tour. Quite high up in New York society, I think. Mr. and Mrs. Van der Leyden."

"What passes for society in New York, you mean," Lady Avebury scoffed. "What did they talk about?"

"They're going to stay at Beningbrough, not far, so I asked them to the garden party."

"The garden party! Some Americans you met at luncheon? Clifford, really."

"I thought Miss Clarke might enjoy meeting some of her fellow countrymen. It might cheer her up a bit, make her feel more at home."

There was a thoughtful silence, the clink of the snifters. "Hmm. You might be right. Anything to help dear Miss Clarke. When do you expect to hear back from her father?"

"Very soon, I'm sure. He must be quite worried about how his daughter is faring, so far away."

"I do hope so. I would like to see everything settled soon."

"Including Cecilia and the future archbishop?"

Lady Avebury gave a happy laugh. "Can you imagine, Clifford? Both our children settled, Danby safe."

Cecilia heard her father kiss her mother. "A comfort to our old age, Emmaline?"

"Not quite so old as all *that*! Should we go to the drawing room now? Everyone will be down soon."

Cecilia heard the door close behind them, leaving her alone again. Well, not quite alone. There was Mr. Brown out there somewhere. She sighed and came out from her hiding place. After a quick glance in the mirror to make sure her hair and gown were tidy, she hurried away.

Redvers stood just outside the doors to the White Drawing Room, holding a silver tray with small glasses of sherry. She supposed she should get used to small glasses of sherry as a vicar's wife; she had heard that was what all the parishioners offered. No more fanciful cocktails for her.

"Thank you, Redvers," she said, taking the largest glass she could see.

"Oh, this was left for you, my lady, on the table in the foyer. It looked as if it was hand delivered." Redvers balanced the tray deftly on one palm to give her a note, folded up small and labeled with her name in dark block letters.

"How odd," she said, puzzled. "Thank you, Redvers."

She turned away to open the plain red seal. The inside was short, written in those same childish block letters, and to the point.

Leave off being nosy, your ladyship, or you will be sorry. None of this is your business.

Chapter Sixteen

The day of Lady Avebury's garden party didn't dare to offend her with bad weather—it dawned bright and sunny, the perfect English spring day, just made for flowers and tea tents and morris dancers. When Cecilia climbed out of bed and pushed back her curtains, she saw endless pale-blue sky with tiny puffs of cottony clouds, amber light glowing on the trees of the park and turning the old stone of the house to a shining jewel.

How could anyone ever resist it all? Especially if they didn't know what lay behind those shimmering windows and ancient walls. If they hadn't received a note threatening them in their own home.

Cecilia turned from the perfect sapphire sky to stare down at the garden, which was a beehive of activity. Great white marquees were being set up on the lawn, rising like old-fashioned, billowing petticoats on the sea of green.

Mr. Smithfield's florist assistants scurried around with huge arrangements that would be set up in those marquees to adorn tables of pastries and lemonade and champagne. Gardeners put the final touches on the beds of tulips and daffodils, yellow and pink and white, while the footmen set up targets for archery, hoops for croquet. All under the strict eye of Mrs. Caffey. She waved her hand, and Paul moved a target two inches to the left.

It had been thus every year for as long as Cecilia could remember. Danby hosted its garden party, the one time all the neighborhood could come to gawk at the gardens and eat some of Mrs. Frazer's famous desserts. Then there would be the grand masquerade ball, exclusive and elegant, followed by the exodus to London for the Season. Even the downturn of the Bateses' fortunes hadn't changed the routine. This year was supposed to be the grandest of all, the year the heir to Danby got engaged.

Apparently, Cecilia was meant to be engaged, too. To Mr. Brown.

She sighed and drew her cashmere dressing gown closer around her shoulders. She looked forward to the garden party every year, the games and laughter, the sunshine, the moment when Danby seemed to really come alive. But it all felt—off this year. Dark shadows hung over it all, a sense of dread, and she couldn't shake it away.

She glanced at her desk, where she had stuffed that nasty little note into her locked top drawer, along with Mr. Hayes's Alice letters. She should give them to Inspector Hennesy, and she knew that she would. Just not quite yet. She and Jane were close to some discovery, she could sense it. But it felt like groping for something in a darkened room, like the priest hole. Something she knew was there, but not exactly how. Or why.

She bit her thumbnail, a bad habit nanny had chased out years ago but which still seemed to plague her at worried moments. Who knew she was asking about Mr. Hayes's murder? One of the footmen? The Byswaters? Lord St. John? Was someone watching her, studying her across the dining table or the drawing room in her own home?

And what about Jane? Was she in danger, too? Cecilia couldn't bear such a thought. Maybe she really *should* give it all up.

But then she saw Inspector Hennesy and Sergeant Dunn making their way across the busy lawn. The sergeant carried a box filled with bottles and slides that Cecilia was sure came from Patrick's laboratory. His precious experiments. Inspector Hennesy looked grimly satisfied, and

Cecilia realized to her horror that Patrick was definitely still in danger of being arrested.

She couldn't give up now.

❧

When Cecilia made her way downstairs to the garden, the arrangements were all in place. The marquees were set up with long tables, tempting with Mrs. Frazer's blueberry tarts and chocolate éclairs laid out like jewels on white damask cloths. The maids waited to pour tea and lemonade, while Redvers managed the champagne cooling in silver buckets. The flowers, nodding lightly in the slight breeze, were a swirl of pink and cream and yellow against the white and red of the archery targets.

She opened her parasol, carefully matched with Jane's stylish help to her pink-and-white-striped muslin dress, and studied the crowds that had started to pour through Danby's gates. She saw Patrick strolling with Miss Clarke, her enormous, fashionably feathered hat of blue taffeta and peacock feathers brilliant against the yellow tulips and the white early roses. The Byswaters sat at a small iron table in the shade of the trees, sipping champagne with Aunt Maggie and laughing. Her grandmother had taken an almost throne-like chair on the terrace, her scarlet suit and black toque a contrast to the bright day. To Cecilia's surprise, Jack and Sebastian, the dowager's temperamental Scottie, sat next to her, as if they were in perfect accord.

Or maybe Jack was gathering new clues? Cecilia wouldn't put it past him.

"Lady Cecilia," someone called, and she turned to see Mr. Brown hurrying toward her. He looked tidy, handsome, and most respectable in his black-and-white suit, his brown hair shining in the sun. She could see why her mother might find him a good possibility.

But what did *she* think?

"Mr. Brown," she said with a carefully not-too-encouraging smile. Yet she *did* admit that he looked terribly attractive in the bright sunlight, so much a part of it all, the fine day, Danby, the neighborhood. His own smile was open and friendly, bright white. It seemed he was the only one not harboring dark secrets of hatred for Mr. Hayes.

Or did he?

"Danby is certainly beautiful at this time of year," Mr. Brown said. "Your mother is a superlative hostess."

"She certainly is. She makes it all seem so easy." But Cecilia knew what happened behind the pretty scene, the rushing and worries. The sort of thing she would have to take on herself one day, when she ran a household.

"And I am sure you will be just as accomplished, when you have your own house to manage," he said, as if he read her doubtful thoughts. "Just as kind and welcoming."

Cecilia laughed. "I'm not sure I could ever learn to manage a home like Danby as my mother does."

His smile turned hopeful at the edges. "You would prefer

something smaller, Lady Cecilia? A manor house, mayhap? Or a vicarage, even? One suitable for a lady such as yourself, of course."

Cecilia thought of St. Swithin's vicarage, a lovely old house of the same golden stone as Danby, pretty, tidy gardens with a view of the village green. "I admit I've never really thought about it all, Mr. Brown."

He laughed. "I confess I haven't, either. When I went to university, I was entirely aimless. No idea what I wanted to do, except maybe write poetry."

Cecilia was intrigued by this little glimpse behind Mr. Brown's perfect smile. "I do like poetry. So how did you come to the church?"

"My uncle had a living to bestow that would soon become vacant, so my parents encouraged me to turn to divinity studies."

"And how do you like the work now?"

"Oh, much more than I would have expected!" he said eagerly. "The opportunity to help people, to be of some real use to them, has moved me greatly. And St. Swithin's is a lovely church, with a fascinating history." He waved at the Misses Moffat from the tea shop, who giggled at him. "Such kind neighbors. I am fortunate indeed." He smiled down at Cecilia. "Just a little lonely at times, but I hope to remedy that soon."

Cecilia felt flustered by his little hint. "Shall we have

some lemonade, Mr. Brown? Or something stronger to drink? I find the day is turning rather warm."

"Of course, Lady Cecilia." Mr. Brown offered her his arm and led her toward the refreshment marquee. Redvers offered them glasses of champagne which did look more tempting than plain old lemonade, and they studied the towering white rose and lily arrangements in silver vases. Mr. Brown chatted about how lovely such flowers would look for the church, and upcoming plans for the fete meant to raise funds for St. Swithin's roof.

Her parents stood inside the entrance, chatting with a couple Cecilia had never met. They were good-looking, gleaming in that way Americans seemed to do, both of them blond and sun touched, dressed in the height of fashion.

"Ah, Cecilia, do come and meet our new friends, the Van der Leydens," her mother said, positively beaming to see her daughter on Mr. Brown's arm. "Mr. and Mrs. Van der Leyden, this is our daughter, Lady Cecilia, and our most excellent vicar, Mr. Brown. Your father met the Van der Leydens while he was in Leeds. They are from New York, on their honeymoon. Isn't that romantic?"

"So delightful to meet you, Lady Cecilia!" Mrs. Van der Leyden gushed. "We always did hear how kind the English are, how welcoming, and we haven't been disappointed. How beautiful your house is."

"And it is lovely to meet you, Mrs. Van der Leyden.

Mr. Van der Leyden," Cecilia answered. "Are you staying in the neighborhood very long?"

"Not long at all, I'm afraid," Mr. Van der Leyden answered. Up close, Cecilia could see that he was a bit older than his wife, his golden hair turning silver, his suit cleverly tailored to disguise a certain girth, but his smile was open and friendly. "We're meant to go to London tomorrow. The start of a European tour. Paris, Madrid, Rome. Wherever Edith wants to go."

"It *is* our honeymoon," Mrs. Van der Leyden giggled. "A rather belated one. We've been married for six months."

Mr. Van der Leyden gave her an indulgent smile. "A most regrettable delay. I had business to attend to in California."

"Are you not from New York, then?" Cecilia asked. It seemed she had heard of California so often of late, thanks to Miss Clarke.

"My family has been there a very long time," Mrs. Van der Leyden said. "And we will make our home there when we return."

"My father built his business in San Francisco, and I must travel there once in a while," Mr. Van der Leyden said. "But my Edith is such a New Yorker!"

"I could be persuaded to try being a European, though," Mrs. Van der Leyden said. "All the history everywhere! I do love it."

"How extraordinary," Lady Avebury said. "We have a

guest staying with us now who is also from California. Miss Clarke. In fact, there she is now!"

Cecilia turned to see Patrick and Annabel had just entered the marquee, Annabel's blue hat and gown brilliant against the white walls, her laughter silvery.

"Patrick, darling, Miss Clarke, do come and meet the Van der Leydens," Lady Avebury said. "They are from New York, on their honeymoon, but it seems Mr. Van der Leyden does business in California."

Cecilia knew her parents had hoped that meeting some fellow Americans would help Miss Clarke feel more at home at Danby, but Annabel did not look especially happy to see them. Her laughter dimmed and she bit her lip. But Patrick led her forward, and she pasted a bright smile on her face again.

"How do you do?" Annabel said, holding out her blue-gloved hand to the couple. "I haven't seen another American in simply an age! Except for my maid, of course."

"You are so lucky to spend so much time here, Miss Clarke." Mrs. Van der Leyden sighed.

"Where is your family from in California, Miss Clarke?" Mr. Van der Leyden asked.

"Oh—lots of places, really," Annabel said with a laugh. "San Francisco mostly, but I haven't been back there in ages."

"I often get there on business," Mr. Van der Leyden said. "Are you related to Mr. Clarke, the mining fellow?"

Annabel's smile froze. "My father."

"What a coincidence," Mr. Van der Leyden exclaimed. "I have often wondered about Mr. Clarke's daughter. I see you are as lovely as rumored. You must know the Goodwards, and the Heywards."

Annabel laughed and twirled her ivory parasol handle. "Oh, I hardly mixed in such daring circles there, we do tend to travel so much! Patrick, dearest, I am quite parched. Shall we find some tea?" She smiled at the Van der Leydens. "So nice to hear an account of home. I do feel I am quite leaving it more behind and becoming more English every day! Shall we go, then, Patrick?"

"Of course," Patrick said, his expression startled, as if he had been far away. He was often that way, caught in his own life, a life none of them could see. Cecilia remembered the inspector carrying away Patrick's samples. "Do excuse us, Mama, Papa. Mr. and Mrs. Van der Leyden. Nice to have met you."

As they turned away, Cecilia was near enough to hear Annabel hiss into Patrick's ear, "Why would Lady Avebury ask such vulgar people here? Asking such prying questions!"

"I thought they were nice," Patrick muttered, and Cecilia thought that, too. They just seemed to be making polite chatter. Were the Van der Leydens really being nosy?

There was a small, awkward silence, before Lady Avebury started chatting about some piece of Danby history, pointing out where the Palladian house met the old Elizabethan gallery.

"Shall we also find some more refreshment, Lady Cecilia?" Mr. Brown asked. "Or perhaps play a round of croquet?"

"I might enjoy watching the tennis," Cecilia said. She studied the game going on across the emerald-colored lawn, doubles with some of the men from the village. It looked so elegant, like a careful dance where first one player then the other glided into place, the ball always in motion. Where one man faltered, another stepped in.

She suddenly wondered if the whole scene in the dining room had not been the work of one person only, but two, working together. Concealing the actions from everyone else. But who would know each other so well to conspire such a dire plot?

Cecilia noticed a man in a dark-blue uniform approach her father as Lord Avebury stood talking with his mother. He handed her father a telegram and then vanished again.

Could it be the message her father was expecting from Mr. Clarke in America? Curious as to what it might contain, she excused herself from Mr. Brown, leaving him to find the Van der Leydens and tell them about the history of St. Swithin's, and she followed Lord Avebury into the house.

By the time she found him, he was just leaving the music room, his expression distracted.

"Oh, Cec, my dear," he said. "Is your mother looking for me? I probably shouldn't have left her alone ."

"Not at all, Papa. You know how Mama is at parties, in her very element. Mr. Brown is with her. And the Van der Leydens do seem nice." She smiled and gently touched his arm. "I suppose we must get used to Americans at Danby now."

He gave her a smile in return, though it looked rather forced to her. "Perhaps. We shall see."

Worried, Cecilia pressed his arm. "Is everything quite all right, Papa?"

"Of course it is, my dear. How could it not be on our garden party day? I really should go find your mother. Will you come with me? I know you always do enjoy the archery competition. Do you have your arrows ready?"

"Certainly. I wouldn't miss that! I just must tidy my hair a bit."

"You look lovely just as you are, my dear. That pink does suit you." His smile turned rather sad. "You know, Cec, that no matter what happens, you will have a safe home with us. I don't want you to worry about anything."

Cecilia thought of Mr. Brown. "I know, Papa. Whatever happens, we are all Bateses, yes? We will be fine."

He nodded and stepped back out into the sunshine, putting on his straw boater. Cecilia made sure she was alone in the foyer before she ran to the music room.

She found the telegram, folded and tucked under a crystal paperweight on her mother's desk. It was quite a long one, she noticed; Mr. Clarke must be rich indeed. She quickly scanned the contents, growing more astonished by the second.

> Such shocking news, Lord Avebury, stop. My daughter Annabel, who has always been of rebellious nature, ran away from home weeks ago, stop. I have sent out detectives with little success, stop. Glad to hear she is to marry, will join you in England as soon as can be arranged, stop. William Clarke.

Annabel was a runaway! Cecilia could hardly believe it. Why on earth would such a lady, an heiress, have to sneak away from her own father in order to marry a viscount? Maybe it was like the story in *Sophia's Curse*, the book about a sweet lady whose cruel father refused to let her wed her true love. The father even threatened to burn down the true love's blacksmith shop, his only source of income, if Sophia married him. So they fled through the winter woods, chased by wolves.

Cecilia shook her head and carefully refolded the telegram. Why would Annabel come to Danby, to Patrick, if she left home for love? Mr. Clarke didn't seem reluctant to add a coronet to his name. There had to be a fascinating tale behind it all.

Or maybe—maybe Annabel was quite right, and someone *was* trying to murder her? Maybe she was trying to hide at Danby, and danger had followed her?

Cecilia determined to speak to Jane as soon as possible. Jane hadn't been Annabel's maid for very long, but servants always knew far more about their employers than anyone else. In the meantime, she knew she had to get back to the party before her mother missed her.

She glanced quickly in a mirror, tidying her hair the best she could and straightening her rose-trimmed hat. She hurried out to the foyer—and ran into Lord St. John, who was half-hidden behind one of the tall Chinese vases.

"There you are, Cousin Cecilia," he said, with one of his unpleasant smiles, as if he saw a cruel joke only he could know. He came close to her, and she smelled the sharp, heavy scent of brandy. He dropped a quiver of arrows at his feet, and his smile widened. "Hiding, are you?"

Cecilia took a step back, bumping into the vase. It swayed, and she feared it might topple, after standing there for two hundred years. It did not, but she was now trapped between it and him. She tried to force the hot rush of panic down. "Certainly not. I merely needed a moment out of the sun."

"You do look quite delightfully flushed," he murmured. "How you do remind me of your mother when she was young. As fresh and delicate as a rosebud, so untouched and sweet. So innocent." He ran the back of his fingers along her cheek.

Cecilia recoiled. "I—I must return to the party."

"Oh, not just yet, surely. We so seldom have the chance to get to know each other. And we are family, are we not? Families should stay—very close."

Before she could see what he was doing, he reached out and grabbed her hard around the waist. His hands were hot and moist through her muslin dress, surprisingly strong. He dragged her closer, until his body was pressed against hers, and his head lowered to kiss her. She saw the beads of sweat on his forehead, the redness of his eyes.

"No!" she cried, tearing her face away. His lips trailed damply, revoltingly, over her cheek, and she tried to slap him. He easily caught her hand in one of his fists, holding her against him with the other. She tried to kick him, but her narrow skirt held her even more tightly bound.

"I do like spirit in a woman." He laughed, and lowered his head to kiss her again.

"Let her go," a low, fierce growl sounded.

As if he was surprised, St. John's grip loosened enough for Cecilia to wrench herself free. She spun around to see Jesse Fellows standing there across the foyer.

He seemed very tall in the moment, very still and calm and focused, like a lion about to pounce. She shoved St. John away and ran to Jesse's side, shaking. She hoped she would not embarrass herself by bursting into tears.

"Don't you ever treat her that way again," Jesse said, quiet, steady. He crossed his arms in his stark black uniform, his gaze never wavering from St. John. "There are many men here younger and far more sober than you who would happily thrash you for such behavior."

St. John smiled and wiped the back of his hand over his mouth. "Including you—footman? What would Lord Avebury say if he knew how you treat his guests?"

"I'm sure my father would promote him and toss you out immediately," Cecilia said fiercely. She was still shaking, but now it felt more like anger than fear.

"That sounds like an excellent idea, Lady Cecilia," Jesse said. "If you pack your bags and leave right now, and never come back to Danby, I'm sure Lady Cecilia and I can be discreet. To an extent."

St. John scooped up his arrow quiver. "I will go. This house is definitely slipping in its standards. But one day, very soon, things will be quite different." He still smiled, but when Jesse stepped forward, fists curled, he turned sharply and went upstairs, vanishing from sight.

Cecilia sighed, feeling suddenly limp and exhausted. "Oh, Jesse. I can't ever thank you enough. How fortunate you were here right now!"

Jesse still watched the stairs. "Mr. Redvers asked me to fetch more champagne." He glanced down at her, a small smile finally touching his face, softening the lion fierceness. "Are you all right, Lady Cecilia? He didn't—hurt you?"

"Oh no, thanks to you. I'm just a little shaken. I may

need some of that champagne!" The few sips she had earlier had quite faded away.

"Then let's go pour you a glass. It's a Piercel Grande Fine, very nice, according to Mr. Redvers, and only to be served to the most important guests. Wouldn't that be you, my lady?" He picked up the case she just noticed on the floor behind him and led her to the empty dining room. As Cecilia watched, he expertly opened the bottle with only the smallest *pop*, just as Redvers did, took a glass from the sideboard, and poured her a lovely, fizzy, golden portion.

"You did that very well," Cecilia said, glad to have something to focus on rather than Lord St. John and his clammy hands. "You're very lucky. Redvers usually lets no one else near his wine."

Jesse laughed. When he smiled, he looked so much younger, more free. And he had the most intriguing dimple, right in his square chin. "I did a bit of wine service at my last position. It interests me. What makes a wine good or bad, how different earth produces such different flavors, even only a mile away, which wine suits which food. I think Mr. Redvers likes teaching about such things, as well. He knows so very much."

Cecilia took a sip of her champagne, and it rolled over her tongue like liquid sunshine. She felt terribly naughty, drinking champagne during the day! Even though they were having it in the garden, too, it seemed quite different in an empty dining room with a handsome man. "It is indeed delicious. So, you're Redvers's protégé now?"

Jesse shrugged. "He's been kind. I don't intend to be a footman forever, you know, Lady Cecilia. Maybe one day I'll be butler at a house just like Danby. Or even own my own restaurant or hotel."

Cecilia took another sip, thinking about how she herself had been feeling lately—a bit uncertain, adrift almost. So many ideas and dreams. What would she do if she could do anything at all, like Jesse and his future? "I definitely think you will. Or if not, you can make a career out of rescuing damsels."

"Maybe I could be an actor on the Lyceum stage? Or in one of those new moving pictures?" He turned to the light to display his profile. She laughed, but he actually *did* look like he belonged on a poster for *Hamlet*.

"Yes, you could do that, too," she said.

"And what about you, Lady Cecilia? What will you do?"

She took another long, thoughtful sip of her champagne. "Right now—I will go back to the party. My mother will miss me soon." Unless her mother was too involved in smoothing things out for Annabel. "Do you really think Lord St. John is gone?"

"I doubt he'd stay. No one here is likely to fall for his drunken seductions, don't you think? And men like him need dalliances to make a house party worthwhile."

Cecilia thought over the women there. Aunt Maggie,

Miss Clarke, Maud, Lady Byswater, Mrs. Van der Leyden. Only Mrs. Van der Leyden didn't know all about him, and she seemed happy to be on her honeymoon. "Hardly. But Inspector Hennesy said no one could leave yet."

"I'm sure Lord St. John would be easy enough to find." Jesse gave her a gentle smile. "Please don't worry about him, Lady Cecilia. His sort isn't worth even an instant of your thoughts."

"I will try not to. Thank you again, Jesse. You have been very, very kind." She handed him her empty glass, wishing she could just stay there with him in that quiet safety all afternoon. "Don't forget me when you're the star of the West End stage."

"I'll try not to, my lady," he answered with a laugh.

Cecilia went outside, finding the archery competition set up on the lawn. The gentlemen's round had just finished, and the targets were being reset for the ladies. Redvers handed Cecilia her bow and gauntlets, and she carefully tested the strings. She'd always enjoyed archery; it made her think of fairy tales she read as a child, with medieval hunters, kings in battle, and Robin Hood. Now she was glad of the chance to let some of her frustrations and anger out by letting arrows fly. Maybe she would imagine St. John's sweaty face on the bull's-eye.

Annabel took up a spot next to Cecilia. She had taken off her elaborate hat and pushed back the flounced sleeves of her silk dress. She looked much happier than earlier and smiled brightly at Cecilia as she examined her bow carefully. "I've only tried this once or twice before. I'm not even sure which way is up!"

"Like this, Miss Clarke," Cecilia said, showing her how to hold it properly.

"Oh, do call me Annabel! We'll soon be family, won't we?" Annabel said with a merry laugh.

"I've always wished for a sister," Cecilia answered carefully. She remembered how moody and erratic Annabel had been recently, and how much danger Patrick was in. That shocking telegram from Mr. Clarke. "Here, if you balance the bow just so between your hands, hold it up—steady now, a little higher than you should at first. Line your sight up along the string, pull back, lower a bit, and then let fly."

Annabel gave an experimental tug at her strings, lining up her sight with a cold, calculating, careful expression on her beautiful face. "Such fun! I tell you, Cecilia—may I call you Cecilia, too?"

"Of course."

"Good! I do have the feeling we are going to be great friends. I tell you, Cecilia, I intend to learn all your English pastimes. Riding to hounds, shooting luncheons, London Seasons. I'll learn to be a great partygoer there! Do you think Patrick will want to sit in the House of Lords one day? I have a bit of a fancy to be a political hostess."

Cecilia tried to imagine her brother giving speeches, hosting London dinners. She almost laughed. "I doubt he would be very interested. Except for Royal Society meetings, he's not much of a London person at all."

"How sad. We'll have to change that."

"Ladies, take your marks," Lord Avebury announced. Cecilia stepped up to her designated mark, Annabel beside her, and Maud Rainsley on her other side. Lady Byswater and Aunt Maggie were just past Annabel. "Raise your bows—aim . . ."

Cecilia set her sight on the center of the target. Only the woods of the park were behind it, a mossy counterpoint to the bright-red mark.

"And fire!"

She loosed her arrow, but her pleasure in hitting the edge of the center ring vanished when she heard a loud scream. She spun around to find Annabel on the ground, an arrow buried in the front hem of her heavy blue silk skirt. She screamed again, one long, agonized wail, her face scarlet.

Cecilia fell to her knees beside Annabel, scanning frantically for any blood. Oh, where was Jesse Fellows now? He would know what to do, just as when Mr. Hayes was ill! Her parents gathered close, along with the ladies who had just shot their own arrows, screaming and murmuring in concern.

Cecilia was most relieved to find the arrow had been stopped by the folds of Annabel's gown and hadn't pierced the leg at all. Her silk stocking wasn't even torn.

"Can someone find Dr. Mitchell?" Cecilia glanced up to see her father and Lord Byswater running toward the woods, and she realized the stray arrow must have come from that direction. There was no way any of the ladies in the line could have fired on Annabel without spinning around in a most obvious fashion.

"I'll find him," Aunt Maggie said, and vanished into the crowd.

Annabel still whimpered. Mr. Redvers handed her a handkerchief, and Cecilia said softly, "It's quite all right, Annabel, you are not hurt. The arrow seems to have been stopped by your skirt."

"But someone shot at me!" Annabel cried. "That makes twice—*twice!*—someone tried to kill me."

Patrick knelt down beside them, and Annabel immediately collapsed in his arms. "You should take her to Jane," Cecilia whispered. "She can help. I'll send the doctor to the Green Chamber." Patrick nodded, and Cecilia watched them leave, the crowd closing behind them. She glimpsed Aunt Maggie leading the doctor toward the house.

She reached for the arrow left on the grass. The light caught on the fletching, the feather a pretty, iridescent peacock green. It was very different from the red feathers of the competition arrows. But where had she seen it before?

"Lady Cecilia? Are you all right?" she heard Philip Brown say. She tore off a bit of the feather and tucked it into the lace cuff of her sleeve to examine later. "May I be of some assistance?"

Cecilia took his hand and let him help her to her feet. She was shaking again and wondered if this strange day would ever end. "I am quite all right. Just a little—upended, I'm afraid."

"What a shocking thing to happen," he said, leading her gently toward the house. Inspector Hennesy stood on the terrace next to her grandmother, the dowager watching the whole dramatic scene impassively while the inspector was turning to rush to the garden.

"Here, do sit down, Lady Cecilia," Mr. Brown said, reaching for one of the wicker chairs grouped around the terrace. "Let me fetch you something cool to drink."

"Thank you, Mr. Brown," she said. She watched as her father and Lord Byswater returned from the woods, empty-handed, their expressions frustrated.

"No signs of anyone there," her father told his mother. He took off his hat and slapped it against the marble balustrade. "We'll have to organize a more extensive search."

"I can assist you with that, Lord Avebury," Inspector Hennesy said.

"Papa, perhaps you could send Mama to look in on Miss Clarke, if she hasn't gone already?" Cecilia said. "Annabel did seem quite frightened."

Lord Avebury sighed. "Perhaps the doctor could give your mother a sedative, as well. She won't be happy her party was ruined again . . ."

Jane peeked through the Green Chamber door at Miss Clarke, who lay under the heaps of brocade and linen and lace in the soft evening light. The maids hadn't come yet to draw the draperies. Dr. Mitchell had been there and had given Miss Clarke and Lady Avebury drafts to help them sleep. Jane had helped Annabel change into a silk nightdress, tucked her in as her sobs grew quieter, and then gone to fetch her some tea.

She tiptoed inside and put her tray down on a green porphyry-topped table. She thought of what Lady Cecilia had just whispered to her in the corridor, about Mr. Clarke's strange telegram.

What did she really, truly know about Miss Clarke? Who would be trying to kill her? Someone who was unhappy she had run away from home? Why?

"Jane, is that you?" Annabel said softly.

"Yes, it's me, Miss Clarke. I brought you some tea and toast, if you can manage it." She poured out a cup, the best Danby Wedgwood of delicate blue and white, and took it to Miss Clarke's bedside. She helped her sit up against the lacy pillows so she could take a sip.

She looked pale, but calmer. "You know, Jane, all I ever wanted in life was to be safe. Danby Hall seemed like a place where someone could find refuge, right? So old. So solid."

Jane remembered what she had read about the earthquake in San Francisco a few years ago, the way the city suddenly collapsed around everyone. She wondered if that was one of the things that bothered Annabel so much, made her go to such lengths to feel safe. "There are bad people everywhere, I'm afraid. That poor Mr. Hayes, of course. No one seemed to like him at all."

Annabel cringed. "He was certainly a boor. I'm surprised someone as nice as Lady Avebury would ever invite him. When I'm the countess, no one like that will darken *my* door. I've had it with bullies."

Jane remembered the argument Annabel had with Mr. Hayes and wondered if it had been more than the way he bothered Rose. She carefully smoothed the covers of the bed. "Did he—bother you, Miss Clarke?"

"He wouldn't! I'm no housemaid, at his mercy. I had to take care of myself back in San Francisco, and I'll do it again if I have to. It's nothing like England there."

"Is that why you left, then, Miss Clarke? A man?"

Annabel took another sip of the tea, her lips twisting. "I wasn't going to stay there forever, with no adventure, no fun. My father just wanted me to marry one of his business partners, a horrid old man, and stay on in San Francisco as his hostess. When I had the chance to come *here*! To be a countess. My father agreed at first, then changed his mind. Who would ever give this up?"

She put down her cup on the bedside table with a click. "You have to grab what you want in this life, Jane. Opportunity never comes twice. Just you always remember that."

Jane thought of Collins asking what it was she wanted in life. "I will, Miss Clarke. I will certainly remember that."

Chapter Seventeen

"I'm so excited your cousin was able to help us, Collins," Cecilia said excitedly, as Collins drove them back to the village early the next day. She was glad to escape the subdued, gloomy atmosphere of Danby for a few hours. St. John had left, at least, cleared out his chamber and departed without a word to her parents. But her mother and Miss Clarke hadn't left their beds, so Jane had to stay with her employer and look after her. Aunt Maggie had been tasked with organizing whist games for everyone else in the White Drawing Room, while preparations for the masquerade ball went on around them. Lady Avebury wouldn't have canceled that even if the plague descended on them. "Mr. Talbot certainly worked quickly!"

"Cousin Harry does have many friends in the business,

my lady," Collins answered. "And it's a small world he works in. They're always happy to help track down an object. I think they like the hunt."

"I can see why." She herself had quite enjoyed fitting little, bright puzzle pieces together. If she could only bring them into a clear image. "But he didn't give you any hint of what he learned?"

"Not a peep, my lady. I think he wants to tell you himself."

Cecilia sat back and looked out the window, adjusting her gloves and the gray felt hat that matched her suit, watching the rainy landscape roll by. She thought of the archery field, the arrow that flew out of nowhere. It had to have been someone who was an experienced shot and knew Danby rather well so they could disappear again. But why target Annabel?

Unless—unless Annabel was *not* the target. Cecilia had been standing right beside her, and there was that note warning her off. What if someone thought the note wasn't enough? It made her shiver.

Collins passed back a fur-lined rug. "It's a chilly day, my lady."

"Thank you, Collins." Cecilia wrapped the rug over her legs, reminding herself she was certainly safe there in the car, the familiar lane to the village sliding past outside.

"So your maid didn't come with you today, my lady? That Miss Hughes?"

Cecilia glanced over to find Collins watching her in the mirror, a questioning look on his face. Or was it even—hopeful? Did Collins *like* Jane, then? Cecilia couldn't help but feel a bit of matchmaking pleasure at the thought. She *did* so want Jane to stay in England, one way or another. It was nice not to feel so lonely, not with Jane to read and talk with.

"She isn't *my* maid, really," Cecilia said. "She's Miss Clarke's. She had to stay with her, after what happened yesterday."

"Oh yes, the arrow. Such a strange thing."

"Indeed. Miss Clarke is naturally rather upset. But Jane was so disappointed not to return to Mr. Talbot's shop. I promised her full details later."

The car turned and slid into the village. Even the lanes and shops there seemed quieter than usual, some of the shutters not even yet raised on the windows. Collins parked behind the shop, and they went inside to find Mr. Talbot behind the counter, carefully examining a small, elaborate Sevres clock of paste porcelain cherubs and rosebuds. Cecilia wondered if she was going to have to add that to her pretty new toilette set.

"Lady Cecilia! I'm so glad you're here," he said happily, putting his magnifying glass aside. "I may have found your box."

"Already?" She eagerly glanced over the cluttered counter.

"Oh, not here, I'm afraid. A friend who owns a shop in

Marylebone knows someone who specializes in Russian art, and he acquired something just like it very, very recently." He searched through a pile of papers until he found a telegram. "Chased silver, engraved in flowers and vines, topped with a cabochon emerald, monogrammed on the bottom with the Cyrillic initial B, hallmark of the St. Petersburg firm of FJR?"

"That does sound like it!" Cecilia cried. "Does he say how he acquired it?"

"A lady sold it, to pay a debt, she said. It seems she cried to part with it, as it was a gift from her husband, but was forced to by finances. An old, sad tale, I'm afraid."

"What did she look like?" Cecilia asked.

Mr. Talbot looked back to the message. "Short, plump, a plain black suit with fur collar, veiled black hat. Hair pinned up and hard to see. That's all."

Cecilia sighed. It couldn't be Miss Clarke, if the lady was short and plump, and how would Annabel get to London and back so quickly? There was that one afternoon she had quite vanished. None of the guests at Danby matched such a description, except maybe Mrs. Rainsley. She couldn't imagine Mrs. Rainsley turning thief and running to a pawnshop, even if she and Maud were not wealthy. Maud's uncle paid her Girton tuition. But *someone* had taken the box from its case and passed it along to be sold.

"I'm not sure who that could be," she said.

"I'm afraid that's all the information my friend had,

Lady Cecilia," Mr. Talbot said regretfully. He and Collins *did* look as if they wanted to solve the puzzle as much as she did.

"I could go to London for you, Lady Cecilia," Collins offered. "If I'm not needed by Lady Avebury. I could catch the ten fifteen to Marylebone station if I hurry and go talk to Cousin Harry's friends in person. They might remember more details, and I could at least retrieve the box for you."

"Oh, Collins! How kind you are," Cecilia said. He *would* be a good match for Jane, so curious and thoughtful, so willing to go out of his way to help someone. "Are you quite sure? I can easily walk home—it looks as if it's stopped raining—and tell Papa you had to run an errand for Mama's party. He would never question that."

"I'll be back as quickly as I can, my lady," he said. He put on his peaked hat and hurried out, the doorbell jangling behind him.

"He's a good 'un, is our Matthew," Mr. Talbot said fondly.

"He does seem to be. He's been so kind, helping me in this strange business."

"He never could bear to let an injustice stand."

"You raised him yourself?"

"From the time he was seven. My father, his uncle, was much older than Matthew's father, who was a cobbler by trade. But Matthew's parents sadly both died young, and only I was left. He was never any bother at all, happy as a clam to go with me to the sales and help around the shop.

He was fixing all the old toys and music boxes from the time he was wee. I'm not surprised he likes his motorcars now."

"We're so lucky he chose to come here, then," Cecilia said, wondering if they were terribly dull next to his Travellers Club employer.

"Indeed we are, Lady Cecilia. Now, do let me show you that toilette set I told you about. Such a pretty thing, I do think it would suit you . . ."

When Cecilia emerged from the shop a half hour later, the pretty antique toilette set boxed up under her arm, the sun had emerged in full and the village was stirring again. She couldn't bear yet to return to Danby, so she went to the cheerful, sugar-scented tea shop instead.

It wasn't yet busy, and soon she was ensconced at her favorite table near the window, a pot of tea and a plate of cinnamon cakes before her. The Misses Moffat, two plump, affable, elderly sisters who had owned the shop for years and given her biscuits when she was a child, kept bringing her more cakes with sympathetic murmurs. She remembered that they, too, had been at the garden party. *Everyone* had been at the garden party.

She tried to imagine one of the sisters shooting an arrow from the woods, but the image wouldn't quite come. Mrs. Mabry, perhaps, or the florist? The dressmaker? None of it fit.

She decided to remember who she could see standing

near the archery lawn and thus could not have been shooting from the woods. But she had been too busy getting ready for her own shot and helping Annabel. She hadn't noticed much at all. Lady Byswater was shooting, her husband watching her from the sidelines; Maud was there, focused on her own bow. Patrick appeared right away when Annabel fell. The gardens were so crowded, so confusing, she had seen no one else in particular.

Except her grandmother, sitting on the terrace with Sebastian and Jack. Cecilia knew the dowager wasn't best happy with an American granddaughter-in-law, but she couldn't picture her going all Robin Hood. Now, if it was twenty years ago . . .

Cecilia sighed and took a nibble of her cinnamon cake. What about Mr. Clarke? Even through the telegram, he sounded exasperated by his rebellious daughter, and he was coming to find her. If this was a real penny dreadful, the villainous father would do away with his scandalous child for not doing his bidding. But that seemed like a lot of unnecessary fuss, considering Annabel would soon be off his hands anyway if she married Patrick.

She thought of the arrow fletching she had found, the odd blue-green color. Who had arrows like that? She was sure someone she had seen did.

Cecilia noticed a group of ladies at a table across the tearoom, watching her over their flowered china cups, whispering. Danby would surely be the source of much gossip and speculation, with a murder and an attempted arrow shooting, and probably would be for some time. It would get even worse if the Clarke marriage never happened. Maybe someone would benefit from Danby's downfall?

The doorbell chimed as a lady came in, her wide-brimmed, stylish hat of amber velvet with a large, striped taffeta bow standing out against all the pink gingham. She turned, and Cecilia saw it was Aunt Maggie, abandoning her whist duties.

"Aunt Maggie, over here!" she called, waving, eager not to be alone with her whirring thoughts for a while.

Aunt Maggie smiled and drew off her gloves as she sat down across from Cecilia. One of the pink-clad servers brought another pot of tea.

"Ah, Cec, dear," Aunt Maggie said as she poured. "I see you felt the need to escape for a while, too."

"Yes. Everyone seems so confused there, everything so dark. I can't believe Mama is going on with the ball."

"You know your mother. She loves to distract herself with working, working, working. Otherwise she'll collapse and Dr. Mitchell will have to give her another sedative."

Cecilia nodded. Running Danby was what held her mother up. "Best leave her to it, then."

"So true."

"No one can stop Mama when she is in party-planning mode." Cecilia took another nibble of the cake and thought of what she had learned from Mr. Talbot. "Aunt Maggie, you said Mr. Hayes was known to have a mistress in London, but you weren't sure of her name."

If Aunt Maggie was surprised Cecilia wanted to gossip about the dead man, she didn't show it. She just looked thoughtful as she poured out more tea. "Even a man like Richard Hayes wouldn't take his light-o'-love out into proper Society. But, yes. We all do rather know one another's business, don't we, even if we don't talk about it."

Cecilia wished they *did* talk about it. It made it so much more difficult to find out anything! "Could she perhaps be named Alice?"

"Alice? My dear, there are surely thousands of Alices littered about."

"Of course there are. But maybe some particular Alice who knew Mr. Hayes?"

Aunt Maggie sipped at the tea, her brow creased. "I remember years ago there was talk of an actress. Alice—hmm, I think Green was her last name. A color name, in any case. White? Brown? I remember for a while, right before my husband died, Richard rather made a nuisance of himself, going to all her performances and tossing flowers onstage all evening. It was thought to be rather odd, because she wasn't even particularly beautiful, being rather plump and dowdy dressing, but her talents onstage were quite rare. A terrifying Lady Macbeth."

The killer queen? A woman who had "given up" so much for an unfaithful, undeserving lover? "That sounds as if it could be her." And then there was the lady who sold the Russian box—short, plump, plainly dressed. Dramatically veiled. "What happened to Miss Green-White?"

Aunt Maggie shrugged. "She left the stage, I suppose. I don't remember ever seeing her again, though my husband died and I was rather distracted. Perhaps Richard's flowers at the theater won her over."

And then ruined her financially. But even if it *was* their Alice Green-White who sold the snuffbox, how did she get it? Did Mr. Hayes steal it and send it to her? How? Or maybe she crept into Danby herself. If she was an actress, she could become a maid or a florist's assistant or something.

"You're certainly very curious about it all, Cec, my dear," Aunt Maggie said.

Cecilia laughed. "Who could help but be? It's like a stage performance in our own house."

"It *is* rather intriguing. Just be very careful who you talk to, darling. I don't want anything else to befall Danby—and especially you and Emmaline."

Cecilia nodded, remembering the warning note, her thought that she had been standing right next to Annabel at the archery. "Do *you* know anything, Aunt Maggie? Something—dangerous?"

Aunt Maggie smiled and patted her hand. "No more than you do, my darling, not about these horrible crimes, anyway. I'm just old and doubtful now, especially when it comes to human foibles. Now tell me, what are you wearing to the ball? I've brought my old Boadicea costume. I've worn it before, of course, but I do love the spear and shield so much. So good for warding off people like Lord St. John."

Cecilia laughed, but inside she shuddered to remember the hot feeling of his hands on her. They chatted about costumes for a few minutes before Aunt Maggie finished her tea and gathered up her gloves and handbag. "I must go, my darling. I'm actually meant to be ordering more flowers for your mother from Mr. Smithfield. Can my driver take you back to Danby?"

"I have a few more errands to run, Aunt Maggie, thank you." As Aunt Maggie kissed her cheek and left, Cecilia checked the little enameled watch pinned to her tweed jacket. She could afford to loiter a bit longer with her cakes. She wished she could wait until Collins returned. She was quite longing to know what he found out.

The gossiping ladies across the room departed, and for a moment Cecilia was alone in the shop, until the bell rang and a gentleman stepped in. Cecilia saw with a burst of excitement that it was the bespectacled stranger. She had him cornered at last! She jumped up and took his arm before he could run away from her, or she could lose her nerve. A lady would never so grab a man like that!

But right now, she couldn't be a lady; she had to be a detective. If she didn't let a threatening note stop her, she wouldn't let social convention.

"How do you do? Won't you sit down, have some tea? It's

still warm, I think." She gently pushed him into Aunt Maggie's vacated chair and slid her own seat around to block the door. "We haven't met. I'm Lady Cecilia Bates. I do enjoy getting to meet newcomers to the neighborhood."

He watched her with a bemused look on his face. "I know who you are, Lady Cecilia."

Cecilia beamed at him. She poured out a cup of tea. "Milk or lemon?" He shook his head, and she passed him the cup. "Excellent. And you are . . ."

"Mr. Blake," he said, most reluctantly.

"And you have important business here, I'm sure. Is there anything I can help you with, maybe? My father is the earl, you know. He does know absolutely everyone."

Mr. Blake slowly reached inside his brown wool coat, and for an instant Cecilia tensed, wondering if he might pull out a gun. He was, after all, a stranger who had started lurking about the village when all this began. Maybe *this* was what Aunt Maggie meant when she said to be careful?

But he only took out a small, silver case. He extracted a card and passed it to her over the teapot.

R. R. Blake, Discreet Investigations, Jermyn Street, London.

"You're a private detective, then?" Cecilia said, fascinated and suspicious all at once. "What brings you here? We are so quiet in our little corner of England."

He flashed a wry smile. "Not of late, Lady Cecilia. In fact, this has turned out to be one of the most interesting things I've done in some time." One of the servers gave him a plate of raspberry tarts and giggled when he beamed at her.

Cecilia folded her hands on the table and stared at Mr. Blake steadily, as her governess used to when she tried to be stern. To outwait Cecilia. It had seldom worked but now seemed worth a try. "And who are you discreetly investigating, Mr. Blake?"

He chewed thoughtfully on one of the tarts and finally nodded. "I think you *can* be of help, Lady Cecilia. I have heard so much of Danby Hall, but it is time to turn to the family. I had a message from my employer just yesterday."

"Your employer?"

"Mr. William Clarke. It seems that, some while ago, he had a dispute with his daughter over a marriage agreement. She vanished, and he only heard of her again when she embarked for England on the *Galatea*. Mr. Clarke remembered then having an invitation for Miss Clarke from Lord and Lady Avebury and realized that must be where she was going. Unable to leave his business in America, Mr. Clarke hired me. I was to find the errant Miss Clarke and discover what sort of situation she was in at Danby Hall."

Cecilia was amazed. Annabel really *was* a runaway heiress! "And what have you discovered, Mr. Blake?"

He shook his head. "I am afraid, Lady Cecilia, that I am

not yet at liberty to say. The terms of my contract with Mr. Clarke, you see, and an agreement with Inspector Hennesy. You will learn very soon, I am sure. In the meantime, I hope you will be very careful indeed. People are so seldom what they seem."

He sounded like Aunt Maggie. Cecilia longed to pound her fists on the table in utter frustration, but she knew it would get her nowhere. "Thank you, Mr. Blake," she said, rising to her feet and tugging on her gloves. "You've been as helpful as you can be, I am sure. May I ask you one question?"

He looked wary. "Of course, Lady Cecilia."

"How does one become a discreet investigator?" She rather thought she might like to be one herself someday. It was quite interesting gathering puzzle pieces, even when people tried to block one's path.

He laughed. "By being incurably nosy, I'm afraid."

Yes, that did sound like a job for her. She nodded and made her way out to the street. If she was to walk home in time to dress for the ball, she would have to hurry.

But she was stopped by Mr. Hatcher, who dashed out of his bookshop as she passed by. "Oh, Lady Cecilia, I am glad I found you! Some of your newspapers just arrived by the last train."

Cecilia ducked into the shop and found a pile of yellowing, enticing papers with fading headlines.

"They are quite out-of-date, I'm afraid," Mr. Hatcher said. "But perhaps you can find something of help?"

"I'm sure I can." She found the newspapers from San Francisco and scanned the headlines for the Clarke name. It was mostly business items about William Clarke, his new endeavors in railroads and steel. Miss Annabel Clarke appeared once or twice in mentions of charitable teas and dances. The best article was only from the last few months, and it had a sketch. "Debutante Ball! The golden Miss Annabel Clarke attends the festivities with visiting British explorer Mr. Richard Hayes."

Cecilia could scarcely credit what she was seeing. The image was in smudged black ink, but the artist seemed quite talented and had captured Mr. Hayes's likeness perfectly. The lady beside him was tiny, barely coming to his shoulder even with her "golden tresses" piled high, and she had a pointed-chin, dimpled, large-eyed, elfin face.

People are so seldom what they seem, Mr. Blake had said, and he certainly was right. Whoever that woman was, who was about to become engaged to Cecilia's brother, it was not Miss Annabel Clarke.

Chapter Eighteen

Cecilia couldn't stop fidgeting as Rose fastened her into her pink-and-blue-striped shepherdess costume for the ball. When she had run into the house with her precious newspaper, the place was in chaos, florists constructing arches of roses and orchids in the White Drawing Room, footmen stringing paper lanterns in the gardens. But her parents and Patrick were locked in their rooms getting ready, and even Miss Clarke's chamber was empty. Jane was nowhere to be found. Rose had grabbed Cecilia's hand and said frantically that her mother *insisted* she dress immediately. Lord Bellham's engagement was to be announced that night.

So Cecilia reluctantly let herself be dressed in the lace and ribbons, panniered confection, her hair curled, until she couldn't stand it for another second. She took the scrap of arrow fletching from her drawer, tucked it in her little lace purse, and grabbed up the newspaper before she ran out of her room.

"Lady Cecilia!" Rose called. "Your hat and crook!"

"I'll come back for them," she answered. As she hurried down the corridor, she thought she smelled a faint burning, perhaps coming from the bathroom, but everything was quiet.

At the end of the Elizabethan gallery, she saw Jane coming toward her, a pleated headdress of shimmering white silk for Annabel's Cleopatra costume over her arm. She tucked it into a basket to be retrieved later. "Oh, Jane," she cried in relief. "You will never believe what I just found!"

"Nor you me, my lady," Jane whispered. "Mr. Collins wants to see you in the music room. He just got back from London. And he's not alone."

Cecilia nodded and followed Jane down the stairs. It seemed they all had big news that night, and hopefully that would *not* include an engagement announcement.

"There was no one in the music room since it won't be used tonight," Jane said. "I checked to be sure, my lady."

The fire was lit in the white stone grate, but there was very little light. It took a moment for Cecilia's eyes to adjust, and she saw Collins standing behind one of the yellow satin settees. Sitting there was a lady, plump and small, wearing a black suit with a dark fur over her shoulders, a black hat on her brown-and-silver hair. Its dotted lace veil was thrown back.

"Oh, you must be Lady Cecilia!" she cried in a lovely, fluting voice. She hurried over to clasp Cecilia's hands between hers. "I am Alice Greenblatt. And I hear I have caused quite a commotion for your family. I am terribly sorry."

Cecilia could see why she had once been an acclaimed actress. Her voice, her concentration, her bright-green eyes were mesmerizing. "You are Mr. Hayes's friend, Mrs. Greenblatt?"

Her expression hardened. "Sadly, yes. What a cruel turn my Richie has given us all, Lady Cecilia! I could barely countenance it when your Mr. Collins came to tell me. It seems he found my flat through that shop. I had to return this in person." She opened her handbag and recovered the snuffbox.

Cecilia took it and turned it carefully on her palm. "So you really are the one who sold it?"

"Yes, but I certainly never believed it was stolen! And from Danby Hall, most shocking. I fear I've found myself in a bit of a pickle lately, you see, and Richie kept telling me he couldn't help me until his book was finished. But he would never sit down and start writing it!"

Cecilia nodded, thinking of all those frantic, angry letters.

"Finally, just as I was about to be tossed from my flat, he sent me that and told me to sell it to pay the rent," Mrs. Greenblatt said. "My Richie, a thief on top of everything else!"

"It certainly is terrible," Cecilia agreed. "Please, Mrs. Greenblatt, you must let us help you with the rent, after your kindness in retrieving the box for us. And stay for the ball! Collins, could you help Mrs. Caffey find some dinner and a place for Mrs. Greenblatt to stay?"

"Oh, you *are* good, Lady Cecilia," Mrs. Greenblatt said with a happy smile. She bustled toward the door, smiling as if her conscience was now clear, if not her finances. Cecilia stopped Collins as he followed and handed him the peacock-green feather from the arrow.

"Collins, I do hate to ask you to perform yet another task," she whispered. "But I know the equipment for the lawn games is kept in the garage. Could you try to match this to any of the arrows used at the garden party?"

Collins studied the tiny fragment carefully. "I think I already know, my lady, or can make a guess. Lord St. John had brought his own bow and arrows, as well as his own tennis racket, and stored them with the others. His arrows had fletching just like that. I remember because no one else's was that shade of green."

And Cecilia couldn't remember seeing St. John after he attacked her in the foyer. He had vanished from Danby. But why would *he* be shooting at Annabel Clarke, who it seemed was not Annabel Clarke? Had he tried to poison her at the dinner, as well? Maybe in his alcohol-soaked mind, he thought he could snatch Danby away with the future countess, but it made no sense to Cecilia.

She nodded, and Collins left with Mrs. Greenblatt, leading her away as she chatted and dimpled up at him.

"Now, my lady, what did you want to tell me?" Jane asked.

"Oh, Jane, you must brace yourself." Cecilia took Jane to the brighter light of the fireplace and showed her the newspaper sketch. "Look at this. Miss Clarke is not Miss Clarke!"

Jane stared down at the paper, turned it over, and then over again, as if she could shake it and change the tale. "Whatever do you mean? Of course she's Miss Clarke! Who else could she be?"

"Oh, Jane. How well do you know her, really? You just met her in New York," Cecilia said gently. "I had Mr. Hatcher at the bookshop order some newspapers for me, so I could try to find out more about Mr. Hayes's travels. Or maybe about Annabel's life in America, since she seemed so sure the killer was after *her*. And look, the two of them actually met on Mr. Hayes's journey to Canada and America! But that is not Miss Clarke."

Jane studied the image in silence for a long moment, her hands trembling on the paper. "I did see this photograph, in a drawer of Miss Clarke's dressing table. Two girls. They were younger, but one was Miss Clarke—*my* Miss Clarke. The other was a small, blond girl, like this one. What does it mean? What happened to this girl?"

Cecilia was worried about the answer to that very question. "We have to find out." From outside the music room windows, they could hear the roar of motorcars arriving for the ball, the music of laughter in the foyer. The house was about to get very full, and surely, Miss Clarke would be downstairs soon for the announcement of her engagement. It seemed a perfect time for a search.

"Come with me," Cecilia said. She led the way into the corridor, where the sound of chatter and laughter was louder, bright with sparkling anticipation. Around the corner, she glimpsed a Queen Elizabeth in black, gold-spangled velvet; a Marie de' Medici in silver tissue and satin; a Henry VIII; her mother in her blue silk Lucrezia Borgia gown.

"I can't be seen upstairs!" Jane whispered. "Mr. Redvers would be so angry."

Cecilia shook her head. It hadn't taken long for Jane to learn the byzantine ways of Danby. But she had a point—no one could see them now, or realize what they were doing. "Let's go this way."

She led Jane into the library. The fires were lit, and red velvet chairs and settees were gathered in cozy little nooks in case guests wanted to escape dancing for a quiet conversation. Inspector Hennesy's work had been mostly cleared away. It was empty of people now, silent.

Cecilia turned toward the spiral staircase up to the minstrels' gallery.

"What is this?" Jane asked.

Cecilia glanced back to see Jane studying the contents of two boxes near the door, apparently missed in the clear-up. Cecilia noticed they were the same ones Inspector Hennesy and his sergeant had carried in from Patrick's laboratory. "Just Patrick's samples, I think. I assume the inspector wants to send them off to test for poisons." Remembering that just made her think of how important it was to find out what was really happening, to clear her brother's name once and for all.

"How odd," Jane murmured.

"I know. No one can decipher it all except for Patrick. All those plants look the same to me."

"No, this." Jane held up a bottle with a cork stopper. Part of the edge was singed, leaving the cork crumbling and charcoal-gray. "I found a bit of this burned stuff in Miss Clarke's drawer, with the photograph. Maybe she stored a bottle just like this one in there, and some of it got left behind."

Cecilia thought of the arrow fletching that Collins said belonged to Lord St. John. Could it all really turn on such tiny, careless things?

She led Jane up the stairs into the gallery and told her about St. John's arrows, about her own idea while watching the tennis that maybe two people were involved in the scheme.

"Lord St. John has traveled to America before," Cecilia said. "He likes to talk about how uncivilized it all is."

Jane snorted. "Not half as uncivilized as groping ladies under the table. Everyone complains about him."

Cecilia laughed, even as she shuddered thinking about St. John's damp kisses. "Exactly. But he could have met Miss Clarke—the supposed Miss Clarke—there, and come up with some plan. Surely, they knew it couldn't last long, though. The real Miss Clarke might show up."

"Unless they did away with the real Annabel, too."

"A terrible likelihood, I agree, Jane. Yet there is still William Clarke. He says he's on his way to England."

She found the hidden door at the end of the bookshelves and pushed it open.

"One of the secret spots of Danby, my lady?" Jane asked.

"Indeed, but I don't use it very much. Just watch your head here."

The light from the library behind them was enough to guide them single file along the small passage. Cecilia had to hold her wide, ruffled skirts close to keep them from catching on the rough plaster walls, and she wished she had worn a more practical outfit for snooping.

They came out near the Elizabethan gallery and turned toward Miss Clarke's Green Chamber. Cecilia couldn't help but think how angry her mother would be when she realized she gave the very best stateroom to an imposter!

To their surprise, the corridor wasn't empty. The door to the Green Chamber was closed, but the bathroom door was open, that strange burning smell dissipating—and Jack sat on the threshold. His marmalade head was held high, his green eyes narrowed in some catlike satisfaction.

"Jack, what on earth are you doing?" Jane whispered. "You can't be here now."

She went to scoop him up, but he eluded her and ran into the bathroom. They had no choice but to follow. The bathroom was all clean white and pale-green tiles, the large, claw-footed tub half-curtained in striped green silk that hid Jack's also-striped tail, shelves along one wall piled high with fluffy white towels.

"What should we do now?" Jane asked.

"Maybe look behind those shelves?" Cecilia said, turning toward the stacks of towels. "Miss Clarke could have hidden something there."

As Jane searched through the towels, shaking out the careful folds, Jack finally emerged from under the tub. He pushed a small bottle, cracked but not broken, half of the tight cork burned away. Was that what she had smelled earlier? Maybe Miss Clarke tried to destroy it in her dressing table and it hadn't worked. He pushed it against Cecilia's silk shoe and looked up at her expectantly.

Cecilia took out her handkerchief and carefully picked up the vial. It only smelled herbal-ish to her, like one of her grandmother's tisanes she always liked to serve at the dower house. A bit of dried green matter was left in the bottom of the glass, but she was sure Patrick could test it to find out what it was. She tucked it into her lacy pocket.

"Good boy, Jack," she praised him. "Come on, Jane, we should try to find Inspector Hennesy and show this to him."

But it was too late. The bathroom door suddenly flew open, and Miss Clarke stood there. She wore her Cleopatra costume, white pleated silk with a beaded turquoise and lapis collar, her dark hair streaming over her shoulders, a golden ankh in her hand. Her cheeks were very red as she studied them, frozen there.

Her gaze swept over Jane and Cecilia, the newspaper in Cecilia's hand. "What are you . . ." She gasped.

Jane and Cecilia hurtled toward the door, yet it was a split second too late. "Timothy!" Annabel screamed, and she used her ankh to shove them backward into the bathroom. Cecilia stumbled over the ruffled hem of her dress and landed painfully on the tiled floor. Jack ducked back under the tub.

"Lady Cecilia!" Jane cried, reaching for her hand. "Are you hurt?"

"I wouldn't be worried about her for much longer, Jane," Annabel said coldly. "If only you had listened to me when I sent you that note, Cecilia! This could all have been avoided. I did try to be your friend, but you have turned against me. And used my own maid to do it!"

Jane stared up at her, her eyes wide. "Who *are* you? I followed you all the way here to England. Surely you owe me that much."

They heard the door open to the Green Chamber across

the corridor, and Lord St. John appeared next to Annabel. He wore his evening suit, the tie askew, his hair rumpled, and he started laughing when he took in the scene before him. Jane and Cecilia crumpled on the floor, Cleopatra wielding her ankh. "My heavens, Amelia, but you do know how to be dramatic."

"So he is your conspirator?" Cecilia gasped.

"He is my fiancé," Annabel, no, Amelia, answered, as if that should have been perfectly clear. "Or he will be, once that wet Patrick is hanged for murder and Timmy is the heir. Now we won't have to meet in secret in the gardens any-more!"

Cecilia remembered that evening she had seen a figure running across the lawn and had imagined it might be the Blue Lady. It must have been Amelia meeting her lover. She shook her head at her own foolishness.

"And, of course, I'm Miss Clarke—just not Annabel Clarke, but I see from that stupid newspaper you knew that," the false Annabel went on. "Dear, sweet Cousin Annabel. Or certainly *not* sweet at all, the harpy. I hope she's happy where she is."

Cecilia swallowed against a cold sense of dread. "And where is that?"

Amelia Clarke laughed, a sound so strange and chilly that even Lord St. John looked at her askance. "Goodness, how should I know. I think she ran off with a Canadian po-liceman when Uncle William wanted her to marry some rich, old friend of his. She always was spoiled. But I'm sure you'll find out everything soon enough."

She nodded at St. John, and he slammed and locked the door behind them, and Cecilia, Jane, and Jack were quite, quite trapped there with two murderers.

Chapter Nineteen

Cecilia felt angry and frightened, but also eerily calm as she stared at the new Miss Clarke. The whole scene was so strange it was almost as if she watched it on a stage, remote from herself. But she knew very well they needed to get out of that room. She pushed herself up and ran for Annabel, no, Amelia, catching her by surprise and knocking her back a step. But when Cecilia tried to grab for the ankh, Amelia hit her with it, and she fell back to the floor, stunned for an instant.

"Lady Cecilia!" Jane cried, trying to catch her.

"Tie her up," Amelia shouted to St. John. "The maid! Use those cords on the curtains. Now!"

Jane screamed when he roughly grabbed her arm and yanked her away from Cecilia. Cecilia remembered how it felt when he touched her, grabbed her, and she wanted to snatch Jane away from him.

She stared up at Annabel—no, Amelia, she reminded herself. Annabel's cousin? Her vision swam for an instant, but she forced herself to focus, to not give in to the dizziness. She had to find a way to get them out of there.

"Surely, you must know the party won't go on forever," Cecilia said. "We'll all be found."

Amelia glanced uncertainly over her shoulder at the door, and Cecilia could see that she hadn't planned for this particular situation. Perhaps she hadn't *really* planned for any of this. Perhaps she had just—run away. Run from whatever unhappiness her past life held, run searching for something new, anything new. Cecilia could understand feeling so desperate.

But she couldn't understand hurting so many people because of that need for change.

"So you killed your own cousin just to come to Danby?" she said, hoping she could keep Amelia talking until a solution presented itself.

Amelia's lips twisted. "I told you! She is not dead. As far as I know. She fell in love with some Canadian, didn't want to marry Uncle William's business partner. Not that I blame her; the man was ancient. But she didn't want to come here, either. That was just silly of her. I thought her stupidity could be my own gain."

Cecilia glanced over at Jane and St. John. Jane's hands

were tied, and she glared up at the man as he watched his lover. He had obviously been drinking again; his movements were slower, uncoordinated, careful, now that he didn't have the element of surprise. He watched Amelia as if he waited for her instructions, but she was distracted by Cecilia. That was a good sign.

"So you helped Annabel run away?" Cecilia said, and she remembered how upset Amelia had been about her lost trunks. More upset than she was by the sinking of her ship. "And you stole her clothes?"

"I did help her! Even though she always had everything, and I was practically her servant. Just because my father fell down a ravine before he could discover a silver mine like Uncle William. She didn't need clothes like that in Canada. And she didn't want Danby Hall. Why shouldn't I have it instead? Uncle William would just wash his hands of Annabel; he wouldn't know or care if she was here or in the wilderness."

"But Richard Hayes knew. He met the real Annabel in San Francisco after her debut."

"I didn't expect that," Amelia said, quietly, almost introspectively. "How could I? I never got to attend those parties."

Cecilia thought of the quarrel Annabel, no, Amelia, had with Hayes, the one she had claimed was because he had harassed Rose. "And so he blackmailed you because he had to pay Mrs. Greenblatt."

"As if we have any money," St. John muttered bitterly. "Not yet." He yanked at the ropes on Jane's wrists, making her wince.

Amelia glanced at him, a soft smile touching her lips. "Dear, dear Timothy. I *did* meet him in America, you know. It seemed like fate when I learned where he was from. Like Danby was truly meant to be ours. With Annabel gone, and Patrick out of the way—Timothy would know what to do."

St. John's expression hardened as he looked at his lover. "Amelia, you never could keep from blabbing everything. What a terrible countess you would make."

Amelia's mouth opened in surprise. "I thought stealing the box and giving it to that nasty Hayes would solve things! But then he wanted my necklace. You were the one who said he would never leave us alone, that we should drug his drink, give him a scare. You didn't say he would *die*."

He waved away her protests. "What did you think would happen?"

"And then you had to make everyone think *you* were the real target of the killer," Cecilia said. "Hence the arrow. I'm surprised you could even draw your bowstring, Cousin Timothy, you were so soused when you kissed me in the foyer. I congratulate you on your aim."

"What!" Amelia cried. "You kissed her? When you are engaged to me?"

St. John didn't look at her. He just watched Cecilia, his

eyes narrowed. "Perhaps my aim was off. I'm not sure. Maybe Patrick would have killed her, as well as Hayes. He would still hang, and I would still be the heir."

"I don't think so," Cecilia said. "You need Clarke money to run Danby, once it's yours. You had to marry Amelia first, get Annabel's money before her father realized it wasn't really her. Then what? Get rid of her, and marry a proper lady? Make sure all evidence of this ridiculous shenanigan was truly buried?"

He laughed merrily, swaying on his feet, as if it was all a fine lark. Cecilia couldn't fathom how anyone could think him a reliable partner in crime. "Maybe I would have married *you*, Cecilia. With your family ruined and Danby mine—how I would have enjoyed your gratitude."

Amelia screamed his name and spun toward him with her ankh. He stepped back—and tripped over Jack, who appeared from nowhere to wind tightly around his ankles. St. John landed with a sickening crack on the tiled floor and went still. Jane, whose feet he hadn't tied, kicked Amelia on the back of the knees and sent her flying into the tub. Cecilia, pulling Jane with her, leaped up and ran to the door.

Her hands fumbled a bit on the lock, but she got it open at last, and they flew along the corridor and down the staircase, shouting all the way.

They found Sergeant Dunn outside the library. He stared at them in blank astonishment as they ran toward him, crying his name, disheveled, dirty, and with a very satisfied cat on their heels. Jack had played his part beautifully.

"I think you had better come with us right now, Sergeant," Cecilia panted. "Your murderers are upstairs in the bathroom!"

Chapter Twenty

Cecilia turned over on her side in the blankets, groaning a bit as her sore muscles protested. She felt terribly battered and bruised, but deeply satisfied. Annabel—no, Amelia—Clarke, along with her injured but breathing lover Lord St. John, had been taken away by the inspector, in full view of her horrified mother's party guests, and Patrick was exonerated and safe. There would be no more poison or flying arrows at Danby.

She carefully eased out of bed and pattered across the floor barefoot to draw back the curtains. Jack was asleep by the fireplace on a pile of cushions, sleek and happy after a feast of shrimp and pâté, rewards for his heroic combat. He peeked at her with one green eye, stretched, and went back to sleep.

Everything else was finally quiet. The guests had gone after all the clamor, filled with delightful gossip, and her furious mother had been put to bed with a draft by Sumter. Mrs. Greenblatt had departed for her train with rent money in her purse. Now dawn was just breaking over the gardens, a glorious pinkish lavender gold that gilded the lawns and flower beds. For the moment, the bedraggled lanterns, the remnants of last night's disastrous party, couldn't be seen. Danby was as serene as ever.

Of course, now that there was no heiress, it was all in danger again. Not of murder this time, but of creeping damp and patchy roofs. At least it wasn't under the power of Lord St. John.

The bedroom door clicked open, and Cecilia turned to see Jane. Despite the early hour, and all they had been through, Jane looked bright and eager, a fresh white apron over her black dress, her blond hair tucked into a frilled cap. She held a tray in her hands, arrayed with breakfast tea and toast.

"Oh, you're already awake, my lady," she exclaimed. She put down the tray on the table next to Jack's bed and fetched Cecilia's dressing gown to wrap around her.

"Oh, Jane, after everything, surely you could call me Cecilia."

Jane's eyes widened. "What if Mr. Redvers heard?"

Cecilia laughed. "Jane. You *are* becoming a true Danby-ite. Maybe you could just call me Cecilia in here, when we're alone?"

"Maybe just in here, then—Cecilia." Jane took a small, tissue-wrapped bundle from her apron pocket. "Collins said Mr. Talbot sent this over. A little present. Everyone in the village is already buzzing about what happened last night."

"Of course they are. Surely, nothing so interesting has happened at Danby since Charles I fled!" She unwrapped the parcel. It was the shepherdess figurine she had seen in Mr. Talbot's shop, her pastel gown and red hair glowing in the new light of day. "Oh, it's beautiful! How very kind of him."

"It looks like you, my l—Cecilia."

Cecilia studied the painted face carefully, her fair skin and painted pink cheeks, her little, secret smile. "I wish I *did* look like that." She carefully put the shepherdess down on her dressing table next to Aunt Maggie's goddess statue and reached for her plate of toast with Mrs. Frazer's raspberry jam. She offered some to Jane, and they ate in silence for a moment, watching the daylight spread its glow across the carpet.

"What will you do now, Jane?" she asked, and poured them some tea.

Jane frowned. "I hadn't really thought about it yet. With no employer, I guess I'll go back to my family in New Jersey. I'm not sure how to find passage."

"I'm sure we can help you with that, if it's what you want. I do understand longing for what's familiar, after all that's happened here!" But Cecilia would miss her too much.

She had only just become accustomed to having an ally, a friend, at Danby.

"I wouldn't mind seeing my family, it's true." Jane stared out the window thoughtfully. "But I can't help but feel there's still more of the world out there."

Cecilia nodded. She felt that way, too. And facing down a murderer—*two* murderers—made her feel that even more. "Maybe, if you liked, you could stay here for a while? I still don't have a maid. I'm not as glamorous as Miss Clarke, but I'm not a killer, either. I'd certainly like it if you stayed."

Jane smiled at her, as brilliant as that sun bursting through outside, and Cecilia smiled back in delight. "I think I might accept your offer, Cecilia."

"Wonderful! I would so miss you and Jack if you left." Cecilia sighed. "Though I fear I may not be able to pay very much. We are quite back to square one here, after Miss Clarke turned out to be the wrong Miss Clarke."

"I don't think I need much right now." Jane stood up and opened the wardrobe doors wide. "Come on, then, Cecilia, drink up your tea, and let's get you dressed. It's time I properly started my new job."

Luncheon was a very quiet affair. Lady Avebury was still locked in her chamber, Patrick had vanished to his laboratory, and all the guests were gone except for Aunt Maggie. She and Cecilia ate alone with Lord Avebury in the breakfast room, after Inspector Hennesy had given the owner of Danby a short report and then departed. The library, the whole house, was theirs again.

"How astonishing it all is," Aunt Maggie said, shaking her head. "I've been traveling the world, and here the greatest excitement of all was right at Danby! False heiresses and murderous cousins all 'round. Who would have thought it? And whatever happened to the *real* Miss Clarke?"

"The false Miss Clarke said she eloped with a Canadian policeman or something, and doesn't care if her cousin took her place," Cecilia said, slicing off a bit of her potatoes dauphinoise. "She simply didn't think about the possibility that someone who knew the true Annabel Clarke might be here. I'm not sure she really thought it through at all; she just let herself be convinced by Lord St. John it would all work, that they could have the Clarke money and Danby, too."

"It seems Mr. Clarke has a private detective in the village," Lord Avebury said. "He is in contact with Mr. Clarke's ship, and his company is ready to send agents to find Miss Clarke in Canada. Hopefully, she is not hurt."

"How very foolish of that girl to ever trust a man like St. John!" Aunt Maggie clucked. "Everyone knows he's been stewing about losing Danby ever since Patrick was born, but surely, it's clear he could never come up with a solid plan for a picnic, let alone a swindle. Unless it was found at the bottom of a bottle. And poor Cecilia! How brave you have been. You must have been so frightened."

"I was, rather," Cecilia admitted. "But they couldn't get away with it."

"You will be the sensation of the Season, my dear," Aunt Maggie said. "I'm sure the change of scene will do you good, too. When are you going to London?"

Cecilia glanced at her father, who was studying her with a small frown on his face. She wondered if he was worried she didn't want to go to London—or worried about the expense. "Oh—I'm not sure what the plans are now. The future seems like a great mystery indeed."

Epilogue

I beg your pardon, my lady," Redvers said, "but it seems a car is coming."

Cecilia glanced up from her book, surprised. Over the days since the party so dramatically ended, everything at Danby seemed to go back to normal, just as it was right at that moment in the music room, the four of them waiting for dinner to be announced. Patrick worked in his laboratory; her mother planned the Season; her father went for walks and spent hours in his library; Cecilia read her books and talked to Jane. Even the curious who had come peeping through the gates for a few days after Amelia Clarke and Lord St. John were hauled off seemed to have vanished.

Now they had company arriving?

"At this hour?" Lady Avebury said, her expression startled.

"It must be someone important," her husband mused.

Curious—and half-afraid of more trouble, after all that happened—Cecilia put aside her book and followed her parents to the foyer. Patrick trailed behind her, still looking a bit distracted by his own reading. He had buried himself in his work ever since his fiancée turned out to be a fraud; he wouldn't even talk to Cecilia about how he was feeling, what he was thinking.

The days were growing longer, and twilight lingered on the Danby gardens, turning the flowers and marble statues and gravel drive to deep purples and mauves. She almost thought she caught a glimpse of the Blue Lady atop a hill, her gown fluttering in the breeze, her hand raised.

But the early evening silence was broken by the purr of a car, the crunch of the driveway under its tires. It was an expensive vehicle, large, silvery, quiet, the windows darkened.

Cecilia watched, astonished, as the impressive car came to a slow halt in a spray of gravel. A tall, stern-faced driver in black uniform got out and opened the back door.

Silhouetted against the fading sun, a portly, impressively mustachioed older man in a gray, fur-collared overcoat stepped out. He offered his gloved hand to a lady, tiny, elfin, and very golden-blond in an amber-gold coat and hat. Her face was shadowed beneath its stylish enormous brim, but when she tilted her head back for a speculative glance at the house, she seemed strangely familiar.

"Lord Avebury?" the man said in a booming voice.

"Yes, I am Lord Avebury," Cecilia's father answered. He made his slow way down the stone front steps.

"I'm William Clarke," the man said. "And this here is my daughter. Annabel."

The girl smiled, and it was bright, warm, gushing, like a burst of summer sunshine. "Oh my! How pleased I am to meet you all at last. I am terribly sorry I was delayed by the wicked lies of my cousin. How shocking it's all been." She turned to Patrick, her smile turning even more blinding. "And I am especially pleased to meet *you*, you handsome thing . . ."